RESIDUAL BELLIGERENCE
THIEVES' GUILD: BOOK ONE

C.G. HATTON

www.6epublishing.net

First published in paperback in 2011
by Sixth Element Publishing
Arthur Robinson House
13-14 The Green
Billingham TS23 1EU
Tel: 01642 360253

Reprinted 2014, 2015

© C.G. Hatton 2011

ISBN 978-1-908299-03-1

British Library Cataloguing in Publication Data. A catalogue record for this book
is available from the British Library.

Printed in Great Britain.

www.6epublishing.net

For Hatt

1

"Where is he now?"

The atmosphere in the Man's chambers was heavy at the best of times, the scent of spices and oils from all corners of the galaxy mingling into a warm intoxicating concoction. The question hung in the air like a wisp of smoke, swirling provocatively between them.

The Man spoke again without giving him time to think up an answer, a warning edge to his voice, "Don't try to read me, NG."

He should have known better but it hadn't been a conscious effort, more a gentle testing of the mood to gauge what the tone of this meeting was going to be.

"We don't know," NG said finally.

"Sit down." The Man nodded towards the heavy set wooden chair in front of his desk. It wasn't often that he'd get summoned to the chambers and only rarely was he asked to sit. He sat.

"Outright war between Earth and Winter," the Man said and shook his head slowly, his hands clasped in front of him on the desk. "Factions finding the audacity to make moves against us. Our own demonstrating questionable motives. And we don't know where he is?"

———————————

There wasn't usually much that could go wrong with an easy acquisition. He wiped blood from his cheek with a shaky hand. Senses still spinning, he tried to lean forward to disengage the drive but the restraints tightened and pulled him back into the seat. An alarm was sounding, distant and irregular, only now becoming an insistent irritant inside his head, which was pounding and wondering where the hell things had gone wrong.

He tried to twist around in the harness to check on the package but his neck resisted and a pain shot through his side with enough

1

bite to make him straighten up and groan. The proximity alarm, he thought. And remembered it sounding much louder not so long ago. It faded as he closed his eyes.

The voice that penetrated the fog was soft and feminine, nudging gently into his awareness. "Hil," she said in persuasive mode, "Hil honey, you need to wake up now."

He could taste blood and smell hydraulic oil. That couldn't be a good combination and his survival instinct was screaming at him to jump up and fight, or run, he wasn't sure which because it was being soundly beaten into submission by his immediate need to fade out again.

"Hil," the voice was louder now. "I need you to get up and help me, hon, because I can't fix this by myself. My suppressant systems are shot and if you don't get back there and do something to control the pressure that is building up, the drive is going to explode and we'll both die here on a godforsaken planet in the back of beyond and no one will care or miss us except for that damn package you had to go get."

It was a dream he had too often so he embraced it and decided to let it run out. Usually he'd wake abruptly and go get a beer to calm his nerves. The nightmares had been more often of late but this was the first that hurt so bad. And the first where Skye was so polite. And come to think of it, the first where he could feel his head spinning from the smell of fumes.

He jerked awake and gasped as the movement reignited all the sparks of pain.

"God damn it Hil," Skye was screaming, "you worthless son of a bitch dragging us out here on a goddamned wild goose chase and dying on me." He'd never heard so much emotion from the ship before.

He couldn't help the smile that crept across his face, sore as he was and in no way sure enough of the state of the ship to be cocky. But he'd gotten hold of the package and made it away. So why was he sitting here grounded on god knows what planet with his wits scattered as far as wreckage from his ship?

The smile faded.

Skye shut up mid-flow. Then tentatively whispered, "Hil, you with me? Hil? Trust me, you need to move. We have three ships moving in on our position and if that damned package means as much to you as you make out, we have to go."

He couldn't even remember what was in the package, but he had a vague recollection of taking the tab and the guild would be unimpressed to say the least if he lost it. The chances that they'd crashed by accident were slim and that three ships were bearing down on them probably meant that someone had taken offence at losing whatever it was that was sitting back there. That wasn't good. And the cold chill of that reality seeped through faster than any nagging from the ship.

Hil freed himself from the restraints and staggered to the back of the compartment. He squeezed into the tiny maintenance area and got access to the main controls, coughing from the smoke, each cough sending a shard of pain spiking through his skull. The bonus in working solo was that the split of credits, both financial and performance points in the guild standings, was always one hundred percent his.

The worst thing, he decided as he hit manual over-rides and released the building pressure in the main conduits of the jump drive, favouring his left hand because the right one didn't seem to be working properly, was that there was no buddy on the way in to pull off a rescue in the nick of time, to clink beers with as the sun set on each close shave. Unlike some people that he didn't have much time for, he'd never worked with a partner, never needed to or wanted to. So as he squinted at the flickering displays, it was down to him and Skye, the ship he'd known and flown with since he was a kid, who was now wittering on about company closing in.

As far as he could tell, the ship was just about intact, the package was intact – if battered – and although they were leaking fuel and the jump drive was burned out, at least it wasn't going to explode now and they should be able to fly out of this and get some place where they could figure out what had happened.

No matter how hard he tried to think through the pounding in his head, he couldn't remember any specifics about the tab he'd taken. The three craft heading for their position might be local farm dwellers come to investigate the crash or they could be bounty hunters out for his head for all he knew.

He paused and tried to clear his mind and calm his heart rate. There'd be no reason why they would be bounty hunters, no one ever messed with guild business. Unless the package had more baggage than had been declared.

He crawled out of the maintenance space and struggled to make it back to the bridge, vision blurred and not helped by the trickle of blood that was running into his eye.

As he passed the stowage area, he paused, one hand resting for balance on the package tied securely into place. He resisted the urge to crack open the seals and take a look. Never interact with the merchandise. It was a guild mantra and one that Hil had only broken a handful of times, all with good reason. Was this one of those times? He stared at it, sitting there in its silver case, sealed with a mark that would get him thrown into the jail on Io Optima for the rest of his life if he was caught with it.

It was about briefcase sized and he had no memory whatsoever of acquiring it, or what could be in it. But whatever it was, he was fairly sure he'd been shot down on his way back in with it.

"Honey, get back up here," Skye said quietly, this time directly into his head through the neural implant embedded beneath the skin on the side of his neck. "C'mon, leave it. We need to get out of here."

She was right.

He grabbed a medical kit from the compartment above it and fell back into his seat. He held a patch over the gash on his forehead and watched nervously as the ship went through the checks, most lights red, some burnt out and safety parameters out of the window but so long as they could fly, they'd fly. He didn't want to encounter the ships that were closing in, friendly or not. He needed a place to hole up, fix the ship for jump and stay under the radar for a while. He'd get the package back, grab the credits for it and take that break he'd been promising himself and Skye for too long now.

Simple.

Taking a package from A to B always gets more complicated when A doesn't want to lose it and C will pay and do anything to get their hands on it. Hil was good, one of the best in the guild. Problem was, he couldn't remember when it had gone wrong.

Skye was being no help, concentrating as she was on outrunning the three ships that were chasing them. She'd said, snapping in frustration at his insistence, that he ran on board with the package, yelled at her to go and then they'd taken a hit after dropping out of jump and crashed.

He couldn't even remember who the client was or where he'd acquired the package. He recalled saying yes to a tab but that could have been three jobs ago. Or three years ago. His memory seemed screwed up and that was more than a bit disturbing. What was worse was that while he knew his guild handler was Mendhel, he had not the slightest detail in his head how to get in touch or get back to base or where he had to take the damn package to.

Skye was getting up some decent speed now. Hil watched the ships lose distance on them then break off, flying away in opposite directions. One shot vertically up, heading for orbit and jump, he reckoned. That was odd. Probably not locals then.

"How far to town?" he said and cringed at how pathetically weak he sounded. He cleared his throat and tried again. "How long 'til we make the space port?"

"Three minutes," she replied curtly. Skye was a typical female AI. They all cared and fretted when they thought you were in trouble and as soon as you were fine, the sympathy evaporated.

Hil sat back. He knew Skye was fast. She'd been built for speed. She was the fastest ship in the guild because they'd refused any weapons. Apart from some light shielding that would barely diffuse the effects of the smallest energy weapons, they didn't even have any defensive measures. His philosophy was along the lines of run to live another day. Hil fought his battles on his feet. If he'd wanted to shoot guns, he would have joined the navy. But fast as they were, they'd taken some serious damage in the crash and bless her for doing her best, but Skye wasn't flying at top notch right now.

Anyone should have been able to catch up with them. So why had the three ships chasing them down suddenly given up the ghost? It was enough to give him a headache. If his head hadn't already been pounding. They'd been called off, he decided, so what now? Should they be expecting a welcome party when they landed?

"I need to contact Mendhel," he said abruptly, out loud, interrupting his own train of thought.

"Not until we reach the guild, unless you have some other way of communicating."

Hil detected a hint of sarcasm. "Skye, help me here. I honestly don't remember where we were supposed to be going," he said. "Where do we usually...?"

"Honey, you just rest your cute butt until I get us to an airfield and a repair yard where we can get some of these systems back online. Then you can worry about getting back and signing in to check your status."

Checking his status. That sounded familiar. Status meant all green, safe and sound, home straight. He'd never had an alert on him. Of course he'd never outright crashed before. So maybe this was what it felt like when the guild put out a red or black. He'd seen poor suckers tagged with alerts before and had felt smugly superior with his spotless record, vying for the top spot, not scuzzing around waiting for an extraction team to haul him back in like he'd seen some of them needing. He'd always been package delivered, thank you very much and onto the next. No matter how tricky – the trickier the better in fact. Thing was, he vaguely remembered thinking that this should have been a walk in the park. Or was that the last job? It was enough to make his head spin. He closed his eyes and let the minutes fly by.

There were two kinds of planet-bound space port that were worth visiting – the big, extravagant, old-Earth style supersizers where you could catch the latest gambling crazes, try out the newest biowares and get cosy with just about any fantasy you could imagine, and the seriously hi-tech Wintran machine shops that were on the fringes of reality, crossing military hardware with upgrades that hadn't even seen a field test yet. He'd spent his fair share of time R&R'ing at the first and spending his hard-earned credits at the second, treating himself and Skye to anything that could keep them a second ahead in the race.

Unfortunately for both of them, this was neither. Skye found them a way in and managed to haggle permission to land at a repair bay. They were dwarfed by a cargo ship on one side and a courier on the other. Both looked to be trash end of the market and Hil felt his skin crawl at the thought of going out there.

"All repairs booked in and authorised," Skye declared. "You go get seen to."

Go get seen to? He didn't want to go anywhere here. Hil didn't move. He couldn't see anything that matched the signature of the ships that had been following them. But that didn't mean they weren't in here somewhere.

"You're still bleeding all over me, Hil honey. I've made a reservation for you at a Wellbeing. It just looks like a small one but they should be able to patch you up."

"Cancel it, I can wait," he said, thinking of the package and trying to remember what the hell he had to do with it.

Skye was a mind reader at times. "They'll help," she said. "You have a concussion and I don't know where we're going so I need you to go get seen to, let them spark that short-term memory of yours back into shape and by the time you get back, we'll be fixed up and ready for go. And the package will be fine in storage."

He weighed up his options. Having full control over life support, Skye could make it impossible for him to stay. Wellbeing it was then. Normally a stay in a Wellbeing of choice was a much anticipated post-tab treat. But even at some of his favourite haunts, there were Wellbeings he'd avoid. Chances of this one being above par were slim but this was purely medicinal, being mid-tab and all, so a quick fix-up wouldn't hurt.

Hil checked that the package was still secure and left the ship on shaky legs, still light-headed and more than a little shocked to see the state of the ship from outside. There were massive scorch marks etched across her hull, Skye's sleek form and elegant wingspan battered from impacts he couldn't remember. Her landing gear was standing crooked and debris littered the floor beneath her. Hil kicked absently at a piece of twisted metal. It was the first time they'd ever got their fingers burnt. But she'd got them here and she'd get them home. Somehow.

He was halfway across the concourse when he got an urgent recall from Skye sounding in his head. He turned and spotted two uniforms making their way towards him, too rapidly to be routine. He turned again, expecting trouble from the other side and saw a guy in a dark business suit standing, just staring at him and intimidating as hell. Hil stumbled slightly as he back-peddled and tried to look nonchalant as he headed back to the ship.

He glanced back and the two uniforms broke into a run so he did too but his flat out was more of a limping ramble. Their outright sprint, guns up, intercepted him before he was anywhere near Skye's on ramp. He stumbled as one of them grabbed hold of his arm and the other wheeled around in front of him. They were probably just grunts from customs, he thought as they forced him to his knees. He could buy his way out of this, but as he opened his mouth to speak, a blow to the back of the head sent his already scrambled senses spinning into darkness.

2

Breathing in the heady air of the Man's private office was giving NG a headache. He sat bolt upright, waiting for the Man to continue.

The Man stared straight ahead, his eyes glinting like tiny black gems catching the light from the many candles that sent shadows dancing around the nooks and crannies of the chambers.

The guild had never before had to deal with a situation like this, one that threatened its very existence. NG kept his breathing calm. It was one that he should have averted. And one that was still not resolved and still had the momentum to inflict more damage.

The fact that their operative, one of the best operatives in the history of the guild, was still missing was unnerving; never mind the financial cost of losing such a valuable asset, losing anything didn't settle well with anyone inside the Thieves' Guild.

The Man reached for a large pewter goblet that was resting on the desk. He poured carefully from a glass jug, dark red liquid that was steaming vapour splashing into the goblet and sending more fumes to swirl between them. He gestured absently towards a second goblet as he raised his own to his lips.

Never one to refuse hospitality, NG poured himself a dash of the wine.

"To the guild," the Man said and drank deeply. "Now tell me everything – from the beginning."

Waking up in a Wellbeing was a warm, cocooned, snug and peacefully slow surfacing to soft cream lights and the gentle awakening of awareness with a nudging from Skye to tell him it was time to get back to work after a well earned rest and rejuvenation. Hil was cold and sore and a pitiful ache deep inside told him he wasn't connected to the ship anymore. Not in a Wellbeing then. It was also sickening to realise that he didn't know where the package was. It was the closest to panic that he'd ever experienced. It was the first time he'd ever been forcefully parted from Skye and the void of quiet felt like it was sucking his brain out into a vacuum.

He gasped and tensed, eyes opening to a harsh white light. He could sense someone standing close by to his right but couldn't move. He was lying flat, wrists and ankles restrained and someone was fumbling to free him. A hand took hold of his arm, pulling it straight, and he was too weak to resist. He felt cold then in the crook of his elbow and a sharp sting followed by a slap to an already tender cheek.

"C'mon Hil buddy, we're out of here as soon as you can gather your butt to move."

The voice was vaguely familiar but Hil felt himself drifting back into the dark.

"God, give him some more, we don't have time for this." The second voice belonged somewhere else and he struggled to place it, female, aggressive and condescending, the kind of voice that was okay in small doses but one you didn't want to be around too long. Another jab hit his arm and as the drug kicked in with a rush he almost gagged. Arms were lifting him up then before he could protest and he couldn't help that his knees buckled as his feet hit the floor. It was distressing to be this helpless but at least he was dressed – coat missing but he was wearing his own clothes. They held him, one on either side, both of them wearing black, lightweight combat gear that he recognised from somewhere despite the lack of insignia. The woman leaned in close and said, "Good god Hil, you're a mess," and there was something about that voice that rankled somewhere deep down.

They hauled him upright and he tried his best to put one foot in front of the other. He couldn't see much past the bright glare of spots in front of his eyes so he put his trust in these two somehow familiar figures that seemed to be rescuing him from he wasn't sure what. He kept trying to reach out to Skye but the void was complete and there wasn't so much as a whisper from her.

They navigated a bright blur of corridors and steps and he still couldn't see or stand straight by the time they pushed through a door to a blast of chill air and he was bundled into a vehicle. He lay back on the cold seat and tried not to throw up as they drove fast, veering around corners and accelerating hard.

Nothing else was said until they came skidding to a halt and Hil's stomach flipped sideways. He could hear launch engines firing up, cracks that sounded like gunfire and someone yelling. There was a sharp metallic impact near his head and he curled up reflexively, rolling off the seat and landing with a groan in the footwell, banging his head and feeling the cut on his forehead open up again. The door near his feet opened and he was dragged out, no apologies, an arm thrown around his shoulders. He was pulled into a run onto an up ramp with bullets impacting around them.

As soon as the arms holding him let go, he sank to his knees on what felt like a loading bay deck and braced his left arm against a cool bulkhead. He heard the ramp slam shut, then footsteps clanging away from him, more yells that he could recognise as the two voices he couldn't quite identify, then the comforting lift of a ship leaving the confines of the planet's surface. No guild monkey ever liked to be planet-bound. The more dimensions you have around you to play with the better. And he was with friendlies. As much as he couldn't place the voices, he knew they were guild and he knew he was in safe hands.

The acceleration was tough. Hil tumbled against the bulkhead as the ship pulled out of the atmosphere. He couldn't stop himself rolling a ways down the deck, wondering vaguely what would happen to him if they went into jump and he tried not to pass out so he could at least attempt to hold onto something.

He passed out anyway and woke abruptly some indeterminable time later to feel the reassuring tug of a restraining harness against his chest and a pressure building behind his eyes. He could hear numbers being checked off, the two voices joined by a third that he reckoned must be the ship.

They were being pursued from the planet and had fighters on their tail from what he could make out. It didn't make sense and he couldn't understand why Skye wasn't goading him into action. Raising a hand up to his neck he felt with horror that there was a bandage patch taped behind his ear. He tore it off and felt the sting of cold air against a wound that was still tender. His fingers came away red with smears of blood. That hadn't happened in the crash. The Senson had still been there, still functional, the implant providing a clear connection to the ship. He'd been talking to Skye before they got to the space port. Crap. What the hell had they done to him?

"Hil, calm down, you're freaking out the ship." It was the woman again. She rattled off more numbers.

Freaking out the ship? He was freaking out himself.

"I just need to know what's happening," he mumbled. "I need to get back to Skye."

"In a nutshell," the woman said, "... ten seconds to jump... you've been extracted. The guild wants that package... five seconds."

The package. That cold touch in the pit of his stomach again.

"Three... two... one."

Then jump. Hil closed his eyes and let the motion of jump pull at his every molecule. He was screwed. He was well and truly screwed.

They made five jumps. And by the time they docked with the Alsatia, they were fairly sure they hadn't been followed. It was the first time he'd ever been here without Skye. The first time he'd ever lost a tab. But crap, that was nothing compared to losing Skye.

Once they'd edged onboard and were given the go ahead to disembark, Hil shook off the cobwebs in his head as he unhitched the restraints and limped down to the airlock without waiting for either of them to say anything. He knew he was being obnoxious and knew he should be grateful for the rescue and humble and patient in his current pathetic state but the cold and aches had turned into anger and he didn't want to talk to anyone. He wasn't sure he wouldn't yell and scream and, obnoxious as he was feeling, he didn't want to inflict that onto the two people who had just saved his ass.

He stood and glared at the red light above the airlock and willed it to turn to green before either one of them appeared behind him.

It was a relief to be home. The Alsatia was a massive wandering cruiser owned by the guild that flitted around known trade routes and uncharted shortcuts, both sides of the line, operating in Earth and Wintran space and the Between. No one outside the guild should ever be able to find them if they didn't want to be found. It had never been attacked, never been infiltrated and it never would be because every single person inside was family, with bonds stronger than blood could ever be. The guild looked after its own and these two people had been sent for him because the guild wanted him back in one piece. And it sucked that he'd screwed up badly enough to need extracting. He'd never needed rescuing from anything.

They'd said the guild wanted the package. The only thing he knew for sure was that the package was with Skye and she was god knows where. He'd lost both of them. Why they hadn't left his sorry ass there and gone after the package itself was beyond him right now. And he didn't feel inclined to ask. The only plan he'd been able to come up with was to grab a ride in another ship and go after her. There were a couple of people he thought he could count on and he was desperately hoping they'd be home.

"Hil wait up."

The damn light was still red.

The guy walked up behind him and caught hold of his arm to twist him around. He resisted because he was still feeling belligerent but it was only half-hearted. He really did appreciate that they'd come after him.

"There's some things you need to know before you go in."

Hil stared. He'd thought his emotions had bottomed out, that it wasn't possible to feel any more cold and sick. He reached a new low at the guy's tone.

"Do you want to come on back and sit down? You don't look so good, Hil bud."

Hil thought he could have been less hostile if he could remember the guy's name. "No," he said and gestured toward the airlock and its infuriating red light. "I just want to go in and get this sorted.

I need to get back out there and find her. Mendhel will set me up with a ride." He trailed off at the expression on the guy's face. He actually didn't know what the procedure was once someone had been hauled in. His reputation would be screwed and his average would tumble but he didn't care. He just wanted to get hooked back up with Skye and rebuild it from there. Screw the standings.

"Hil." The guy looked uneasy as hell. "Mendhel is dead and LC is missing."

3

"Losing Mendhel has been a blow," the Man said slowly, every word resonating. "The guild must be seen to be invincible – on both sides of the line. I trust that action has been taken."

NG didn't answer straight away. He wasn't sure that an answer was necessary. He held the goblet and felt the warmth of the wine. Mendhel had been more than just one of his best handlers, he'd been a good friend.

"The guild is as strong as it's ever been," he said quietly. He swirled the wine gently around the bowl of the goblet and watched the vapours rise. It was true, the guild had survived, but the cost had been far higher than anyone had realised. It wasn't just that it had unbalanced their standing in the complex and delicate political situation between Earth and Winter. The guild thrived on the paranoia and hysteria that rumbled between the two. No, it was the repercussions of the conflict this whole incident had sparked within the guild itself that had hurt.

Thinking back, he'd known right at the start how much certain individuals, key individuals, had been tempted by the chance to use the situation to force a shift in power.

The Man smiled and shook his head. "It's not wise to get caught up on hindsight," he warned gently and filled NG's goblet to the brim. "This turn of events was unexpected but such is the nature of man. The greater our understanding of that capricious nature, the more we can exploit its strengths to our own end." He paused and directed his gaze directly at NG once again. "Tell me more."

Mendhel dead? It didn't register. Hil felt wide-eyed and stupid as the words simply didn't register.

"The package was switched on you, buddy," the guy said. "We have

15

Skye, and the package you put in storage is phoney baloney, bud. NG is seriously pissed. We've all been played for fools. The guild has lost its best handler, its best field-op and its second best has been severely fucked with. We were lucky to get you out of there, Hil. We've had teams all over looking for you." He paused then repeated the only bit Hil could grasp. "We've got Skye, Hil. She's as screwed as you are but we're hoping we'll be able to recover from the two of you what's actually happened. Because NG wants that package and he wants LC back."

"What's happened to Mendhel?" Hil said, a chill clutching at his stomach.

"Hil," the guy said, "that's not your biggest problem right now, trust me. NG wants to know what the hell you were doing out there."

"I don't remember," Hil said, frustration fuelled by obnoxious belligerence and every hurt yelling at him to fight back. "I don't know where I've been. I don't know what I was doing. I don't even know your name."

He didn't get an answer before the woman stomped up next to them and gave him a disgusted look. "God, you people are so damned cocky when it's all tickety-boo. It's pathetic to see you like this." She hit the button. He hadn't seen the light turn to green. "Go, scoot. Get your ass up to Medical. I'm sure NG will send for you when he's ready."

He had a dozen questions on the tip of his tongue but he couldn't formulate a whole sentence. He kept his mouth shut and was halfway down the tube before he thought to turn.

"Thanks for the rescue," he said and went home.

Medical was the last place he wanted to be. Hil checked the docking schedule but there was no listing for Skye. If they were bringing her in, she hadn't got there yet. He had to get to Acquisitions if he was going to have any chance of finding out what had happened to LC and Mendhel. His nerves were trembling, from the crash, the drugs or what, he couldn't tell, but he felt edgy and uneasy as he'd never experienced before at home. Home was a secure, safe place but something had changed. He tried to remember exactly what the guy had said but the words slipped out of his memory and were gone, try as he might to bring them back.

The dock area was busy. He didn't want to be around people who would ask him awkward questions and he didn't want this nightmare making public. He knew that Skye always logged in their successful deliveries and let him know if there were any urgent requests for him to contact Mendhel. He could remember that much even if he couldn't remember anything from this latest job. Usually coming in after a big tab involved checking the bank account, picking up any messages and heading out to R&R. Downtime on the Alsatia between routine tabs meant time in the Maze, training, getting to grips with any new upgrades to bioware or just flat out pushing to get fitter, faster, stronger and better for the next one. Coming home was usually a cocky checking of the standings before waltzing out on the next tab. But not this time.

Hil slunk into the lift and kept his eyes on the floor. Three dock jockeys edged in after him and he squirmed, expecting a hard time but either they hadn't heard or they didn't recognise him. They pushed the button for three and two grunts entered the lift between the closing doors. Hil pushed his back against the back wall and let the lift take him up. They reached three and the doors opened. The three dockies jostled each other out and Hil made a move to push the button for ten. He was pushed aside by a black armour-clad arm that pressed twelve. He could see the grey insignia of the Watch – guild internal security – so they weren't just grunts from the guild's militia wing, they were here to pick him up. Shit. They turned to face him as the doors closed and the lift started to rise.

NG was waiting for them as the lift doors opened. NG was the guild's head of operations, head of the guild effectively because no one else ever actually met the guild's council of elders. The Man was the only one of those mysterious figures who ever visited the Alsatia and he only dealt with NG. It was NG who knew exactly who was where, what was what and where they were going. Why everyone called him the New Guy was a mystery because he'd been there as long as Hil could remember.

NG was rumoured to have a sixth sense and it was a relief to see him, to recognise the face and be able to put a name to it. Hil almost fell towards his outstretched hand.

"It's good to have you back, Hil," NG said softly. "We're in the shit and I really need to know what you can remember."

It was like clutching a warm surge of electricity when you shook hands with NG. The guy was an enigma. He was like everyone's big brother but no one knew anything about him. Kase and Martha must have reported in already, Hil realised, suddenly remembering the names of the two extraction agents who had rescued him. And realising who it was who had been sent to extract him sent a chill right through him that set him off shivering. He tried to calm down – this wasn't a good place to go into shock.

NG put a hand up to the back of his neck and nudged him gently into motion down the corridor. That warm hand was reassuring and Hil felt his heartbeat settle slightly. He couldn't help raising his own hand up to the patch behind his ear, awkward and embarrassed.

"I… they… NG, I'm sorry, I don't remember anything straight." He was rambling like a fool so he took a deep breath that caught in his chest. "What happened to Mendhel? Has someone told Anya?" He didn't even know where Mendhel's daughter had been living recently.

NG shook his head. "We'll go through a full debrief later. Right now I need to know whatever you can remember. You okay for this?"

They stopped at the door to the conference room.

No, Hil was screaming inside his head. "Yeah," he said. You never said no to NG, he had a habit of hearing yes anyway.

There were four people sitting at the round table. All display screens were off and there were no recording devices evidently out. Chances were the monitors were off too – that was a bad sign. That meant that they didn't want a word of this meeting going any further.

Hil sat down and tried hard to place the faces looking at him.

Section chiefs. He was sitting with the five most important people in the guild. Oh crap. And he hadn't even had a chance to wipe the blood from his hands. A simple screwed up tab wouldn't warrant this kind of inquisition, surely? Or was this what happened to all the suckers hauled in after screw-ups?

NG took his place and started up proceedings. "Chief," he said to the huge man sitting opposite Hil, "do you want to take this up?"

Chief was the chief of Acquisitions. He was the only section chief known as Chief, the others referred to by their section. Acquisitions looked after all the handlers, field-ops and security. The Chief was a good guy but Hil had never had to talk to him before without Mendhel smoothing the way first.

He took a deep breath, the loss hitting hard and the loss of memory of recent days making a confusing swirl of empty cold deep inside. He tried to sidestep his emotions and take control. He was with friends here. These people were on his side.

The Chief shook his head, placed his huge hands out flat on the table in front of him and leaned forward. "Where the hell have you been and what the hell have you been doing?" he said coldly. "We get word Mendhel is dead, your emergency beacon yells for help and suddenly we can't contact LC. We were hoping he was with you but obviously not." His voice turned icy. "Tell me the three of you weren't out on a tab that we didn't know about."

What? Hil blinked and felt a pulsing tick above his eye start to flicker. No one ever took an unauthorised tab. Not ever.

"We've found evidence of a tab at Mendhel's safe house on Earth," Legal piped in. She was a smart, black-clad woman who everyone said had connections to the Assassins. Hil had never seen her this close up. She was stunning and scary as hell. "He was handling an assignment that had not originated from the guild. What do you know about that?"

There was silence as the accusation swirled around the room. He didn't know what to say.

"Do you fully appreciate the consequences of this?" Media was another woman, softer in appearance but with an even more scary reputation. "I can't believe Mendhel would do that. We need you to detail exactly what Mendhel gave you, where your pick up took place and what the instructions were for drop off because I am very disturbed that one of our handlers could have been acting independently. What did he say to you?"

The room went quiet and Hil looked from face to face. Science was sitting there, a stony look on his thin face, fidgeting with a data board in front of him like he couldn't believe they were wasting his time with this.

Hil fumbled inside his brain for a set of words to string together into a sentence. He opened his mouth before anything was ready and shut it again when he realised he couldn't remember the question.

He was saved by the Chief who pushed back from the table and stood up. "Let me set this straight," he said. "You left here with LC. That's logged. It is not in dispute and don't deny it. What the hell were you two doing?"

What?

He must have shown something in his face because NG shot a glare straight at him.

"You don't remember leaving with LC," NG said quietly. It was a statement rather than a question and he had it right.

Hil tried to set his face to neutral. It was hard not to fidget. He had dried blood under his fingernails still and his face must have looked a mess. Beyond the pounding in his head, he felt nauseous and the more he concentrated the more he could feel each twinge of pain, in his ribs, his right arm, left ankle, that cold spot behind his ear. He didn't know what had happened so he didn't know what to say. He'd never faced this before. Mendhel had always handled the fallout from any little upsets his ego had gotten him into. He felt distanced from it all – it all seemed so unreal.

Legal pushed a data board across to NG, the thin display screen flickering. Hil squinted at it but couldn't make out any of the text on it and he looked to NG, feeling more and more helpless.

NG glanced at it but didn't say a word.

Hil looked over to Legal and saw that she was staring at him, eyes cold and distrusting.

"It took us five days to get to you," she said. "After we picked up Skye's distress beacon, it took us five days to find you. Can you account for that time?"

He shook his head miserably. It hadn't felt like five days.

She looked to NG again. "We still haven't been able to identify ownership or allegiance on the facility where he was eventually found. I have some leads but nothing substantial as yet."

Hil felt disgustingly tainted. God knows who'd had their freaking hands on him. He wanted to go and shower, feeling more and more uncomfortable.

"...and that leads us onto the other matter," Media said, "the implant. That was a Senson Six, right?"

He stared, and absently reached up to his neck.

"Whoever took that has violated the guild. We cannot underestimate the damage that can be done because of the loss of that implant. That technology is military grade hardware and anything even approximating its capacity is not expected to be available commercially for at least another two years or more."

"A year at best," Science said.

"Regardless, it still means the loss of a distinct advantage across all spheres of our operations. Whoever took it must have been one helluva bio-engineer," Media said. "We had protections on it, I assume."

Hil felt distant from the conversation. They were talking about him as if he wasn't there. He'd answer their questions if he could but they weren't giving him time to think.

"Of course, we did," said Science, with disdain. "We wouldn't send out such a valuable asset unless it was absolutely secure."

"So what consequences are we looking at here?" That was from Media he thought but their voices were merging and he couldn't see straight.

Hil faded out, like he was sitting in the centre of a bubble that was shielding him from everything outside.

A hand gripping his shoulder shook him back to the room. He braced and tried to focus as the Chief helped him up. "Let's get you to Medical. We can go over this later."

4

NG took a sip of the wine. It was hot and strong, and even that small sip burnt his throat.

*"LC Anderton and Zach Hilyer are our two best operatives, by far,"
he said. "They've made acquisitions no one thought possible. There
have been jobs I almost turned down and there have been items that
departments within the guild decreed that we needed that I almost vetoed,
but in every case one of those two has successfully pulled it off. No one
else is near. Their instincts are astonishing. They never work together,
they're very different and they're fiercely competitive. Mendhel was the
only handler who'd ever been able to keep control of the pair of them."*

*He paused to take another drink. The Man was sitting quietly,
unmoving, keeping his full gaze focused. It seemed to be getting warmer
in there, if that was possible.*

"In your judgement," the Man said, "was there a risk?"

*"Their loyalty to the guild was never a concern to me," NG said.
"They came to us young and they both knew they'd found their home
here. Their aptitude for our area of expertise is inherent. But I can see
now it wasn't surprising that when an entity outside decided it was going
to cross the guild, those were the two targeted."*

"Hil honey…"

The moment of impact crashed through his bones and sent a
spark of pain drilling through his skull. He jerked awake again at
the voice, expecting smoke and engine oil and the taste of blood.

"Hil, we're home. Calm down that heartbeat or they won't let
you go."

Instead of a hard, cold console, Hil felt pillows.

"That's better."

"Skye?" he thought and reached up to feel smooth intact skin behind his ear, just the vague feeling of an implant beneath his fingers.

"We've both been through the mill, honey but we're home now."

"God, Skye, I've missed you." He felt breathless. The shock of losing contact with her was sinking in worse now that she was back, as if he hadn't let himself feel the full effect of it.

"I know, honey. When I lost touch with you, I thought... I thought they'd killed you, Hil."

It hadn't occurred to him to consider what Skye had been going through. He tried to take a deep breath but his chest was hurting. "What happened? They said I was there for five days."

"Whoever they were on that planet, they impounded me, hon. They broke in and busted open the package. There was nothing in it, Hil. They were really angry. They just left me there. And I couldn't find you."

"The package was empty?"

Hil sat up, favouring his left arm to lean on. There was a brace on his right wrist and the pain had numbed down to a throbbing ache. His head felt better though, a little woolly inside but more settled than it had been. He was in a private room in Medical, white walls and sparse furniture with racks of medical equipment that were beeping at him erratically. Apart from routine exams, he'd never spent time in here. He'd never had to and he didn't know what he was supposed to do.

"We're in trouble, Hil," Skye whispered. "I've been locked down. They won't even start repairs yet. They don't know what happened and it's scaring a lot of people. Can you remember anything?"

"We crashed," he said.

"No, honey, before that. I'm missing a memory module, hon. How did that happen? How could I not know? They've told me I'm out of action until we find out what happened. Did they tell you about Mendhel and LC?" She sounded scared. How could an AI sound so scared? "What were we doing, Hil?"

He rubbed his left hand across his face, and felt the tug of an IV line. It was irritating so he pulled it out and dropped it to the floor, holding a corner of the sheet against his hand until it stopped bleeding. He felt rung out but he wasn't going to sit there like an invalid.

They were in the shit. His head wasn't scrambled that badly. He could remember what Kase had said and how NG had reacted. He'd been hauled in front of the section chiefs, for god's sake. Skye was a mess too, they'd said. She was worried and scared for him.

Hil clambered out of the bunk, trailing wires he hadn't realised were attached to him. He pulled loose and looked around for his clothes. The things he'd been wearing when he was extracted were bundled into a locker by the bed, filthy but it was all he had. He rummaged through the pockets and swore as he realised his toolkit and knives were missing. They hadn't just taken his Senson then. He instinctively checked his left arm, the nondescript-looking band still snug around his forearm. It might not look it but it was his favourite piece of kit. The dull black metal band concealed a lock pick, hidden flexed along its edge, and the band itself was an intricate piece of bio-engineering that included an automatic sensor to warn of contaminants and toxins. It had cost him a small fortune, saved his ass several times, and thankfully, whoever had nabbed him had been stupid enough to overlook it.

"Hil, I've heard rumours that Legal want you thrown into the brig," Skye said. "They're saying we've gone rogue. Have we? Why don't I have any record of LC being with us on that last trip? What was he doing?"

"I don't know, Skye," he said, aware that he was being sharp with her and he tried to be patient, but he didn't know. How many times did he have to say it?

He pulled on his shirt and combat pants carefully, trying not to flare up the sore spots he could feel through the drugs they'd pumped into him. He put on his boots, not bothering to lace them to avoid bending over any more than he had to, and checking as he did that his knife was still hidden there – it was, they'd missed that too. He pulled it out and sat staring at it, tracing a finger over the delicate pattern of etchings worked into the hilt and weighing up its perfect balance. Mendhel had given it to him a long time ago.

LC had one that was identical, Mendhel swearing it was a crime to split up the matching pair but what else could he do with the two of them so close in the scores? Throwing it with astonishing accuracy was about the only thing Hil could beat LC at. That and poker.

His hand started to shake.

He slipped the knife back into his boot and stood up.

"What are you doing, Hil honey?"

"I'm leaving," he said. "How long have I been here?"

She didn't reply and that wasn't exactly reassuring.

"Skye?" he thought, and looked up as the door opened.

A medic stepped into the room, flanked by another two security personnel, both armed and wearing armour.

Hil stared at them. They weren't Watch; these guys had the giveaway red flashes on their armour that tagged them as the Man's personal guard. What the hell were they doing here? It seemed excessive and the medic seemed unimpressed by the state he'd left their equipment in.

"Mr Hilyer," she said, "I see you've decided to leave us." She looked him up and down. It was disconcerting, like he'd been caught trespassing, and with a slight shake of the head, she handed him a data board and pen. The two guards had stationed themselves at the door, but whether they were stopping someone from getting to him or stopping him from getting out wasn't clear.

"Skye," he sent, going through the motions of reading the information on display on the board. "Why the security detail?"

"Honey," she said, "I'm trying to find out but I told you, I'm locked down here. I don't have access to anything."

Crap. He glanced up at them while he scribbled his signature with his left hand, twice as big as it usually was. He put a cross-eyed angry face in the descending 'y'.

"Is that it?" he said, looking back at the medic and giving her the board. "Don't I get any instructions to ignore? Am I done?"

The medic looked at him like she was used to patients being assholes when they left. Maybe she'd dealt with field operatives before.

"You're welcome to leave," she said.

"Free to leave?" he asked, glancing from her to the armoured figures at the door.

She waved the board at him. "You're released from Medical," she said and smiled. "What they do with you from here is up to them."

He narrowed his eyes and walked to the door. They parted and let him pass, taking up position slightly behind and to either side, following as he walked into the corridor.

At the lift Hil pushed the button for level ten and glared at the two bodyguards he seemed to have acquired, waiting and daring them to over-ride it with a twelve. They didn't and as the lift took them up towards Acquisitions, it was hard not to wonder what the hell was going on.

Walking out onto ten, Hil felt about as low as he could go. The atmosphere in the halls was muted. Respect for Mendhel, curiosity about himself and LC he supposed. He couldn't remember it ever being this quiet.

The guild's massive cruiser had subcultures within subcultures. Acquisitions was the cold steel walkways of the barracks and spooksville, dominated by the endless depths of the Maze, where he spent every spare minute, and the noise of the mess with its rowdy bar and the always looming and ever changing board showing the standings, where every field-op was listed by points. It was a place of gambling and risk, rough and tumble amongst the grunts of the guild's militia and fierce competition between the field-ops.

Each section in the guild had its own atmosphere and way of life. Legal had three decks of marble hallways and oak panelled staterooms. They controlled the library, the real library with the books crammed into aisles of wooden shelves. Dusty artefacts of long ago and hardly necessary when anything you wanted was at your fingertips through a data board but the library epitomised the compulsive nature of the guild to hoard. It wasn't often that the field-ops got to visit the library but Hil had occasionally and it was an awesome collection. They had all that as well as the billions of items of electronically-stored information. Legal kept the maps and the star charts and the manuals. The guild owned the history of the human race, from Earth to all the colonies and out to Winter; knowing everything gave them a power that was almost unmatched.

Legal was the intelligence arm of the guild, gathering data, recording information and negotiating contracts.

Media was more superficial and more insidious even than Legal. Media was effectively the espionage branch of the guild, all comfy sofas and real coffee pots with a finger on the pulse of the future. It didn't predict trends, it created them and used them to manipulate the colonies with a voracity for change that unnerved anyone caught in their vicinity for too long. They didn't inspire, they dampened individuality and spontaneity by feeding the masses exactly whatever it was they decided was the current in, creating and destroying on a whim. Acquisitions collected. Legal controlled. And Media frog-marched them into the future.

Science was the fourth of the big four. They had a sphere at the very centre of the Alsatia and no one that Hil had ever met on board had been in there. They came out occasionally but any damage caused in there by their many explosions and accidents were dealt with by their own. Science kept to themselves except when they hurled a fast ball of evolution out to the field-ops to try in the outside. Science was also the main drop off point for in transit acquisitions. It was rare for a tab to go straight to the client; more often packages would go through Science first then back to the beyond. That way the guild made much longer term acquisitions itself than purely the price paid for the tab. It was simple and devastatingly effective.

When he tried to turn into the barracks corridor, a gentle push on his arm kept him from turning. He wasn't feeling up for a fight so he let them lead the way. They took him straight ahead.

The Chief's door was open. Hil hesitated at the threshold. He'd only ever been in there when he was in trouble and then that was only after Mendhel had cleared the air with the Chief. He'd never appreciated until that moment how much of a pain in the neck he'd always been to his handler. It was a horrible feeling to realise that he'd never be able to make it up to the man, who had always been more than a handler and more of a father figure to them all. He wasn't sure if he could face the Chief.

He took a step into the room and the door closed behind him, leaving the security guys outside.

The Chief had his back to the door, standing over by his planning wall, wire frame outlines of maps, charts and lists moving constantly over its smooth surface. "Sit down, son," he said and moved a hand over the control board – it all faded to black, leaving the room darker but easier on the eyes.

Hil sat on one of the three chairs in front of the massive black desk that dominated the room. He kept his head down, and scuffed his boots along the lines in the metal deck, trapping the trailing laces of one foot with the other.

The Chief walked over and sat in his chair behind the desk, quiet for a long time.

"I've managed to keep your ass out of the brig," he said eventually, "for now. But I have to tell you, Hil, you don't have a lot of friends on this cruiser right now."

Hil looked up, his eyes hooded. "I don't know what to say," he said, trying not to sound as defensive as he felt. He didn't want to let Mendhel down. "I don't remember what happened."

The Chief had a data board on his desk. He flicked through a few screens. "The staff in Medical have confirmed that you've had concussion with probable related amnesia. However," he said, still looking down. When he looked up, he was frowning which was never a good sign. "They don't think that the head injury completely accounts for your memory loss. They can't even identify half the substances you had in your system when you got back here, Hil. What the hell were you doing?"

Hil rubbed absently at the brace on his wrist. "I don't remember," he said again, knowing how lame that sounded.

"Well, as far as the official report goes, you have amnesia. That gives us some time. But I have to tell you, Hil, I'd rather hear what happened out there from you than from some wiseguy in Legal if they get to the bottom of this before you manage to get yourself together enough to remember. Legal are having a field day with this. They've been muttering for a while that we're too easy on you guys, that we give you too much leeway because of your particular talents. We've been holding them off because you've all been delivering the goods. This could tip the balance. The last thing we want down here is for Legal to be pulling the strings of our operations. We're all shocked to have lost Mendhel. You should know that people have been sent to investigate the circumstances of his death. If you have anything to add to that investigation, bring it here first. That will be the only way I can protect you, do you understand?"

Hil nodded, not really understanding at all.

The Chief stood up. "You're off the list and confined to Acquisitions."

That meant no tabs and pretty much house arrest. He'd had in the back of his mind that he'd be going out after LC.

"But…"

"No buts. Medical won't clear you to go out and I don't want anyone else to get their hands on you. Take it easy, Hil. Get back in the Maze. Keep your head down, get yourself back up to full fitness and we'll take it from there. I've lost one of my best operatives – I'm not going to lose another."

5

*"And do you see now why it was imperative that we place Hilyer under
protective custody?"*

*NG nodded reluctantly. "I would never have predicted the animosity
that a situation like this could create within our community." It was
the one thing that had affected him the most in all this and it was the
hardest to admit. "I should have known. I don't find it easy to see the
worst in people."*

*The Man smiled. "Why should you? You can read their minds.
You see their hearts. You are a unique individual amongst your race,
NG, with an extraordinary talent. You choose the best people and
put them in the most appropriate positions for the good of the guild.
For anyone to turn against us... that cuts deep. When one section of
our guild finds satisfaction in the distress of another, we cannot help but
feel anguish at the betrayal. Yet..."*

*He picked up his goblet and drank deeply. "Yet we place each and
every individual under immense strain to perform and we set them
against each other in competition that is bound to create stresses and
weaknesses. Why then should we be surprised when cracks appear?
Losing Mendhel and Anderton in such circumstances was bound to
create tension, a catalyst for action against the arrogance that had been
growing. Admit it, an arrogance that we had been nurturing."*

*"Every section in the guild has a degree of arrogance. They deserve
to," NG said. "We do bring in the best. And we push them to become
better. Maybe we push too hard."*

Back in the barracks, Hil left his escort keeping guard at his door,
showered and fell into his bunk. He slept fitfully for a time and
woke up in a cold sweat with no memory of the nightmare that

had left him feeling on edge. It didn't feel worth the effort to try to get back to sleep so he got up and made his way to the Maze, acknowledging a few friendly faces on the way but not lingering long enough to get caught up in any debates. He was thankful no one tried to waylay him into the mess.

His two security shadows stopped at the entrance and nodded respectfully as he went in. Only field-ops ever entered the Maze.

He logged in and got changed into the black work-out kit that he kept in his locker. Fliss was in there already he noticed from the log. She was the only one and it would be company he didn't mind.

He checked the environmental control settings. Fliss had a habit of screwing with the norms and the last time he'd followed her through, she'd wound the temperature up, the gravity down and set a sprinkling of electrobes lose, to 'give her a buzz' she'd protested. The last thing he needed right now was a breath-full of those damned things. Someone had said once that the microscopic organisms that were the by-product of AI thought processes were going to take over the universe and wipe out all other life forms. He hated them and hit the reset, purging the system of any traces. Felicity would have to get her buzz another time.

He pulled his belt tighter, realising for the first time how much weight he'd lost, and took his time warming up, feeling the strain more than usual which was a real bitch because he'd been getting faster before that last tab. He shrugged it off and went for the Straight.

The Maze was a training ground for the field-ops and there were various routes through it, the toughest being the Straight – the most direct, difficult, treacherous, fastest route. LC was the only one who'd ever finished it faster than him and the two of them were the only ones who could complete it.

It was irritating to struggle and damned frustrating every time he lost his grip and fell, or lost his balance and tumbled, or most embarrassing just couldn't catch his breath as he climbed and clambered. He ended up sitting atop a beam across the vast space that was known as the Void.

Skye was quiet, but then she didn't usually disturb when he was in the Maze.

The dark stretched in every direction.

He almost fell off when a figure landed next to him and threw her arms around him in a hug that he hadn't realised he needed.

"God, Hil! What the hell happened out there?" Fliss was small and slight and desperate to make her way up the standings. She was about fifteenth last time he looked and probably didn't have a chance of getting higher. Except of course that was before one and two had just tumbled out of the picture.

"I don't know," he said simply, not even trying to dig into his memory. He was tired of trying to think about it.

She stood up and pulled on his arm. "C'mon, come with me." She winked and dragged him forward.

Precarious as his balance was he almost pulled them both down into the hole but her forward momentum kept them on the beam and she led him out and up the shaft towards the Sphere.

"Hang on," he protested when he saw where they were going, not sure he could stomach zero-g.

She glared at him with a piercing stare and gestured to the opening, flashing that sweet smile she liked to turn on and off when it suited her. The grunts fought over that smile. How could he refuse?

The Sphere was a massive dark chamber of artificially controlled gravity that hung in the centre of the Maze, directly in the path of the straightest route through. Hil paused at the entrance, holding onto the cold metal of the doorframe. It was the fastest way to get from one side of the Maze to the other, if you could handle the inertia and not break an arm. Usually they'd fly across it in one trajectory and tumble out of the far doorway in a roll. This time he eased himself in and kicked off gently into the zero-g.

Fliss floated up to the centre of the Sphere and twisted around to look at him. He floated up and enjoyed the moment for a change, turning head over heels and just letting go. Fliss caught his arm and pulled them both together.

"We need to talk," she said. "Hil, how much do you remember? Because there are some scary ass rumours floating about."

He didn't feel like talking and just drifted there in the centre of the sphere.

She whispered in his ear, "They've taken you and LC off the standings board."

"What?" The cold knot in his stomach clenched uneasily. No one was ever taken out of the standings – unless they died. "They can't do that. The Chief said I was off the list, but off the board? Who the hell is top?"

"Hil, it doesn't matter. What happened out there?"

He tried to pull away but she squeezed his wrist.

"Who said we're off the board?" he demanded.

Fliss glared at him and narrowed her eyes. "Hil," she said, "they can do whatever they want. But if you must know, Sorensen is top and he's being a pain in the ass. Everyone else is saying what the hell do the standings mean any more if they can ditch you and LC so easily." Her gaze softened. "What happened?"

He put aside the gut-wrenching ache from being dropped – she was right, it didn't matter any more – and tried to sift through the mess of memory that was left rattling about in his head.

"I got the tab, picked up the package and crashed," he said eventually. "Dropped out of jump and got shot down. We crash landed on some planet. Someone was after the package. I thought maybe they were just upset to lose it or set someone on my tail to get it back."

"The package was switched," Felicity said.

"I know, Kase told me. I didn't know. I don't know how it could have been. It was a clean grab, Fliss, honestly, the acquisition was as simple as they go."

"You remember that?"

It was surprising to realise that he couldn't recall any details, just a clear notion that it had been simple.

"Do you know what they're saying?" she asked and squeezed his wrist again to emphasise the question.

He shook his head.

"They're saying that LC has screwed the guild over. They sent out Kase and Martha, for god's sake, with six other teams. No one ever gets seven teams sent after them, no matter what they're caught up in. We couldn't believe it. We all thought you'd just had an accident or something, but for Kase and Martha to be sent out, good grief Hil, they've not pulled a run-of-the-mill extraction in years, not since they were bumped up to spec-ops. I knew something was wrong when they were sent out after you. There's some crazy talk going around about who the client was and what the package was."

"Like what?" he said, feeling cold again at the thought that it had taken Kase and Martha to pull him out of whatever it was he'd been caught up in.

"Like, you don't want to know because if it's true, you're going to wish you'd never been found."

He couldn't help pulling away then and the motion sent them off at different tangents. Fliss caught hold of him and they tumbled together.

She glared at him. "Hey, I'm a friend here. And if things go the way I think they are heading, you're going to need a friend, Hil. Mendhel was murdered. Did they tell you that? Someone even said it was LC that killed him, Hil. How mad is that? That's the kind of rumour doing the rounds. We're the Thieves' Guild, Hil. We look after our own. And we're the ones doing the taking, no one takes from us. No one messes with the Thieves' Guild. No one."

She pulled him close and kissed his forehead gently.

He pushed her away. "What about LC? Does anyone know what happened to him?"

She traced a finger along the bruises on his cheek. "There's no sign of him. He's vanished, no tags or entry docs anywhere with any of his codes. They've been checking airfields and orbitals all the way to Earth. People are saying that you left together on the same tab. Do you remember that?"

"No," he said, honestly. If he'd hooked up with LC on the same tab, it must have been one helluva job. They'd always joked they'd be invincible if they worked together. He had a pang of regret that he didn't remember it if that was what had happened. It would have been awesome.

"Something could have happened to him, have they thought

about that?" he said. "Why is he being tagged as the bad guy here? This is LC we're talking about."

Fliss shrugged. "He's dropped off the radar – that's never going to look good whichever way you look at it. I'm really sorry, Hil."

And she did look it. The cold spot deep inside flared up again.

Fliss hugged him tight. "I know, it's a mess," she said. "I've heard that there's a price out on him."

She paused and his heart sank further. If bounty hunters were after him, LC wouldn't have a chance.

"And it gets worse," she said, hesitating.

He wanted to throttle her. Worse? How could it get any worse?

"We've been assigned a new handler," she said. "It's Quinn."

Quinn? That wasn't going to happen in a million years. No way would he work with Quinn. Why hadn't the Chief mentioned that? He began to shake his head but Fliss shushed him.

"Fight me," she whispered. "We have to move around or they'll start to wonder what we're doing in here." And she spun backwards using his body for leverage and aimed a vicious high kick at his shoulder.

She kicked his ass and didn't hide the fact she was enjoying it so much. Kick a man when he's down, why don't you. Hand to hand in zero-g was one of the hardest things they trained for. She'd never beaten him before and she'd never do it again once he got back up to speed. He limped the rest of the way out along the easiest route and picked up his two security guys who were waiting patiently. They didn't object when they made their way to the barracks and he didn't resist when Fliss kissed him before leaving him at the door to his quarters.

"Get some rest," she said. "I'll let you know if I hear anything."

It couldn't have been much rest because he was still aching from the work out when he was woken up by Skye.

"Hil, honey, NG wants to see you in his office."

He crawled out of his bunk and fell asleep in the shower.

"NG wants to see you now, Hil," she sent, more forcefully that time as he was enjoying the heat of the water and the oblivion of the moment.

"Skye, have you found out what happened to Mendhel yet?" he asked, drying off and searching around for clean clothes.

"I'm not getting through to anyone on that, hon, sorry but it looks like the ranks have been closed on us."

"I need to talk to Martha then." It was awkward but she'd be the only one who could help. She'd found him and he needed to know where the hell he'd been.

"I don't think that's a good idea, Hil honey."

"Skye, it's old history. She'll talk to me. Where is she?"

"Hil, get your head straight. NG wants to see you in his office, now. Maybe he knows something."

She sounded stressed again.

Hil pulled on a jacket and headed out. The two guards fell in on either side. He took a look at each of them in turn as he walked through the still eerily quiet corridors of Acquisitions. They may or may not have been the same two guys as before but they were both wearing red flashes. The elite of the elite. The Man's own personal guard. Whether they were there to protect him from harm or guard him from escaping still wasn't clear. And it was unlikely they'd speak to him however much he goaded them.

"So does this new status I have come with a pay rise?" he said. They ignored him so he picked up his pace and raced them to the lift. They didn't rise to it and let him get ahead, but watching their reflections in the polished door of the elevator, he could see them both put a hand on their side arms. He punched the call button, tempted to make a run for it, just for the hell of it to see what they'd do. He'd had run-ins before with the Watch, most of them had, tempers and emotions ran hot in Acquisitions, but he'd never been this close to the Man's own guards before. That they were here meant the Man was on board and that he'd assigned two of his guards to babysit Hil for some reason meant that Hil was attracting attention that was unwanted and unlikely to be in his best interest.

The lift doors opened and Hil slipped inside, hitting the button to go down. The two guys were still walking, still some distance away and as the doors closed, Hil couldn't help the cocky smile. It faded as the doors jammed half open and half closed. There were rumours that the Man's guards had complete control over every system on board the Alsatia. They hadn't even twitched.

Hil frowned and stepped aside as they entered the lift, one of them pushing him against the wall and saying, "Don't try that again," the voice deep and throaty through the armour, as the other one hit the over-ride.

"Neat trick," Hil muttered. He needed Skye and all her resources hacked into a system before they could do anything like that. He'd never thought of the cruiser in terms of somewhere he could break into, but now the idea was there, he started running scenarios through his head. And each time he came up against a brick wall. He looked at the two guards as the lift rose up through the ship.

There'd be a way.

NG's domain on twelve wasn't a usual haunt of the field-ops. But it had a welcoming feel that made him relax. It had soft carpet on the floor, not hard metal deck, and pictures on the walls, huge images of places he didn't recognise. It was warm and quiet and the two guards manoeuvred him to a row of chairs. He didn't need the hand on his shoulder to encourage him to sit, his head was still pounding and there was a weakness in his knees that was sapping his energy.

One of NG's staff brought him a cup of something hot and sweet. She winked at him as she handed it over and he smiled as he watched her walk back to her desk, short skirt swinging. The two guards watched as well, he noticed, so they were human after all.

When he turned back, NG was at the door, beckoning him to go inside. NG's office was cool and dimly lit, spotlights shining on key features around the room. Hil had been in there before and knew there were banks of data walls and planning tables off to one side, a massive desk in the centre and a round wooden conference table to the other side. Bookshelves stacked with artefacts from across the galaxy lined each wall. It was an eclectic mix of textures and technology that reflected every section and aspect of the guild's operations.

NG directed him towards the conference table where a soft light was casting shadows over a pile of books and data boards. The woman sitting there stood up as they approached. She was wearing travelling gear, had a gun in a holster strapped to her thigh, and as she reached out her hand to greet him he almost recoiled when he saw the flash of the embossed silver badge attached to her belt that identified her as a bounty hunter. She held his grip more firmly than she needed to and smiled at him. She might as well have pulled out the gun and held it to his head.

"Hil," NG said, "this is Sean O'Brien. She's going to bring in LC and I want you to help her find him."

6

The Man laughed, a deep throaty chuckle. "Sean O'Brien," he said. "You have style, NG."

He'd never heard the Man laugh like that before. "Desperate times," he said, placing his goblet on the desk. "She's done good work for us before. I thought she might bring Hilyer to his senses."

The Man nodded slowly and threaded his fingers together. He looked up, solemn again. "Your report suggests that he was held captive after his crash. Why could we not identify his captors? The extraction team found him easily enough."

"They found him in a facility not far from the location where Skye set off her emergency beacon. The place was an anonymous holding facility. There was nothing to identify its owners or most recent occupants. Our priority at the time was to get him back. The teams that went back in afterwards found it deserted, sterilised. I should have questioned Wibowski and Hetherington. That was an oversight that cost us badly."

"You're too hard on yourself at times, NG." The Man leaned forward and topped up both goblets, a splash of wine bouncing onto the surface of the desk with a hiss. He wiped it away. "Bringing in the bounty hunter was a good move."

"We needed outside input. I had everyone on this and it wasn't enough," NG said, reaching for his wine. "And our resources are still stretched. This has been hard on all of us."

She was armed, in NG's office. That was unheard of. Not that he'd ever heard of NG entertaining bounty hunters before. And when Fliss had said there was a price on LC's head, he hadn't realised it was the guild that could have put it there.

"We leave right away," she said.

"We?" Hil said. He'd been planning to get back out there but for god's sake, not with a freaking bounty hunter.

"The trail's cold already. You're going to give me a head start, the insight into where he'll have gone." She had an air of confidence that rankled in a way that was too familiar. She even stood in the same confrontational way that Martha had a tendency to adopt around him.

Hil looked at NG, reluctant to cause a scene in front of an outsider. But there was no way he was going with this woman. No way that he was going to rat out LC to a bounty hunter. He had no memory of what they'd done or where they'd been but whatever had happened, this should be dealt with by the guild, not some mercenary outsider.

She smiled at him again. "You want him back, work with me. It'll be far better for him that I find him before," she paused for effect, "certain other practitioners of my profession."

She reached towards NG and shook his hand. "You'll hear from me as soon as I have something." She looked back at Hil. "I'm docked in bay twenty four. Be there in half an hour."

NG saw her to the door, leaving Hil to stand stranded by the table, looking surreptitiously over the documents there trying to figure out what they'd been talking about. He scowled and threw the board he was holding onto the table as NG came back.

"Full cooperation, Hil," NG said. "You want us to treat you like one of the best operatives we have, start acting like it."

"I can't believe you're asking me to work with a bounty hunter."

"We often work with outside agencies. Put aside your prejudices and work with her. I want LC back, here within the safety of the guild."

"How do we know she won't sell us out once she has her hands on him?"

"Hil, give me some credit here. How much do you think we're paying her?"

"The Chief said I was grounded," he said, feeling unsettled and out of his depth.

"He's aware of the new situation. He wants LC back. We all do.

We're looking into what happened, Hil. And I have to say, there are some people calling for me to throw you into the lock-up. Concussion aside, Legal don't believe your story. Being out there with someone I trust is the best place for you right now."

Skye was horrified that they were sending him out with a bounty hunter. "Good gods, Hil, what are they doing to us? Why don't they send out the extraction teams?"

He threw some essentials into a holdall and rummaged around his locker. He'd lost his favourite coat and the only other one he had wasn't as warm. He checked the pockets. It would have to do.

"They have," he said. "They're doing everything, Skye."

"She's registered with Earth. Can we trust her?"

"I trust NG and he's told me to go. What else can I do?"

"I've heard that her ship has a terrible reputation, Hil. Their apprehension record is phenomenal but over eighty per cent of her captives log an injury on deposit. I'm sorry but I don't trust her to look after you, honey."

"If I walk up into Legal right now, they're going to throw me in jail. Which do you prefer?"

She went quiet.

"Exactly," he said. "I have no choice." He slammed the locker shut and kicked the drawer closed.

"Hon, I've been told to give them whatever information they need on you and LC. But I can't tell them what I don't know, Hil honey, can I?" she said, distressed at having to talk about him to people she didn't know.

It sucked. And he knew that sitting there in lock down was tough for her. Not being trusted by the guild was tough on both of them.

"Just keep your ears open, Skye. I'm sure LC is laying low somewhere. See if you can find out what happened to Mendhel. I'll be back soon, I promise."

The engines were already firing up as Hil walked on board. The ship talked him through their procedures and told him where to stash

41

his gear. Edinburgh was a small two-seater with a holding cell in place of a cargo bay and it was strange being a passenger but he was still tired so he just buckled up and closed his eyes. Apart from a couple of curt, polite comments, the bounty hunter ignored him until they were about jump distance away from the cruiser.

"It's Hil, right?" she said. "That's what you prefer?"

He knew she was looking at him so he nodded.

"The more you help me, Hil, the faster we'll find him."

"I don't know where he is," Hil said stubbornly, repeating the mantra that had been his only answer since he'd been picked up after the crash.

"Yeah, yeah, amnesia, I know, they told me all about that." Like she didn't believe him. "So where first?"

"Abisko," he said without thinking. It was in the Between, not far from the system where he'd been found. Something that no one else knew, not even Mendhel, was that the two of them had a series of drop boxes hidden on orbitals across the galaxy. If LC was alright, he'd leave a message in one of them at some point. And one of the boxes was on Abisko station. It was a long shot but hey, where the hell else was he supposed to start. "There's a bar we know. We'll try there."

"Be straight with me, Hil," she warned. "I don't tolerate time wasters."

"I'm not a good team player, Ms O'Brien," he fired back. "I'm sure they told you that about me."

She smiled. "They told me a lot about you."

That didn't bode well.

"You're a lot alike, you and LC, according to everyone I've spoken to. That should help us find him."

He frowned. He wasn't anything like LC. They were a similar build, that was all. Slender and agile, but then so were a lot of the field-ops – it suited the job. Apart from that, they were nothing alike.

Sean laughed. "Yeah, they said you'd deny it too."

"I didn't say anything."

She laughed again. "Defensive, arrogant, fearless. Same height, same weight – give or take a few pounds, same average for a hundred metre sprint, same Paninski profile. Same hungry look in the eyes. You're both near as dammit ambidextrous, except that LC is naturally left-handed. The only thing I can see that separates you both is your arrest record. You get into more trouble than LC."

"They give you our whole freaking personnel files?"

She threw a board over to him. "The whole caboodle."

She had everything. Not just personnel notes and training logs, the board contained full ID data, DNA tags, fingerprints, retina scans, photos. A chill gripped his stomach.

"This is private," he said quietly.

"Not any more."

Guild field operatives didn't exist. They were all issued with a different ID and documents every time they went out on a tab. No one anywhere knew anything about any of them. Wrong, no one outside the guild should have known anything.

"There's already a contract out on Anderton," she said. "With a price that's attracting attention. There's a basic physical description in the public domain. But that's all. So that gives us an advantage. I take it he's smart enough to change his appearance if he doesn't want to be found?"

Hil shrugged, still irritated that she had their personal data and disturbed that she'd confirmed the rumour that there was a price on LC's head. "I don't know why he's disappeared so I don't know what he's thinking. Has anyone considered that he might be hurt somewhere?"

"Your guild is checking out that possibility. I've been hired to assume he's on the run." She leaned forward and entered the coordinates for the jump. "Edinburgh, start jump procedures. Hil, don't worry, that information's not going anywhere except with me."

Hil liked Abisko. That was another reason it had come to mind as the first place to look. Abisko was a mining colony. Neutral alliance, tough environment with most of its deposits under hundreds of metres of ice, and one of the best rec scenes on any of the orbitals in the Between. The planet also had some kind of research status so the station teemed with science types as well as the mining facility operatives. And working in those kinds of harsh conditions meant everyone was up for a good time when they had leave. They had some good friends here and if nothing else, he thought, downing the last of the amber liquid in his glass, they had good whisky.

O'Brien had caught hold of his arm and ticked off her rules before they'd left the ship.

"Stay out of trouble," she'd said. "Check your contacts and get back here in two hours. In the one in a million chance that Anderton is here, bring him back to the ship. There are too many people interested in this contract. Don't get their attention. No drinking, no fighting. And call me Sean, for Christ's sake."

They'd left the ship separately and he'd hightailed it straight to Polly's. She'd given him a hug, said she hadn't seen LC and had let him into her stockroom to climb up and break into the station's maintenance core. The drop box on Abisko was simply one in a bank of lockers used by the orbital's crew. It was easy to get to. Some of their boxes were hidden in ridiculous places that no ordinary person could even hope to reach. He couldn't face a climb with his wrist in the state it was, so again this was a good place to start.

The box had been empty.

Polly pushed across another whisky and took his empty glass. She was wise enough not to ask any questions but she'd held his hand and brushed a finger over the scar on his forehead, and looked at him disapprovingly.

"Mendhel was a good man," she said.

Polly was one of only two people outside the guild that he'd trust with his life, that even knew what he really did for a living. She ran the bar with an iron fist and a warm heart, and every patron knew with absolute certainty that their secrets were safe.

Hil nodded and drank the shot down in one. Polly topped up the glass, looked up over his shoulder and nodded. "Watch yourself, babes," she said and turned away.

He watched the guy approach in the mirror behind the bar,

saw the glint of silver at his belt. The bounty hunter sat down on the stool next to him and waved to catch Polly's attention.

"Whatever he's drinking," the man said, waving casually towards Hil.

Polly brought over the whisky bottle and another glass, filling it and leaving the bottle by Hil before backing off and making it clear that she was watching.

Hil downed his and filled it up again.

"You came in with Sean O'Brien," the man said, picking up his own glass.

"You're mistaking me for someone else," Hil muttered.

"No," he said loudly. "You see, I know Seanie and I saw you leave her ship. So what's the story?"

The man had ruddy cheeks and carefully groomed stubble. And there was a pistol at his waist next to the badge.

Hil let his left hand wrap slowly around the base of the whisky bottle while he took a drink with his right, holding the glass as well as he could with the restriction of the brace. As he put it down, the man's left hand shot out quickly and pinned Hil's wrist to the bar, squeezing hard. Pain shot into his hand and up to his elbow.

Hil raised his head, winking at Polly as she edged sideways towards her alarm button by the till. She rolled her eyes and hit the button anyway.

The bounty hunter stood up, moving closer, leaning his weight into the bar and increasing the pressure on Hil's arm.

Hil let himself relax completely. "You really don't want to make a scene in here," he said quietly, fingers tightening around the bottle to his left.

In the mirror he could see two of Polly's guys moving in, one on either side. Polly was reaching under the counter.

A voice at his shoulder broke the tension and he had to shift his weight slightly to see Sean standing behind him.

"McKenzie," she said over-cheerfully. She put a hand on the guy's back and leaned in to pop a kiss on his cheek, whispering, "What the hell are you doing to my little brother, McKenzie?"

Hil grinned at him and shook the hand off his arm, still smiling as he slipped his arm under the counter to nestle in his lap. Crap, that had hurt.

McKenzie opened his mouth to speak but Sean shushed him with a finger to his lips. She turned to Hil. "Time to go, little bro. Get back to the ship. I'll see you there."

She edged her way in to the bar, putting her body between him and the other bounty hunter. Hil stood up, still grinning. Polly waved off her guys and leaned over to hug him across the bar. "Be careful, babe," she whispered. He kissed her on the cheek and pushed away from his stool.

McKenzie was glowering at him. Hil waved a sloppy salute at him and grinned at Sean. "See you there, sis."

One of Polly's bouncers followed him to the door and stopped him outside. "Look out for yourself, Hil. A lot of people have been here asking about LC," he said quietly. "What the hell are you into?"

"You don't want to know," Hil said. "Look after Polly. Tell her we'll be back once this has blown over."

"Do you know where he is?"

Hil looked into the guy's eyes. Tavner was one of Polly's long time protectors, closer to her than a member of staff should be they reckoned, and he'd known him a long time but there was something in his eyes that made Hil feel more uneasy than he'd ever felt here. This was supposed to be somewhere safe.

He shook his head. "I don't and don't ask me again."

7

The Man stood up and wandered off around the room to light more candles. "Never in our history," he said, "has the Federation of Bounty Hunters dared accept a contract on one of ours. Why now?"

NG twisted around in the chair and watched as the Man shuffled from shelf to shelf, the glow in the room brightening as the scent of oils deepened. The answer was a difficult one to voice. And in thinking it, he'd already replied.

The Man turned and smiled. "My ego is not so great that I can't face our limitations, NG." He returned to his seat behind the desk. "So, there are petty factions of men who consider themselves powerful enough to take on the Thieves' Guild?"

"There always have been," NG said. "It doesn't usually take long for them to realise the error of their ways. But occasionally, circumstances collude to create momentum that it takes time to overcome. We can't be everywhere, all the time. Human occupied space is extensive and we have allies but there will always be individuals that have ideas beyond their abilities. They tend to have great influence over the weak and such mob-mindedness is always going to be dangerous."

"And our efforts to countermand the contract?"

"Legal started to fight it as soon as we became aware it was out there but someone was determined to keep it alive. And with that much money on offer, it grew into a legend of its own. The more effort we put into closing it down, the more infamy it seemed to gather. And ironically, the harder it got to find LC."

He could tell Sean was fuming when she got back to the ship. She threw her coat into a locker and glared at him in the same way Martha always used to when he'd been an ass.

"Are you insane?" she said.

He assumed it was a rhetorical question and yawned.

Sean frowned. "God, they told me you were hard work – I didn't think you'd have a death wish. I thought I told you not to drink."

"Sean," he started and decided he didn't know what to say so he shut up. It would have been rude to visit Polly and not stay for a beer but he didn't expect her to get that.

"The contract out on LC is going to be very lucrative for whoever takes him in," she said. "Do you understand what that means? You look a lot like him. McKenzie was trying to figure out if your hair is naturally that colour or whether you could actually be LC. NG trusted me to take care of you, Hil. I can't do that if you take off and risk running into money-grubbing bastards like McKenzie."

Hil yawned again. He couldn't help it. He was tired and the whisky hadn't mixed well with the painkillers that Medical had given him before they left.

"Well, LC's not been here," he said. "We should go to Redgate next."

Sean clenched and unclenched her fists. He smiled at her.

"My life has gone to shit," he said sweetly. "Polly's been like a mother to us both for a long time. I trust her. And besides no one on board the Alsatia would let me near a drink."

She let out the breath she'd been holding and sat down. "Okay, okay." She watched as Edinburgh started up the engines then turned to him. "Tell me more about LC. I have to figure out where he's going to be. McKenzie being this close, this soon is not good for any of us."

It took twelve hours to fly into Redgate from the jump point. Sean woke him up when they were less than two hours out and threw a ration pack at him.

He'd woken with a headache and swallowed down a handful of painkillers as he tried to make his way through a squeezy pack of soup that was making his throat protest.

Sean watched him struggle and laughed. "Hangover?"

"Headache," he mumbled.

"So you really have no memory of what happened?"

He shook his head, not wanting to go through it all again. She had all the information from the guild – the report would be in there.

"You don't talk much, do you?" she said.

"What do you want me to say? I've never worked with a bounty hunter before."

"Hil, apart from a few early training runs you've never worked with anyone," she said, nodding towards his file as if to re-emphasise there was nothing about him she didn't know.

He frowned and bit down on the belligerent reply that was his first response. He paused and she smiled at him in the same knowing and annoying 'I know what you're thinking' way that Martha always did and it suddenly hit him. She was toying with him in the same way Martha used to. Used to? Still did. Pushing his buttons to get him off his guard, although to be fair, Martha didn't actually have to do a lot to push his buttons.

"Okay, so you know all about me, I get it," he said grudgingly. "Seems a little unfair, don't you think? What about giving me some background on Sean O'Brien? How come you're working with the guild? I thought bounty hunters were one step short of law enforcement. For NG to call you in at all must be pretty exceptional, never mind for him to say he trusts you."

"Fair enough, we're going to be together a while," she said smiling. "I've done some work for NG in the past. As far as being law enforcement, the badge is tolerated both sides of the line, more as a necessary evil than an officially sanctioned service. It has more influence in some systems than in others." She looked away briefly to check some displays then turned back to him and the smile had gone. "And in some, they don't recognise it at all. Tell me why we're going into Redgate."

"We have a contact there."

"What are the chances that LC is there?"

Hil shrugged.

"What kind of contact?" she asked, sounding frustrated. "Hil, work with me here. Right now we have no idea who initiated the contract or why. That puts me in a difficult position and gives us a time frame that could rapidly diminish if more information on LC appears on the grapevine. I know you're feeling like shit, but help me here."

"The guild has a deep cover intelligence agent in there. He…" It was weird talking to an outsider about all this but NG had told him to so what the hell. "He gets information for us. If LC needed help, he'd come here."

"And where is this guy? Last I heard, Redgate wasn't terribly hospitable."

He shrugged again. "They don't know which side of the line they want to be on. It doesn't bother us. We're never exactly legitimate visitors."

"This contact – what's his name?"

"Badger. He works out of the North Shore of the capital."

"Nice area. You have a way in?"

Hil closed his eyes and leaned back. "Course I do."

"We go in together on this one. And we get in and out fast. I don't want to spend more time in there than we need to."

"Don't worry," he said. "This isn't going to be a social visit like Abisko. Badger doesn't like company." And they didn't have a drop box there. If LC was there, he'd be with Badger; if he wasn't, Badger would know if he'd been within fifteen systems of the place. The guy had access to the best material the guild's techies could supply on top of all his own sources. And they had no way of communicating with him, except physically flying in and fighting through a war zone to get to him. Badger listened and watched, he didn't broadcast. That was how he'd managed to stay hidden so long. And he was not going to appreciate Hil trooping in there followed by a host of bounty hunters. "It might be best if I go in alone," he said.

Sean hit him on the arm. "No way. I'm not letting you out of my sight again."

He sat up and looked at her. He didn't have much choice in the matter and he knew it. "We go in silent," he said. "No electronics, no wacky devices for anything. I know what kind of stuff you people use. You have to go nakid, nothing live at all or he'll spook and we'll never find him. And if he's got LC with him, we'll have no chance."

"What about weapons?"

"Everyone carries weapons in Redgate. He won't care about that. But you'll have to lose the badge. And if you take so much as a whistling key fob, he'll know."

It was unsettling to be going in there without Skye. She always gauged the situation and gave him the rundown on troop movements and current politics before he went in anywhere.

"Can you monitor chatter from the surface?" he said.

The ship had been quiet but she piped in then, "Of course we can. What do you need to know?"

"We'll have to wait for a ceasefire. And we need to check who's in control of the area around the airfield. Bring up maps of the city and I'll show you where we're going."

He followed Sean through the terminal, glad he'd put on extra clothes, and uneasy to see so much security.

They had waited for two days while reports of escalating trouble came out of the capital. Redgate had been enjoying a precarious rumbling peace, rumoured to be at the behest of some Wintran corporation that was looking to invest in the city. Hil couldn't see that there was much of a city left to invest in and according to the reports that Edinburgh was picking up, the Earth Empire loyalists had ducked for cover and were trying to build a case to blow off the deal. What a corporation would want with the place, he couldn't fathom. It was lousy timing that they'd arrived just after a band of loyalists had attacked a Wintran envoy and sparked a new round of hostilities.

They'd watched the reports and finally Sean had declared that they couldn't wait any longer. Hil had reluctantly agreed. Usually he had an unlimited time frame in which to operate. Timing was everything and waiting for conditions to be right was a key part of every tab. This time, they had no time and he had to give in and take a chance.

He'd told Sean to wait until the city was on the darkside to start their descent. Edinburgh had flashed up more information than he could digest and he'd had to harry her to condense it all to the facts they needed. Sean had laughed and asked her ship to behave. It felt like he was outnumbered and like he was the butt of a private joke between the two of them.

From the data Edinburgh had gathered, it was cold in the northern hemisphere and the temperature in the capital had dipped well below zero.

"Tell me there's somewhere warm next on your list," Sean had grumbled, pulling on extra layers and cold weather gear.

"LC likes the cold," he'd said. "I'm thinking Winter itself next," and she had looked at him like she thought he was insane, or maybe she'd been thinking that she was insane to be there with him.

The papers she produced cleared them through customs, with only a short delay while the official decided whether the bribe was adequate, and they took a taxi into the city. A light snow was falling and the vehicle was freezing cold despite the proud reassurance of the driver that his was the warmest car in the rank. Smoke was trailing skywards from bombed out buildings and the car passed tanks and armoured soldiers at each street corner.

"Wintran militia," Sean said. "Their gear sucks. See, they haven't even got full body armour."

They were stopped at two roadblocks before they reached the city centre and the massive warehouses bordering the river. It would have been better to get further in but the military presence was getting heavier and they needed to duck out of sight before someone decided to put a tail on them. They had about an hour before curfew, less than that to disappear.

They pulled over and he watched the street while Sean paid the driver. Half the buildings didn't have lights and most of those that did looked like they'd been damaged. It was worse than the last time he was here, but for the moment it was quiet. They walked briskly for about half an hour, the pavement getting increasingly icy, their breath frosting in the chill air. The main street was deserted already and they walked along it, travelling parallel to the river, seeing glimpses of it to the north between buildings. There were more potholes and bomb craters than he remembered and all the shop fronts that weren't boarded up had broken glass in their windows.

They were running out of time and it was tempting to run but twice, armoured vehicles crawled past them, soldiers sitting upright on top tracking them with rifles. There was always tension in the Between, lots of skirmishes and rebel actions but it wasn't often that outright war broke out. Redgate was different and it had always been different. It was the forgotten frontier, the last way point between Earth and the colonies that had been bypassed and abandoned long ago as the jump range of ships increased, except by the people who lived here who had pledged their allegiance to one or the other and who were stubborn enough to keep on fighting. For the guild and Badger it was the perfect place to monitor both sides of the line.

The snow began to fall in heavy billowing flurries and it was a relief when finally the faded sign of the tube station appeared up ahead. Hil led the way down icy steps to the underground system. It was damp and cold. Most of the lights were out and a heavy odour of unwashed bodies and smoke held in the air. A prickly unease nagged at the back of his neck and his eye caught the twitch of a surveillance camera swivelling to focus on them. It had been burnt out but new wires showed that someone had bothered to fix it.

"Something's wrong," he muttered.

He slowed, feeling the chill seep through his joints despite the layers of clothing. He'd wrapped a black thermal bandage around the wrist on his right hand, finger tips to elbow over the brace, and even that wasn't stopping the bone deep ache that was setting in.

Sean was pushing through the abandoned barriers. Something in the air was setting his nerves on edge. "Wait up," he hissed. Faint voices echoed up to them from the stairs ahead. Angry voices. She stopped and looked back at him, pulling the pistol from her leg holster.

Someone was in trouble down there. The underground tunnels were the only way across the river without getting shot at or targeted by mortars, and as much as every sense he had was screaming at him to back up quietly and head for the surface, and leave whoever it was to their fate, he knew they wouldn't make it to the next station before curfew.

There was a shout and sounds of a scuffle.

"We have to go back," he whispered and pulled out a knife, holding it loosely in his left hand.

Sean backed up to stand beside him and they turned.

Shadows moved. Hil took a step back and an arm grabbed him from behind, tight around the throat, as a hand grasped his wrist and twisted.

Sean cursed and struggled against the figure that had caught hold of her, and as their eyes met in silent agreement to break free, another figure emerged from the shadows in front of them, gun up and a shit-eating smirk on his face.

"What do we have here?" the newcomer said. He was wearing body armour but it was a mishmash of pieces strung together over dirty fatigues. He waved the gun casually. "Lose the weapons."

Hil relaxed, shoulders dropping, and he let the knife fall to the floor. His captor frisked him, pulling his coat aside to take the gun from his waist and the other knife from his belt, the hand clamping firmly around his neck again.

"We have business here," Sean said calmly, relinquishing her pistol without argument.

The man smirked. "I know exactly what kind of business people who run around in the snow at curfew are after. Ditch the vest as well."

Sean shrugged out of her coat and let her armoured vest drop to the floor with a clatter. The guy holding her was wearing a massive rain cape, hood up, that still dripped with melting snow. He produced a wand that he waved up and down over her body, careful not to stand in his boss's line of fire. The wand beeped once. He grinned and reached into her trouser pocket to take a small knife that he threw down onto the floor. Once satisfied, he shoved her aside and moved to Hil.

Hil smiled softly and balanced his weight. "I heard the mutants had taken over the sewers this side of the river," he said.

The guy in the cape growled and the hand from behind tightened around his neck.

"Shush now," the guy with the gun muttered, taking a step forward to look into Hil's face.

He thought for a second that he'd got their attention away from Sean but the guy stepped back abruptly, increasing his angle to cover them both. So they weren't all stupid.

The wand beeped only at Hil's wrists as he was checked again. Cape guy pulled up Hil's sleeves, satisfied that the brace on the right and the band on the left were no threat and stepped back with a guttural grunt.

A scream echoed up from the station below them.

The main man smiled and waved his gun again, gesturing towards the barriers. "Shall we go and join the party?"

Hil braced himself as the guy behind took hold of his arm and tried to turn him. As the pressure on his throat eased up, he pushed sideways and dropped his weight, throwing the guy off balance and sending them both tumbling.

He heard Sean yell, gunshots echoing loud in the confined space, then he was rolling free. He managed to get to his knees, pulled the knife out of his boot and threw it in one fluid motion, the projectile leaving his fingers an instant before the guy tackled him and threw him down.

For a moment his vision swam as his head hit the floor and the guy pummelled a fist into his face. Hil tried to curl up and tensed but the weight vanished, Sean leaning in close to hold a hand gently against his cheek.

"Nice throw," she said and pulled him to his feet.

He groaned and looked around. The two bodies of the heavies were still twitching but the bossman was dead, Hil's knife embedded in his throat.

"Come on," Sean said, "we should go."

Hil walked unsteadily to the guy he'd killed. He looked down. It wasn't often that he'd ever need to go to those extremes and it made him queasy.

He knelt and pulled the knife out, wiping it on the guy's sleeve.

He stood and twirled the knife slowly between his fingers, staring at the body. "Shit."

Sean put a hand gently on his shoulder. "Come on. We're going to have to risk the surface. You up for a race?"

8

"Speaking of Legal," the Man said, pausing with his goblet half way to his lips, "did you know they were battling on two fronts?"

NG slowly traced a finger around the rim of his glass, feeling the warmth rising from the wine. "The section chief in Legal hasn't been in post long," he said carefully. "She has ambition and drive. And, as much as her appointment was risky, her background was too intriguing for me to let her pass. We make full use of her connections with the Assassins and she is completely loyal to us. That I do know. Whether she's loyal to me is another matter and that changes on a whim. But yes, I was aware of the internal quarrelling. Rather than a distraction, it served to spur on certain parties within Legal to increase their efforts. That our people still feel the need to prove their abilities will never be detrimental to the guild. It's the model we rely on."

A candle to their left flickered and died, a trail of smoke winding upwards into the embrace of the darkness. It was warm in the room and the loss of that small circle of light seemed to darken the mood.

"We sit," the Man said, "between Earth and Winter with a multitude of other potential allegiances at every turn. The Assassins, the Merchants, the Federation – each vying for power across the line. You say Hilyer took O'Brien to Redgate. That very colony itself illustrates the fierce fighting nature of man that we aim to harness. Look at the voracity with which they protect their own. Imagine the possibilities if they were to be delivered a real enemy to fight."

They ran through the snow, keeping close to the walls and ducking into side streets whenever the roar of a vehicle threatened to close in on them. Lights pierced the whiteout and they heard the whine of sirens behind them. At one point, vehicles screeched to a halt up ahead, skidding through the deepening layer of snow covering the road. Doors slammed and there were yells. Hil grabbed Sean's arm and pulled her into a doorway, fumbling with his lock pick to open the door. They fell through into a dark and musty hallway. Numbered apartment doorways loomed on both sides of a long corridor, half of them open, hanging off hinges. They ran through to the back and broke out into an alley, a whistling wind hitting them hard and whipping at their coats. An aircraft screamed overhead and distant blasts echoed eerily as one side or the other began their nightly bombardment of the city.

They ran on and made their way back to the main street, watching as carefully as they could in the blizzard before breaking out onto the wide boulevard. Hil still wasn't back up to a hundred percent after the crash and breathing got hard fast, an agonising stitch in his side sending sparks of pain through his recently battered ribs every time he slipped on a patch of ice. They stumbled into the tube station, soaked through, bitterly cold and breathing heavily.

Hil doubled over, wheezing.

"Hey, you're not as fit as your file claims, superstar," Sean said, slapping him on the back.

"I told you before, you shouldn't believe everything you read," he muttered.

She laughed and gave him room to recover, stamping her feet and blowing on her hands. He watched her scout around with a flashlight, making sure they were alone. She was a lot like Martha, he thought, but she was more lively, cheerful in a way that Martha could never quite manage around him. He shivered and stood up.

"C'mon," he said. "We need to get across the river."

This station wasn't as badly damaged but it was a mess with shattered glass and rubbish strewn across the tiled floor. He led the way down three flights of stairs that stretched down to the tube tunnels below. The air was stale and damp. The last time he was here, the trains were still running albeit infrequently, dilapidated carriages with haunted faces at each grimy window, keeping the southern part of the city mobile. The blighted area had spread and it looked like the no man's land of the North Shore had stretched its fingers out to embrace the southern banks of the river, both sides fighting over land that wasn't worth the effort. Based on the state of the stations here now, they were going to be lucky if they managed to find an intact tunnel to get across.

They moved quickly and quietly. Twice more he saw cameras, black and twisted boxes that twitched almost imperceptibly as they passed.

"Someone's watching," he said under his breath. "It was always difficult to get to the North Shore, but it looks like someone wants it cut off completely."

Sean had her pistol out, holding it loosely by her thigh. "This might seem obvious to you, but why didn't we just land on the north side of the river and come south into the city?"

He laughed. "You've not been here before, have you?"

"No," she said matter of factly. "Anyone that wants to lose themselves in this shithole are welcome to disappear."

"The Merchants' Guild operates the airfields," he said. "They have some kind of neutral status. Trying to fly in anywhere else on this hemisphere will get you shot down by one side or the other. Entering the city legitimately through the Merchants then disappearing is the only way to get in."

They came out onto a level with tiled archways that were pitted with bullet holes and turned a corner.

"I hope Badger is worth this," Sean said, staring at the collapsed tunnel and mangled train in front of them.

Hil jumped down onto the tracks and shone his flashlight at the seemingly impenetrable mass of the train.

"I can get through there," he said. "You want to stay here?"

"You're kidding me?" she said from the platform. "I've heard all kinds of crap about you guild guys but this I have to see."

It wasn't the hardest thing he'd ever done, not by a long way, but crawling through the twisted metal and trying to make sure Sean had a way through too wasn't easy, especially with one arm throbbing and refusing to take his full weight. He was also cold and wet and hoping like hell that it was worth it. He was starting to get flashes of memory, glimpses of LC that were making him think that they'd been in trouble before he'd ended up crash landing alone on that planet.

The carriages were abandoned and in parts the train had been crushed by the collapse of the tunnel. If the train hadn't been there, there would have been no way for them to get through. As it was, the strength of the frame of the compartments had braced the roof fall in places. He wriggled through a gap, pushing metal bars and seat debris out of the way, and hung upside down in an open space that looked like it was the front control carriage. The window had shattered. Hil manoeuvred himself carefully and braced his feet so that he could take his full weight on his legs, dangling backwards, leaving his left arm free to squeeze out of the gap and bring the flashlight up. Through the train's warped frame, he could see that the tunnel ahead was clear, the faint light of the torch fading into the distance. He swept the beam around, saw the reflection bounce off flood water and caught sight of the smooth motion of the auto-sentry a fraction of a second before it swivelled round and opened fire.

He yelped and curled back up into the gap, scrambling backwards as rounds impacted on the front of the train.

He almost yelled as Sean grabbed his ankle from behind. "Who the hell is that?" she whispered loudly.

"It's a freaking auto-sentry. Someone really doesn't want anyone using these tunnels." He squirmed backwards to find more space and twisted around to check his hand where he'd felt the sting of an impact. It was bleeding but was just a scrape, shrapnel. He hated auto-sentries almost as much as he hated electrobes.

"Here," she said, nudging his leg again.

He reached down and took a small metal cylinder from her. "What's this? We could bring the roof down if we throw a grenade."

"It's a concussion grenade," she said. "Neural flash-bang, no collateral damage."

"A concussion grenade won't take out an auto-sentry, they're designed to withstand hi-explosives."

"No, it won't take it out, but there's a chance that if you drop it close enough it might disrupt its sensors long enough for someone to get to it and disarm it."

"And the someone would be?"

"Well, you're up front, superstar," she said, smiling at him in the torchlight.

"How much of a chance?"

"A small one, but I figure it's our best shot unless the gun's really sophisticated, which it isn't – otherwise it would have hit you with its first two shots. And unless you're packing an EMP generator to fry its circuits, we really don't have much choice."

He looked at the grenade dubiously and began to shimmy back into the gap.

She tugged his ankle. "Make sure you throw it as far as you can – it has a decent radius."

He stretched forward, trying not to lean on his right arm that was aching in the effort to hold the torch loosely in numb fingers. The minigun began spitting rounds at him as soon as he cleared the gap. He flinched, dropped the flashlight and threw the grenade from his left as best he could. There was a splash and a flash and a sharp agony speared through his eyes to the back of his head.

He was vaguely aware of someone climbing over him. He managed to squeeze open one eye and through the pain and rapidly diminishing vision he watched a pair of exceedingly fine hips sway their way casually towards an auto-sentry desperately trying to reboot itself. He tried to move and his world went black.

Someone was holding him and stroking his head. Hil groaned and moved slightly, even that small motion sending sparks flaring behind his eyes.

"Hey there, superstar," someone said from somewhere above him. Sean, he remembered vaguely. He opened one eye to darkness, a faint beam of light illuminating a mangled mass of metal.

"Come on, Hil," she said, ruffling his hair. "Time to move. I've frozen my ass off here waiting for you to stir yourself. How about it?"

He lifted his head and squinted into the darkness. It was quiet.

"It worked," he mumbled.

"Yes, it worked. It doesn't always. Fortunately for us it was junk, scraped together from salvaged parts by the looks of it. What did I say to you about the range?"

She was way too much like Martha.

He lay there and pinched the top of his nose, trying to relieve some of the pressure.

"But hey," she said, "you gave me enough time to push past you and get to it."

Hil stood up unsteadily. Any glass that had been in the window frame had gone. He picked up the torch and picked out the sentry. The barrel of the gun had flopped down listlessly.

"It's disarmed?" he asked and felt a trickle run from his nose. Sean stood up and shone her light in his face. He shied away, closing his eyes instinctively from the glare. She reached a hand up and pressed a cloth against his face.

"Your nose is bleeding," she said. "Don't worry, it'll wear off. The headache will take a while though. And yes, it's disarmed."

She turned the beam onto the window and cleared away the remaining shards of glass from the edge. "After you."

They splashed through the tunnel, moving quickly to warm up. The river was seeping in, flowing down the walls in sheets and, in places, torrents, and it wouldn't be long before the tunnel would be completely flooded and impassable. The cold sapped their stamina and they were both tired before they reached the first North Shore station.

"How far once we get to the surface?" Sean asked as they climbed out onto the platform.

"Another mile or so east. If he hasn't moved."

The station was burnt out but the stairs this side were clear and they jogged up, feeling the air get colder as they approached street level.

"No crazy shit from here on in," Hil said. "Badger micro-monitors a one mile radius around himself. If he spooks, we'll never find him."

"Will he know we're here?"

"Probably been watching us since the train."

"If he's watching, won't he see it's you?" she said. "I thought you knew this guy."

"Yeah, and he'll see I'm with you. Did I forget to mention that Badger doesn't like strangers? I'm hoping he'll be curious enough to give us a chance to explain."

Out in the street, it was quiet, soft white snowflakes drifting down like ash from a fire. They walked swiftly through the dark streets, keeping to the buildings, both with weapons out but they didn't encounter anyone. Not a soul. This side of the river was deserted. It set the back of his neck tingling again.

"It's not always this quiet," he warned as Sean started to drift out into the open. She came back to his side, in the shadows. He'd seen militia raids on this shore before, fast and violent attacks on the pockets of resistance that kept a hold here. It wasn't something he'd want to get caught up in.

They triggered three alarms that he was aware of before they reached Badger's building. He hit the buzzer with numb fingers and the door clicked open.

"Don't be startled by anything that happens," he said and crossed the threshold.

Immediately, a score of bright blue beams scanned him from head to foot. He stood patiently, only stepping forward once they had receded. He beckoned Sean to enter. She holstered her pistol and stepped in. The beams lingered on her longer and he could see that she was starting to get irritated when they shut off abruptly and the door at the far end of the hallway opened.

"Welcome to the Badger's set," he said and led her through a warren of corridors and stairs as doors opened for them and the guild's deepest and most elusive agent let them enter his domain.

9

"I understand she's still working for us."

NG nodded. "She's good. If she wasn't so well known, I'd ask her to come in. As it is, she's probably more useful to us maintaining her position within the Federation. She's registered with Earth but I know she's worked across the line and is as popular on both sides. She has a natural charisma. I've heard it said that some fugitives have given themselves up for a chance to travel with her a while."

"A rare quality."

"It is and one that we've exploited on a number of occasions."

The Man smiled. "We incubate extremes of temperament in our people. That is when man truly reaches his potential. Adversity and necessity – it has been proven time and again throughout the ages. A content man is a being in decline. Survival of the fittest was sorely damaged in the burgeoning of man's technological advancement, in man's striving for soft comforts. It is fortunate that man's own nature tends towards jealousy and insecurities."

NG sat back and the need to defend humanity was too great to resist. "The colonies have known hardship," he said.

"No one in this galaxy has known hardship," the Man said. "That is why we must prepare. That is why, NG. A million threads of destiny must be brought together. I will not be defeated again."

Badger was sitting in the centre of a mass of monitors and banks of equipment tapping away at a board on his lap. He didn't look up as they walked in.

Badger looked thinner and more wild than Hil remembered, dark hair sticking out in all directions, dark glasses perched on the edge of his nose.

"The shower's on the blink," Badger said without looking up, "but it works if you hit it with a wrench. There's food in the kitchen. Grab some beers, will you?"

Hil smiled and steered Sean in the direction of the bathroom. It was surprisingly clean and there were towels heating on a rail.

"Nice," Sean said. "Do you mind if I…?"

"Make yourself at home. There's a drier in the corner and I'm fairly sure Badger doesn't have cameras in here."

He left her to battle with the shower and wandered into the kitchen. He wound up the gauge on the heating panel and shrugged out of his wet coat, leaving it draped over a chair to dry. There was a pot of chilli bubbling on the stove. He grabbed two beers and went back to the main room.

Badger glanced up then. "You won't believe some of the stuff that's going on. What the hell have you been up to?"

Hil edged his way through to the table in the centre of the room and pulled out a chair laden with data boards and electronic gizmos. He piled the gear onto the floor, sat and leaned his arms on the table, resting his head down and letting some of the tension in his shoulders relax. "I was hoping you could tell me."

"It's all kicking off. You're taking a big risk working with her."

Hil looked up. Badger was still working, maps and lists flashing across the boards he had spread in front of him.

"Badger, what have you heard about Mendhel?"

"From the guild? Nothing. They're keeping closed on that. They've sent agents to Earth and requests for information all over the place but they're not giving out anything."

"What about from elsewhere?"

Badger stopped and looked at him. "It was a hit but it wasn't the Assassins. I'm sorry."

Hil bit his lip and popped open the beers. He sipped at his, feeling sore and cold, and let Badger busy away with whatever he was working on. His eyes were starting to close when Badger said, "Here," and pushed a board across the table to him.

"What's this?" Hil said, trying to figure out what was in the blurry image on the screen.

Badger cast his eyes over to the door and leaned forward suddenly to wipe a hand over the screen.

"It's nothing," he said and grabbed the board back.

Hil looked over his shoulder to see Sean standing there watching them. He turned back to Badger and mouthed silently, "Was that LC?"

Badger nodded.

Hil said quietly, "Help me here, Badge. NG told me to work with her."

The agent pushed across another board, this one clearly showing a star chart with Palmio at the centre. He wiped its screen as soon as Hil had glanced at it.

"The contract on LC has been posted by a corporation but they're using a bitch of a system of bypasses and subversives to hide its origin," Badger said. He pushed his glasses up his nose. "I haven't broken it yet but I'll get there. In the meantime, I'll keep watching out for him." He looked up at Sean. "You watch out for yourself, Hil."

"I'm trying to," he muttered.

The heat from the shower took a while to work itself through the cold in his joints but by the time he'd dried off and rescued his clothes from the drier, he was starting to feel more hungry than tired. Beer on an empty stomach had been a bad idea.

There was a bowl of chilli waiting for him, still steaming, and another beer already open. Sean and Badger had finished theirs and Sean had spread a cloth out on the table and was carefully stripping and cleaning her firearms.

Badger looked up as he sat down. "The guy you killed in the subway was a sub-commander in a band of rebels. They're not much more than a gang of thugs, more talk than action, and there are people who'd thank you for it. But even so, you'll need to watch yourself going back."

Hil reached for the beer and Sean pushed the bowl across to him. "That was an impressive throw you pulled off," she said. "How come their wand didn't find the knife?"

"It's not metal."

The chilli was good. He knew he was eating too quickly and it burned the inside of his mouth but he didn't care. Crashing out at Badger's place was a safe and familiar routine that was helping him get his head straight.

Sean was looking at him quizzically. "Neither's mine but those detectors still pick up polycarbons."

Hil reached down and pulled the knife from his boot. He placed it on the table. "It's made of stone."

She picked it up and turned it, feeling along its blade.

"It's one of a unique pair," Badger said. "Mendhel had them made for a competition he set his field-ops. No one knows what kind of stone it is and Mendhel would never tell anyone."

"You have two?" Sean asked, handing it back with some reluctance.

Hil shook his head. "LC has the other one. He was beating me but he can't throw a knife for shit – even if his life depended on it. I caught up to him right at the end and Mendhel decided to split the prize."

Sean picked up her pistol and wiped it with a cloth. "I need to know things like this, Hil. Is there anything else?"

He thought about it while he spooned in another mouthful of chilli. "LC's got a weird memory. He denies it's eidetic but he only needs to see something like a map once and he knows it. If he sees you anywhere twice, he'll remember you. You need to be careful with that or you'll spook him."

"What else?"

Hil smiled. "Poker. Don't ever get caught up in a game of cards with LC, he'll take your eyes out."

She put down the cloth and looked at them both. "Anything else?"

Badger laughed. "You need to know that you're not going to find LC until he decides to let you."

Hil smiled and pushed his bowl away. He flinched as an alarm sounded loud against the gentle hum of machinery. "Crap, what's that?"

Badger leapt up and tapped a data wall behind him, the smooth surface coming to life with flashing lights and streaming data. "West Bridge," he said. "Son of a bitch. You know, one day these people are going to wake up and decide this pile of crap planet isn't worth fighting over."

"What are they fighting over?" Hil asked, not really caring but guessing that Badger was done talking about guild business. It was getting warm and he was starting to feel sleepy. He resisted the urge to rest his head down on the table.

"It's the nature of the Between, Hil. Everyone wants a piece of it. Earth isn't ready to let go and Winter won't back off. The latest," he said, swiping a finger over the wall and creating a blur of images that made Hil wince, "is that some hotshot entrepreneur from Winter is looking to rejuvenate the whole planet as a centre of excellence for bleeding edge technology. Of course, those rumours set Earth off on a defensive 'but we always valued Redgate' campaign. It's laughable."

The alarm went off again, louder.

Sean stood up. "Are we in danger here?"

Badger ignored her and switched the content of the wall to another mix of images.

The alarm faded.

"What's really sad," he said, "is that Earth and Winter are both embarrassed by the situation. Neither want to commit resources to a place they abandoned but there are too many misguided fools here holding onto an age old allegiance with blind loyalty and as soon as one side twitches an ounce of support in this direction, the other jumps up and makes a noise because it can't be seen to be losing face. Or losing ground, that no one wanted in the first place. It's absurd. You should see some of the stuff that's coming through here. It's the only outright war in town and they get to try out all their new shit on the guinea pigs in the field here."

"I just want to find out what happened to Mendhel," Hil said, resting his head down. "And find LC. 'Cause I have a feeling the guild isn't going to let me back out there until I do."

He woke up abruptly from a nightmare, the adrenaline of running through never-ending smoke-filled passageways receding slowly. His neck was stiff and there was a numbing tingle in his arm. He rubbed his eyes and clenched his fist trying to get some feeling back into his fingers. Someone had cleared the bowls away. Sean was standing with Badger arguing quietly about something they were looking at on the wall.

"Hey, sleepy," she said, turning to him as soon as he stirred as if she had some motion sensor tagged to him.

"We need to go," he said, yawning.

"Yes, you do," Badger said. "You've been recalled. The guild wants you back on the Alsatia."

He sat up. "What?"

"They've sent out an alert on you. A Black. They want you back and they're letting everyone know they want you back."

Shit. Hil stood up, feeling all the aches twinge afresh. "What time is it?"

"Two hours past dawn," Sean said. "Badger here is showing me some of his insights into the political situation across the Between and the nature of the influence the corporations are building within a climate of structured innovative anarchy."

Hil stared at Badger. The guy had a shy almost embarrassed look on his face.

"He's not letting me anywhere near any of his really juicy stuff," she said smiling at them both. "But hey, we have all day. We're not going anywhere while it's light, Hil. You might as well go crash out and get some decent sleep."

By the time they got back to the airfield and Edinburgh, Sean had admitted that Badger had told her nothing that could lead her to LC.

"I thought I had him," she'd said grudgingly as they trudged back through the snow.

"I can't believe he showed you anything. Are you always that charming or does it depend on how much you're getting paid?"

She'd feigned hurt and shoved him in the ribs and laughed.

She wasn't that similar to Martha he'd decided; MJ was never that light-hearted.

They took off after an argument with the overly defensive air traffic controllers and jumped back to the Alsatia where Edinburgh docked only long enough for him to disembark.

Sean walked him to the airlock and caught hold of his arm before the ramp opened. "I need to know where I'm going next," she said softly.

Part of him wanted to shrug her off. He shook his head. "I don't know where he is."

"But you know where he might go."

"Sean," he started but didn't know what to say. Going with her to a couple of places was one thing, giving away their favourite haunts and having no say in what she might do there was another.

"There are bounty hunters like McKenzie getting close to people you both know," she said, "and with that much money on offer, guys like Polly's friend might not be so loyal as you'd hope they'd be."

That hit a spot deep inside. He'd seen the look on Tavner's face and he knew she was right.

"Palmio," he said reluctantly. "There's a club there called Joanna's. And the station at Sten's World. I've never been there but LC mentioned it a couple of times. He knows a girl there."

She smiled and squeezed his arm gently. "You guys hang out in the most pleasant of places. What's her name?"

It felt like he was betraying LC as he said, "Olivia. She runs an escort agency."

Sean nodded. "Don't worry, I'll find him and I'll bring him back safely."

Hil walked off Edinburgh into a chilly dockside that was bustling with too many people to be routine. Two of the Man's guards were waiting and they picked him up straight away, without a word, one falling in to either side of him as he walked across the dock. He frowned at them.

"Hil," Skye greeted him immediately, the connection sparking to life with a welcome warmth that relaxed a tension in him that he hadn't realised was there.

"Skye, what's going on? Have they started repairs yet? Are they letting us go out?"

"No, honey, we're not going out." She sounded sad. "NG wants to see you in Ops."

Ops was where they were given the details of their tabs. It was the domain of the handlers. NG didn't interfere with Ops unless something was wrong.

"What's happened, Skye?" he said, panic starting to clutch at his stomach. "Have they found LC?"

"No," she said again, lighter that time and he forced his heart rate to calm. "I don't know what's happening, honey, but NG is in Ops with Mr Quinn and they're waiting for you."

Quinn. Crap. Hil hoisted his bag over his shoulder and edged past the crews of dockworkers throwing boxes of supplies onto loaders headed for the ships. Some of the extraction teams were there supervising and as he caught sight of Martha, he stopped, wanting to talk to her but not here, not surrounded by her freaky extraction buddies, not in the cold public space of the docks with two of the Man's personal guards at his heels. He watched for a moment as she ticked off items on a clipboard and argued with the dockie who threw up his hands and shook his head. She laughed and turned and stopped as she caught Hil's eye. The laugh faded and instead her face broke into a wide grin. And it wasn't a happy to see you kind of grin. She said something to the dockie and left him to it, walking over with long strides and a look in her eyes that he couldn't fathom.

"You are in a world of shit, sunshine," she said.

He bit back the irritation at her tone and the fact that she knew more than he did.

She waved the clipboard at him. "You and LC both."

"Martha, we need to talk," he said quietly, knowing they had a growing audience as more people stopped what they were doing to look over at them.

She shook her head and rested the clipboard against his chest.

"Whatever it was you went after out there, Hil, you'd better hope your ass that LC has it and he comes in." She walked away, and said without looking back, "Quinn wants you in Ops."

She'd cut her hair since the last time he'd seen her and it bobbed as she walked, soft red curls bouncing on her shoulders. Hil bit his lip. Skye was right, she was still pissed at him.

He stood there amid the stares.

"Now, honey," Skye interrupted, "you really need to get your cute ass to Ops. Mr Quinn is getting impatient."

That was the sarcastic Skye he knew and loved. Quinn could wait all he wanted. The man was a toad sucking, lackey of a scum dweller. But keeping NG waiting was never a good idea.

He burst through the door into Ops with a temper building at the thought of having to deal with Quinn. Mendhel had always been a superstar who knew exactly how to wind them up, calm them down and get the best out of all his operatives. It wasn't a coincidence that the top six field-ops had all been Mendhel's. Quinn was an upstart who'd never done anything to impress anyone so why the hell was he being handed Mendhel's people? The Chief should have had better judgement than that.

He was pointed in the direction of a briefing room and he went in, leaving his two newly acquired bodyguards waiting outside.

Quinn was sitting at the head of the table, alert and pretentiously formal. NG was perched nonchalantly on the bench along the side wall, flicking through data boards. Hil pulled out a chair and sat down, looking to NG for a lead in.

Quinn cleared his throat and opened his mouth to speak but NG threw a board down onto the table before he could get a word out.

"Mr Quinn here is your new handler," NG said. "You have a tab."

10

NG eyed the jug and tried to calculate how much wine was left and how many goblets it could fill. His head was starting to feel the effects of the alcohol and a tingling in his cheeks gave away the fact that there was more than mild inebriation at play in here.

"Tell me about Badger," the Man said.

It wasn't often that the Man took an interest in individual guild personnel, but then it wasn't often that individuals in the guild put so much at stake.

"He's one of our best," NG said, swirling the last of his wine around the goblet. "It was worrying when he disappeared. But he's easily spooked and this business has upset the equilibrium surrounding a lot of our people. He sent word that he was going to disappear for a while so I'm hoping that he's either resettling somewhere and will be in touch soon or he's waiting this out before returning to Redgate."

The Man sat and watched, waiting and NG tried to figure out how much to say.

"It was a good place for O'Brien to go," he said finally. "If there was ever anything going on in the Between, Badger knew about it. He scrounged together technology and developed systems that Science would be envious of. With hindsight, I should have pulled him back here but as it was, he was too valuable to us on Redgate. I think he knew where LC was. The danger was if someone else found out that he knew."

Hil felt broadsided. He'd been expecting an introduction to Quinn, not a tab. What had happened to being off the list? And Skye wasn't ready.

NG carried on before he could say anything. "Skye isn't ready, we know. You'll be going out with Genoa. Kase and Martha will be running escort for you. This isn't a usual tab. These aren't usual circumstances."

Hil picked up the board. It had the usual details on it and even looked run of the mill but he wasn't ready. He still couldn't support his weight on his right arm and he hadn't been able to keep up with Sean without having to stop to catch his breath and ease the stitch in his side. How could he go out on a tab? With a ship he didn't know? The panic that rose up was unfamiliar and that panicked him even more. He put down the board before the shaking in his hand became too obvious.

He said, "Am I back on the list? The Chief said I was grounded."

NG jumped down and pulled up a seat at the table.

"This isn't a normal tab," he said again. "This has come from the same source as the one Mendhel was handling from Earth."

"How do you know what, where…?" Shit, he couldn't think straight.

"We know. Don't ask how, it's complicated. But we know. Trust us. We know that it was a professional hit on Mendhel. And we haven't been able to contact his daughter."

NG let that hang in the air. Only a few people in the guild had ever met Anya. Mendhel was fiercely protective of his only daughter. They all were. This was getting worse and worse.

"You left here with LC presumably to meet Mendhel about this tab. He turns up dead, Anya is missing, LC is missing and we're still trying to piece together what that job actually was," NG said. "We want to sort this out. No one messes with the guild. We're not going to let them get away with this. This new tab is definitely from the same source. And they're asking for you, by name."

That in itself was massively suspect. Clients didn't request operatives by name. No one from outside should even have known his name. It was disturbing on a whole new level that made Hil feel queasy beyond his upset stomach and throbbing headache.

"How do they know who I am?"

"Hil, like I said, this isn't an ordinary tab. Whatever happened with Mendhel, these people now want you. We want you to take this tab and then we'll see what happens."

"So I'm bait?" The words popped out before he could decide not to say it out loud.

"Yeah." NG was nothing if not blunt.

"Does the Chief know about this?"

"It's not his decision. We want LC back and we want that package. You know what we have to do, Hil. You know we won't let anything happen to you but the integrity of the guild is everything. You know that, don't you?"

Yes was the only answer, again. He nodded reluctantly. Arguing that he didn't work well with company, or need an escort, wouldn't stick because right now, he didn't know what he needed. Food and more sleep were high on the list.

"Legal are trying to trace whoever is behind this but they're embarrassed at how long it's taking them to get anywhere," NG said, standing up. "And as far as this tab goes, Quinn will handle things from this end."

He looked at them both and walked to the door. "I'll leave you to sort out the details. But be aware that we are still investigating Mendhel's death and we're running an internal investigation. And however this goes down, we won't be losing anyone else."

He left the room and Hil could see him talking to the two guards. He watched, ignoring Quinn, feeling even more like he was under arrest or something. Like he'd done something wrong and it was his fault Mendhel was dead. It might be, for all he knew.

Quinn had stood up and walked around behind him before he realised. Quinn was a big man and one of the few handlers who'd never worked field-ops themselves. He was a pusher, not a doer and that was why it was tough working up any respect for him. Mendhel on the other hand had gone through the wringer as much as the rest of them before some injury had sidelined him. He never went into it, just impressed on all of them to keep their fitness up and take care. He'd always mother-hen'ed them and at the same time goaded them into being better and faster and never to shy away from a risk.

Quinn tended to take easy tabs for his guys, easy successes but low rewards. The big man was out of his depth here.

Hil twisted around out of his chair and squared up to him. He wasn't going to be intimidated by a wanna-be.

Quinn was trying to dominate at full height, leaning forward to tower over him. "Mendhel was a fool to let two numbskulls like you and LC run rings around him," he said. "He deserved what happened to him. It was always coming. He was a naïve fool to think it was him handling you and not the other way around. Things are changing around here. You're mine now."

Hil stood his ground. "What the hell did happen to Mendhel?" he said angrily. "No one will tell me a thing."

"He was stupid and it cost him. Trusting you two maniacs was stupid and he died for it. He broke all the rules to protect you and got himself killed on Earth in that safe house he was foolish enough to think he could keep secure."

Scenes flashed through Hil's mind but there was nothing he could pin down. He'd been at the safe house before with LC and Mendhel many times and a memory that sparked up, of sirens and smog-heavy rain, could have been from any time. Except he flashed on a look on LC's face, LC scared and hurt. LC was never scared. Hil tried to grasp the scene around the brief memory but it was fleeting and gone before he could hold onto it.

"Mendhel was shot in the head," Quinn said. "God knows what guild material he had stashed in that house that was compromised."

"Nothing!" Hil snapped back. "He kept nothing there that had anything to do with the guild. It was a safe house." He took a step forward and Quinn glowered at him. "You wouldn't know, because you never leave here. We go out there and we do our stuff and Mendhel was always there when we needed him."

Only he hadn't been.

Quinn saw his hesitation and pushed him back, pushing out with the flat of his hand against Hil's chest. Bad move. Hil resisted, balancing his weight on his back foot ready to fight back, fists clenching by his side. He heard the door open and Quinn broke eye contact to glance over. Hil tensed, ignoring the door, weighing up his chances against the bigger man and reckoning it would be a breeze to knock him down.

NG came into his line of sight behind Quinn and the moment was gone. Quinn stepped aside and Hil relaxed, feeling the shakes start again.

"Sit down," NG said to Quinn. "Hil, go up to my office and call into Medical on the way for some painkillers, for Christ's sake."

It seemed like an age, waiting outside NG's office, but it gave the meds time to work their way into his system and ease off the aches. He was still wound up from the confrontation with Quinn but pacing up and down had only irritated NG's staff to the point where they threatened to throw him out. So he sat down and bounced his legs up and down against the deck and flexed his wrist trying to decide if he could take the brace off yet. His two bodyguard buddies watched from a distance.

NG turned up eventually and showed him inside.

"Sit down," he said in a softer tone than the one he'd used with Quinn.

Hil sat.

NG sat down and rubbed his eyes wearily. "I need you to work with Quinn, Hil. I know your history with him and I know Quinn's reputation. But he's our best handler right now. Forget anything that has happened previously. Just get out there and let's see where the flak flies." He paused and his dark eyes looked up suddenly, and when NG looked right at you, it was hypnotic.

"We have concerns over Mendhel's recent activities," he said finally. "We still don't know who put out the contract on LC and we don't know yet whether he is on the run from us or from some other party."

Or dead in a ditch.

"And to be honest, Hil, there have been concerns voiced over you and your position in this."

That cut deep and Hil had to stop himself from jumping up and telling NG to go shove it.

"You can't be serious," he said calmly.

"There are inconsistencies."

"In what? No one has explained anything to me yet." Except what Kase and Fliss had thrown at him before he was sent out of the way with Sean.

"Where did you go with LC when you left here?"

Hil straightened up, feeling the atmosphere switch. He didn't feel up to an interrogation but he sure as hell wasn't going to slink away while god knows what was said about him behind these doors.

"I don't know," he said stubbornly.

"You two are the best operatives we've ever had and you've both always outright refused to team up then you suddenly take off together without a word to anyone. What did you do with the boards for the tab you took?"

Data boards were always copied onto the ship's logs then left in storage with Legal. "I don't know," he said again belligerently, knowing fine well that he hadn't done that for some reason. It was just the reason that was eluding him.

NG looked exasperated. "Hil, calm down. There have been concerns voiced. Not in this office. I'm not accusing you of anything. We know you left with LC. There were no boards because the tab didn't originate here. We want to know how that information was passed out to you."

Blank on that.

"Really, I don't know," he said feeling foolish that he'd over-reacted. "I can remember being with LC on Earth, at Mendhel's place. But I don't know if Mend was there or not, or what. It's coming back slowly, in bits."

For all he knew, he might have just signed his death sentence, admitting to that.

"Something was wrong," he said. "LC was upset about something." But beyond that, he couldn't remember a thing except now he had a really unsettled feeling inside that it hadn't been a routine tab, it hadn't been an easy grab and whatever had scrambled his brain had done a really good job of blanking out any memory of a situation that had gone badly wrong.

"We have people trying to find out what happened, Hil. Trust me. Liaise with Quinn, go out there and we'll be watching closely this time."

"Why Genoa?" Hil said, hearing himself sound petulant.

"She's a good ship, Hil, and she volunteered. Just go and do the job. We need to find out who these people are. Come home safe and trust us to sort the rest. I've told Quinn to meet you in Acquisitions. Legal are getting more material together for you. Take your time. Work on it for a couple of days and try not to come to blows."

Hil stood up. "Do you trust LC?" he asked before he turned to go.

"I do," NG said. "But there are parties in the guild who don't. Someone has got through our defences and it's unsettled everyone."

11

The Man poured himself another goblet of the wine and held it in the palm of his hand. "Did we err in allowing Mendhel to stay on Earth?"

It wasn't often that the Man would ever consider the possibility of an error. In his eyes, every contingent was planned and any deviation was simply a new avenue to explore. It didn't bode well if he was thinking they'd made mistakes — that NG had made mistakes. The guild operated like a massive family, all living in each others' pockets, devious and closely guarded, every department working on a thousand different projects that all impinged on each other. It was his job to maintain coherency and avoid dysfunction in that huge living entity of incredibly talented and equally fragile human egos. It wasn't simple and he had made mistakes.

He set his own goblet on the table. The wine had already warmed its way down to his knees and he knew too much more would begin to cloud his judgement. The field operatives and their handlers were at the very centre of the guild and were the most difficult.

"Mendhel's relationship with his brother," NG said carefully, "gave us an in to both sides of the line. Pen Halligan is well established in Wintran territory. Mendhel having insights into Earth itself and Winter, through Pen, has given us an advantage for a long time. Yes, it was risky. But it was a danger that we all cultivated. Somewhere at some point we got it wrong. We just didn't know at the time who it was that had managed to break through."

They spent three days in Ops squabbling over the plan. Quinn had no finesse. Hil always went over every detail himself, by himself, until he could see every possibility. And Quinn wanted to know exactly what he was thinking and why, picking holes in his reasoning. It was driving him mad. Mendhel always gave them free reign. That was where the magic came from – when pure initiative was in play, anything was up for grabs. Hil argued his corner and walked out twice, disappearing into the Maze for a couple of hours each time to work off his frustration.

The tab looked straight forward enough but as well as having to deal with a new ship, he'd have a scary ass, trigger happy, extraction team looking over his shoulder. Acquiring any item from any source was a delicate balance of timing, skill, luck and barefaced bravado. But this tab had too much baggage attached to it for it to be anything other than a massive risk he wasn't sure he was ready to take.

The package to be acquired was in a high security lab on Io Maximus. That was solidly in Earth territory and would be a bitch to get into. Their route in according to Legal was specified in the tab – a pick up point would provide ID and access codes. He hated the sound of it. Hated relying on exterior intel to provide him the means to get in. But it was very specific. They had to fly out to Abacus A, which was a colony in the Between, to make contact. Hil had been there before and the idea of going back made him feel sick. And they were asking specifically for him. He almost baulked there and then and the urge to yell for NG to pull him from the tab was overwhelming. He threw a board across the room instead. Quinn smirked and Hil had to resist another urge to throw something at him.

There were no details on the package itself but the lab was a corporate bio-feedback facility that was heavily guarded. Hil never tried to second guess the focus of a tab and it was driving him mad that Quinn was quibbling about what it could be. Considering the circumstances, Hil didn't expect to make it past the initial encounter. The whole thing was yelling set-up. There probably was no package. There'd be no codes just god knows who waiting for the guild to deliver him up to them.

The plan for Abacus A was simple. Make contact with the go-between, leave with the codes and avoid getting arrested for drunken brawling like last time. The go-between was supposed to make themselves known once they docked. He didn't like the sound of it, didn't like taking advice from Quinn and he didn't like relying on anyone other than Skye.

It sucked.

By the time they'd been through all the data that Legal had provided Hil was tired, hungry and had reached the point where he simply phased Quinn out of the equation.

"You're not listening to me," Quinn said.

Hil closed one eye and squinted at the big man through the other. He threw the board he was holding onto the table and stood up. "I'm done," he said and walked out.

Something had been niggling at the back of his mind since he'd sat at that table with the section chiefs, since Martha and Kase had pulled his ass from wherever it was that he'd been. And that was it. He didn't know where he'd been. There was a whole chunk of time missing from his memory and during that time someone had screwed with his mind. He'd been so messed up he hadn't even thought to question it before now.

He walked past the Man's two elite bodyguards, mumbled something about food and needing a break and led them into the mess. It was busy and as they joined the queue, Hil glared around the room, looking for a certain redhead, daring anyone to make eye contact.

"Skye, where's Martha?" he thought, not seeing her there. He spotted Sorensen at the same time the new number one field-op saw him and rose to his feet. Sorensen was the last person he wanted to speak to and Hil turned, muttered that he needed to go clean up, and was half way to the washroom before Sorensen intercepted him and caught hold of his arm. The two guards were right behind and they stepped in close, one with a restraining hand on the guy's shoulder.

Sorensen ignored them. "What the hell happened to Mendhel?" he hissed.

Hil shook free. Skye spoke softly when she sent, "She's in Legal."

People were looking their way. Hil looked at Sorensen and saw a couple of other field-ops standing up. He made a snap judgement and stepped forward, grabbing hold of Sorensen's shirt and pulling him close.

"Whatever you've heard, LC hasn't betrayed anyone," he said quietly.

Sorensen tried to pull away, anger showing in his face. It wasn't surprising. All of Mend's field-ops had been dedicated to the man, above and beyond. Micah Sorensen was one of them and he was due an explanation. Except Hil couldn't give him one.

The two guards took hold of Hil's arms at the elbow, one on either side. "Break it up," one of them said.

"Trust me," Hil said to Sorensen and he could see the anger turn to hurt and confusion. He didn't know what else to say.

Sorensen narrowed his eyes and opened his mouth to speak but one of the guards pushed him aside. Hil let go as they pulled him away and he walked out with them, seeing Fliss stand up on a table off to one side and mouth "Don't worry," to him. He smiled faintly and let them escort him out.

He wasn't going to have much say in anything, that was clear. And there was no way they'd let him walk up to Legal so Martha was going to have to wait.

In the corridor, they backed off and let him walk, stepping in close again as another field-op approached them.

"Hey Hil," she said, eyeing up the guards and shrugging, "I just got in from Redgate. Badger said you'd left this at his place a coupla days ago. He asked me to give it to you." And she held out a necklace, a knotted lace threaded with an elaborately engraved shark tooth.

He took it without hesitation. "Right, I knew I'd left it somewhere. Thanks."

"Badger was really worried you'd forgotten it. You know what he's like and man, I've never seen him so agitated. You don't wanna go out without your good luck charm, huh?"

She smiled and wandered off. He had no idea what the hell it was as he tucked it in a pocket and walked on, shadowed by the two bodyguards who were seeming more and more to be his own personal jailors.

He went down to the dock to see Skye before he had to leave with Genoa. They could talk from wherever he was on the Alsatia but it wasn't the same as being close up. She was upset, upset that he was going without her, upset that he was going back to Abacus and he'd better mind his butt and his attitude and stay invisible this time, upset that he was going with Genoa and upset that her own sorry ass wasn't ready. The Chief had given the go-ahead for the repairs at last but they'd only just started and anyway, they'd need to visit one of her favourite yards to get everything back in shape.

He sat on the bridge and kicked his feet while she let off steam. Then he pulled the necklace from his pocket and held it up. She stopped mid flow.

"What is that, honey?"

He didn't need to ask if they were secure, she always talked on a tight link when he was onboard. No one could eavesdrop.

"I don't know," he sent, "but I need you to find out."

"Hold it still."

It didn't take her long, then she whispered, "Where did you get that? Hil, what's going on?"

He shook his head and caught the shark tooth up in his hand, wrapping the black thread around his fingers. "What is it?"

He felt a subtle change in the atmosphere as she kicked in shielding. If anyone was watching them, trying to listen, they'd be a black spot in the centre of the repair dock. Suspicious as hell. Like it could get any worse.

"There's something etched into the pattern," she sent.

"What?" He squinted at it and saw nothing but swirling lines.

"Oh Hil, what is this about?"

"Skye," he sent, exasperated. "What is it?"

She flashed up a magnified scan of the tooth, spinning it round and zooming in until he saw the wording. Scrawled in tiny letters, etched in Badger's meticulous handwriting along a swirl, was a warning – 'guild compromised, trust no one'. It wasn't signed. Hil felt sick to his stomach. If it was a joke, it was a bad one. And if it had come from anywhere else at any other time, he would have laughed it off. But now, after everything that had happened and with his memory still screwed so badly he couldn't even remember where he'd been, it was too much.

He threw the necklace into a locker. Mendhel was dead, LC missing and someone was calling for him by name. What the hell choice did he have but to play along?

One thing that Hil was great at was compartmentalising. When his head was straight. It was frustrating as hell to have a whirlwind of crap whistling around his mind. He paused at the ramp and let his shoulders drop, felt the tension ease, let the pain bundle up and wisp away. He hadn't worked with Genoa before but he wasn't going to let that get to him.

He closed his eyes and let the dark embrace him, felt it warm and comfort him through to the bone. Going out on a tab was an awesome mix of apprehensive yearning for the thrill of the test and a quiet inner calm that came only from knowing you could handle whatever the tab threw at you. Invincible. The cockiness that Martha hated so much came later when you had that package bagged and tucked up under your arm running for the touchline. This was no different to any other tab he'd ever run. Hil took a deep breath and shunted back an edge of panic that this was not just another tab, that his world had gone to shit and his brain was scrambled. He almost wished he could forget what he'd seen etched on that swirl. It changed everything and suddenly the Alsatia seemed a dangerous place to be. He let calm not panic flow over him and stepped onto the ramp.

The connection with Genoa initiated as soon as he entered the ship. Skye was gone again but this time he knew where she was, knew she was in good hands and he let her go willingly. Genoa was quiet while he stowed his bags and headed to the bridge. She was a much bigger ship than Skye, bigger and slower but capable of longer jump distances. He had extraction teams going out with him and whatever happened he would be pulled in. Not an ordinary tab in the slightest but hey, this was where he was so he settled in for the ride.

He sat down and strapped in, refusing to acknowledge the faint tinge of irritation at the unfamiliar layout of the console and the too small space to stretch his legs.

Genoa was still silent. He didn't know how to start up a conversation so he sat and stifled a yawn. It was tempting to nap so why not?

She woke him with a klaxon.

"Undocking in three, two, one."

The ship disengaged from dock with a reverberating shudder. She accelerated too fast away from the cruiser and had to adjust her trajectory to wait for the others.

"Genoa," he said finally.

"Zachary," she replied curtly.

No one called him that. Not since he'd run away from the latest in a long line of foster homes for the last time at the age of eleven.

He felt awkward and didn't know what else to say. He'd never worked with any ship other than Skye. She knew him inside out and when he worked she was there with him every step of the way. Sitting here with Genoa made him feel like he was a passenger. Passive and helpless.

He ignored the chatter as Martha called in to discuss numbers with Genoa. He didn't care how they got there, didn't much care what they did when they arrived. He was being fed to the wolves but he was away from the guild and as soon as he could meet up with LC, he'd catch up on what was what then. There was a dropbox on Abacus. Whatever had happened to LC, if he was okay there was a chance he would have left a message in one of the boxes. Hil just had to get to it.

12

The Man leaned back in his chair. "Your decision to use Genoa for that particular assignment was regarded in many circles as foolhardy, NG. Why is that?"

He'd been dreading the topic of Genoa, inevitable as it was.

"You have to understand the delicate relationships that can develop between our people and the AIs they work with," he said. "Hil especially is close to his ship. Skye is his partner. They've worked together for over ten years. It's hard to recruit AIs and we don't have many. They demand high pay and deservedly so. Not all our operatives team up with an AI. Anderton never has. And we have some AIs, like Genoa, that prefer to work freelance wherever they're needed." He paused and considered his next statement carefully. "The issue of AI personality and allegiance is tricky. You talk of man but we mustn't underestimate the AIs. They have a place in society now that is still becoming established, even as a minority. They have rights and they have emotions that can be as raw as any human."

The Man sat quietly and NG stopped abruptly and emptied his mind of any thoughts except this room, right there and then. A whisper of a breeze set the candle flames dancing and a hint of sweet incense swirled across the desk.

"What happened?" the Man said softly, well aware that this was an area NG didn't want to address.

"I can't read the mind of an AI," he said, uncomfortable in having to admit it. "I had no idea."

It just took one jump to get to Abacus A. That was unsettling in itself. The Alsatia spent time on both sides of the line and wandered, a self-sufficient colony, that had been deep in Earth controlled space last he knew. The massive cruiser must have shifted some to get them that close to the Between. And the fact that it had positioned itself firmly in the Between, rather than letting them jump there themselves, made him uneasy. Field-ops didn't often have the entire guild baby-sit them through a tab.

Genoa went in first and docked, Martha and Kase due to follow after a discrete enough gap. Hil didn't wait for Genoa to give him the go ahead to leave and she didn't offer him any words of encouragement or even reassurance that she had his back. As a guild support vessel, she was equipped to track him, hide his signature, open doors and get clearances for him. He took all that for granted and he assumed nothing. She'd screw up or she wouldn't. He didn't intend to rely on her.

The dock was busy. Abacus was a hive of machine shops and repair docks. Hil stalked through the security channels onto the station, glaring daggers at anyone who so much as looked as if they were going to stop him or question his clearance. The IDs issued by the guild were pure gold at places like this. Even the military shouldn't look at him twice. Of course, that only worked if you kept your nose clean and respected the local customs. Last time hadn't been so clear cut and a spell in the detention centre was not something he wanted to repeat.

He was kept waiting in line at entry control and it was cold enough that he started to regret not putting on another layer. But Genoa had cleared the way through for him and it didn't take long to get to the lift and up a level to the recreation deck where the temperature rose to an almost unbearable heat with too many bodies enjoying themselves for the aircon to handle. It was shift change and the grimy corridors were packed. Hil slipped through easily. He broke out onto the main stretch and wandered nonchalantly into the first bar, not the one they'd agreed to meet in, an unmistakable sense that someone was following him tingling at the back of his neck. Crap, he hadn't expected to be picked up this quickly. He edged his way through the crowd and made for a gap at the bar.

"You have company," Genoa said quietly in his ear.

He didn't reply. He was watching the mirror behind the bar and planning a route out. The guy next to him bumped his arm and spilled beer. Someone nudged into his back and a woman leaned across in front of him, a stench of perfume mixing with the bitter tang of alcohol. He saw his way out and moved quickly, weaving through the throng of bodies and ducking out of a staff-only door in the back. Someone yelled after him but before they could get to him, he was away and up through a vent in the dingy ceiling. Old stations like this were playgrounds for field-ops. The basic beam and vent constructions were riddled with access ways, ladders, tangled networks of pipes and walkways covered with thin veneers for bulkheads covering pockets of comfortable living space and utilitarian working places.

Hil took his time working his way around and up to the next level, flexing his wrist, glad that he'd left the brace on. He got his bearings, made his decision and without a word closed off the connection to Genoa.

Whatever had happened, he couldn't trust anyone out here. Delivering himself up to whoever was not an option. Someone had killed Mendhel and Hil knew without doubt that it hadn't been LC. His memory from that cold dark night on Earth was still patchy. They'd flown in together, LC with him and Skye. And they'd met Mendhel but something had been very wrong. He flashed suddenly on LC stumbling to the floor and his stomach turned to ice at the thought. It hadn't been Earth. It had been someplace else, a lab or a research station. Cold corridors teeming with electrobes and a fight to get back to Skye. Back on Earth, before or after he couldn't tell, and Mendhel saying they'd been set up and he had no choice. He was sorry but he had no choice and LC saying they'd do it, of course they'd do it.

Oh crap, what the hell had they gotten into? Hil sat on a meshmetal walkway and let his legs dangle. Sounds from a club on the deck below drifted up, chatter and the thump of bass. He leaned his left arm on a pipe that was warm and comforting, right arm hurting and nestled in his lap, and settled his head down, closing his eyes. He couldn't pull it together, couldn't get it in the right order or time frame. The tick above his eye started up again. Mendhel had been alive when they left Earth, he was sure of that. And LC? Hil could vaguely remember an explosion but that might have been the crash. Heat and a jarring hurt. No, it was an explosion then the crash after that. He'd been with LC when... when what? But however much he racked his memory, he couldn't pull up any names or details.

He had two choices the way he figured it. He could either go down there and meet the contact and leave his fate to the guild or he could climb up to the drop box and see if LC had managed to make it this far. Otherwise there was Aston and Pen – that would be the next step, and one that he hadn't been able to bring himself to mention to Sean. As much as he wanted to run back to the safety of the guild, as much as it hurt to think it, he didn't know how safe that was any more and he had to find LC.

The box was in an impossible to reach location off a ventilation shaft above the military base on the other side of the station.

Getting through to that side of the station was tricky because of the military barriers and seals in place but it wasn't anywhere he hadn't been before. The final obstacle was the vertical climb up a wire cable that was a magnitude more difficult than he remembered. Hil paused half way, out of breath, sore and hurting. He wrapped his foot around the cable so he could stop and rest. His wrist was throbbing. The walls of the shaft were too far away to reach and there was nowhere he could go but up or down. The air here was thin and cold with a metallic taste to it but nothing set off the band on his wrist tingling in warning. He could hear the whine and whirr of machinery from the base.

Gritting his teeth he set off again and hauled himself up, catching hold of the cross beam with relief when he reached it. He climbed up and crawled across the beam to the inset cubby hole by a thick twist of cables. With trembling fingers he pulled out his lock pick and made a botch job of opening the tiny metal box nestled in there. The mechanism was one of LC's favourites and it was a bitch to crack at the best of times. With the fingers on one hand swelling beyond the restriction of the brace on his wrist and the other feeling cold and numb, the freaking lock refused to give until finally he heard that wonderful click and felt it release.

The box was empty. No note, no data sticks, no message. If LC was okay, he hadn't been here. Hil sat back, deflated. Crap.

Getting back took twice as long. He fell twice, the second time from a narrow ledge to tumble down a height and slam onto the deck leaving him stunned and shaken. Best in the guild, my arse, he thought.

He sat. Reconnecting to the ship was tempting but he couldn't face Genoa's silence. Kase and Martha would be wondering where he was. And if NG could see him now, he wasn't exactly being an honest and open guild operative. NG would be within all rights to consider him rogue. He had no leads and apart from NG, he didn't know who he could trust without finding LC himself. Anya missing could mean she was with LC. They'd always had a thing going on between them that they'd denied enthusiastically and Mendhel had all but forbidden but they could have gotten together. In which case, he could go back to the guild and leave them to it. They'd be fine. They could be on a beach together somewhere. But a niggling thought that was attached to a memory he couldn't pin down gave him a bad feeling that Anya had already been missing when they met with Mendhel. And when he left LC, cocky invincible LC was in a bad way. He had to find them both. Before McKenzie or any other of Sean's bounty hunting buddies.

He made his way back to the recreation level and nonchalantly slipped into a rest room. Holding his hand and wrist under cold water brought on shivers but numbed the swollen joint somewhat. It was time to face it. He took a deep breath and renewed the connection to Genoa.

She didn't jump straight into a friendly conversation the way Skye would have but she'd alerted Kase and Martha because the pair of them were waiting when he emerged from the bathroom into the bar. They ignored him when he looked their way so he walked past and headed for an empty table. He didn't make it as two beefy guys in black suits, who looked like they could have been clones of each other, sidelined him and took up an arm each. He tried to shake them off but that wasn't going to happen easily and as he glanced back over his shoulder, another three were blocking any attempt Martha and Kase could have made to get to him. Okay, this wasn't part of the plan but it wasn't entirely unexpected.

Hil looked around for anyone else from the guild but couldn't see any familiar faces. They'd be there and they'd make sure he got back to the guild in one piece, taking care of whoever it was along the way. That was how the guild worked. No one messed with the guild.

"Hey, no one messes with us, y'know?" he muttered and one of the corporate gorillas grasping his left arm twisted and squeezed just enough for him to know that conversation wasn't going to cut it.

They took him through a back door and up some stairs.

"Genoa, you getting this?" he sent through the connection, more desperation creeping into his intonation than he intended.

"We're right with you, Zachary," she sent back coldly. "Don't worry your pretty little head."

As much as he knew that the teams from the guild were some of the best it was possible to work with and that NG had given explicit instructions that his safety was priority, it was hard not to panic. His expertise, same as all the field operatives, was to get in quietly, get out unnoticed and interact with no one, no exceptions. Dealing with people was something left to Legal or Media. He felt exposed and vulnerable and ego aside, it was unsettling to think that he couldn't just up and flit away.

They walked him to a lift and before the doors opened, a heavy hand slapped against his neck right where his implant was. He felt a numb quiet encapsulate his mind. Hil didn't see any other people around and couldn't hear Genoa as much as he yelled at her to respond. She couldn't possibly be such a bitch as to ignore him now. He was shielded somehow.

So he was alone.

He tried to reach a hand up to his neck but they were holding tight.

"That's not freaking legal," he protested, realising as he said it what a stupid thing it was to say.

They didn't respond. The lift doors opened. It occurred to him that he might have been acquired by station security again but these guys weren't wearing uniforms. Whoever Mendhel had been dealing with, they'd sent in a tab to the guild and had asked for him personally. Well, they had him. This wasn't about codes. This was about that last tab and whatever the hell had gone wrong, it was still happening and he'd just walked himself straight back into it.

Alone in the lift, they pulled his arms behind his back and clasped restraints on each wrist, pulling tight.

"C'mon guys, is that necessary?"

There was still no response. He slouched his shoulders and waited until they were done then set about testing the cuffs. From what he could feel, they were the same type LC had shown him how to bust out of one time they were messing about in the Maze. LC could break free in seconds – Hil had never beaten him and given the state of his wrist he wasn't sure he could manage it at all but it was worth a try.

The lift dropped down and Hil started to get a bad feeling as it dropped and dropped and about the only place they could be going was the docks. Leaving the station was definitely not in any plan. The doors opened and Hil braced himself. The guild would be watching the docks, they wouldn't just let these guys walk him into a ship and leave.

The lift deposited them in a private area manned by similar looking corporate security. He bided his time as he was marched through gates and check posts and by the time they reached a walkway adjacent to the public terminal, he still hadn't seen any guild. There was no one watching his back. He couldn't believe there was no one watching his back. It was time to look after himself. He slowed the adrenaline, subtly manoeuvred his left arm and dislocated his thumb with a snap, twisting his hand out of the restraint, shouldering one guy aside and slamming his left fist back-handed, into the other. They were good but he was fast. He bolted for the main concourse and weaved through a thinning crowd, desperately looking for a friendly face. If any guild teams were there, he couldn't see them. So much for covering all bases. Quinn and all his micro-managing was just as crap as he knew it would be.

Hil dropped and rolled under a barrier, staggering up from one knee with less finesse than he would've liked. Genoa was berthed in twenty seven. From the signs, he was up in the fifties and doubling back to the hub would be the fastest way round but not necessarily the smartest. He stayed close to the walls and looked for an access hatch to duck into. The two he bumped up against were locked and would take too long to open. He ran on and looked for an opening to ditch out of this area.

There were more people around as he moved down towards the docks so he blended in and walked alternately with running and avoided any security.

He was beginning to think he could make it when there was a yell and a wall of guards appeared up ahead. He wheeled around. The two corporate guys were behind him, pushing past people. Hil broke right and barged his way through a door, shouldering it open and bursting through into a narrow corridor. If he could find a hole to hide in, he could lose them. Otherwise he was wide open here.

The door crashed open behind him and something hit him solidly in the back between his shoulder blades. With a yelp, his knees buckled and Hil hit the floor, out cold.

13

"I hesitate to ask but how wise was it to send Hilyer back out on his own?"

NG watched as the Man refilled the goblet and pushed it across the desk towards him.

"With hindsight," he said, reluctantly taking the cup and taking another sip, "we could have acted differently. He had a serious concussion and other injuries. We train our people well and we push them hard. You know that. Hilyer is one of our best and he's stubborn – he pushes himself more than anyone could ask. I made the decision that we couldn't afford to give him time to recover. And don't forget, at the time we didn't know what the item in question was, or who had initiated its acquisition." He didn't want to sound too defensive. The Man always leapt on any weakness. "No one anticipated its importance. It was only later that Science realised the meaning of the rumours that Media were bringing in." And there was the problem. He'd missed it. The entire guild had missed it until it threw itself upon them like a curse and inflicted more damage than they'd experienced in over three generations.

"You should have known," the Man said sombrely and NG felt the nudge inside his mind. It was tender but deeply disturbing and as physical as if the Man had reached out and pushed him. He resisted the urge to push back and retreated. He should have known. It was undeniable.

"I know," he said, the words unnecessary but out there in the open anyway.

The Man held a hand over his goblet, fingers twirling to disturb the steam, sending it swirling up in spirals. "Every action has repercussions. Every inaction has the potential to precipitate our downfall. We need to extend our influence so that this will not happen so easily in future."

"To be fair," NG said, downing more wine in one go than he intended, "it would have been nigh on impossible to predict the alignment of factors that coincided to lead to this outcome. In fact, as random occurrences go, this could turn out to be one of our best."

He came to as they hauled him back towards the dock. The freaking sons of bitches had shot him with an FTH round and with neurons firing randomly and uncontrollably, there was nothing he could do to resist.

The painful tingling didn't wear off until they were on board a drop ship headed for the planet. It was a corporate transport, plush interiors and soft padded seats but the drop was still as vicious as any military or cargo vessel. The two apes had shoved him onboard and retied his hands, fastening the restraints to the arms of the chair he was pushed into. It wasn't like he could go anywhere but they weren't taking any risks now. He smirked at them and they sat back glowering at him with their guns held firmly in their laps.

Hil relaxed his breathing and tried to shake feeling back into his limbs. They'd resented the fact they'd been stupid enough to let him get loose and had made him pay for his efforts on their way to the ship and he couldn't count the number of bruises he had now. Nowhere along the way had he seen any guild faces at all. So much for all their protection. Badger had said trust no one but to distrust the whole guild was impossible, however paranoid he wanted to be. The guild looked after their own and he'd done nothing to change that, not really, as far as he knew. Doubt crept in as he sat there feeling miserable and angry. He'd known this tab would be a trap. But Quinn had refused to listen and if anything, they'd agreed that it was the only way for them to find out who the hell could be asking for him by name and what they might have to do with Mendhel. But Hil still had no idea what was going on and now it looked like even the guild had abandoned him.

They hit the atmosphere with a jolt and glided down to the surface. It was higher gravity than he was used to and he made no effort to move once they'd come to a stop. It was raining heavily, grey and oppressive and the rain hit the craft with the force of hailstones. They taxied and eventually stopped. He watched as they hooked up with a tunnel leading directly indoors, nothing too good for these corporate types.

His new friends weren't gentle as they freed his arms and pulled him up. Hil felt like he'd put on pounds. He hated high gravity – it made him feel sluggish. The two guys still didn't say a word.

Hil couldn't resist. He looked from one to the other. "I know cloning's come a long way but do you guys share just the one brain cell?"

He got a slap to the back of his head and the muzzle of a gun nudged firmly into his ribs. He sucked in a breath. The Fast Takedown round had been bad enough from a distance so he shut up. The 'H' was supposed to stand for "Humanitarian" but it was doubtful if whoever had named it had ever been on the receiving end. He'd always thought the "Fuck That Hurts" definition was more apt.

Ways to escape were limited. His arms were pulled back behind his back and the gun stayed in place as he was pushed out of the ship into the adjoining tunnel. Thinking back to all the crap predicaments he could remember, this rated as bad, one of the worst. Not counting whatever had happened with LC, probably. So not the worst then and he took comfort from the thought that whatever had happened then, he'd got out of it. Which meant he could get out of this. Somehow.

He watched closely as they marched him down more corridors but there were no signs, logos or corporate branding anywhere. There was nothing to suggest where he was or which corporation it was. The place was sterile – white walls and grey floors, numbered doors. It was kind of chilly in an air conditioned way and not so oppressive suggesting they had gravity control.

He was taken into what looked like a meeting room that was empty except for a round table and eight chairs. They took off the cuffs, took his coat and frisked him for weapons. Sloppy procedures, they should have done that as soon as they'd taken him. Civilian then, not military or law enforcement and not used to dealing with situations like this. He tried putting it into context with what he knew. These guys were probably some suit's personal bodyguards, more used to standing around looking menacing and as much for show as for any real security work. These guys were a fashion accessory. Ex-military or law enforcement would have taken no chances but those guys who were on the real front line of personal protection worked for another guild not entirely unlike his own and clowns like these would never have made the grade. Still, he thought as he considered his bruises, they were pretty effective as hired muscle. It made him wonder again just who he was dealing with. People with money. Lots of money, but not much experience of handling people like him. The kind of people who thought money solved everything and paid others to do their dirty work, like hiring the guild.

He watched them as they worked. The two clowns were getting a buzz out of all this. They were way out of their depth and didn't even realise it. They missed the tiny knife hidden in his boot again, making him wonder if these were the same guys that had nabbed him after the crash, and they left the band on his left wrist. Amateurs. Once done, they manoeuvred him roughly into one of the chairs and left.

As soon as he was alone, Hil jumped up and tried the door, locked, and scrounged around looking for anything that could be a way out. The walls were smooth, the ceiling was one solid expanse and there was no keyhole or locking mechanism in the door. It was the most pleasant, secure jail he'd ever been held in. He pulled off the dampening patch attached to his neck and yelled out to Genoa but she was either too far away, still on the station probably, or the room was shielded.

There was no point expending energy when it was clear he was stuck here so he sat down and rested his head down on folded arms on the table and snoozed.

They woke him up setting down a tray of sandwiches and drinks. He looked suspiciously at the woman who sat down opposite him. She was tall and thin and looked like she shopped on Earth, expensive tailoring that the colonies had never mastered. He stared at the tray. If they wanted to drug him, they could have just stuck a needle in his arm.

The woman pushed the tray towards him. "Go ahead," she said, accent not quite something he could place. "It's real coffee."

He took a cup and slowly tasted it. Real coffee was unheard of this far from Earth. Mendhel had a liking for coffee. There was always a fresh pot on the go at the safe house. Hil put the cup down.

"Your pet gorillas shoot me and drag me off the station and now you give me coffee?" he said. "Why the charade of the tab? What do you want with me?"

He pushed the tray back across the table. She leaned across and not so gently touched his arm right on the spot where the brace wasn't exactly doing its job. It was hard not to wince.

"Do you need a medic?"

"I need you to let me go, give me a lift back to the station and freaking leave me alone."

She picked up her own cup of coffee, looked up towards the door and nodded to a guy in a suit standing there. He walked over and smirked at Hil, piercing grey eyes cold and smug, and for a second there was something about him that was irritatingly familiar.

The man threw a data board onto the table and sat down next to Hil. The board was playing some kind of recording, poor quality and no sound but the image was clear enough. Hil stood up and grabbed it, stomach going cold at what he could see. He looked up at the woman who was smiling at him over her coffee cup, wisps of steam swirling up in front of her face. She took a sip and watched him as he watched the scene as it replayed over and over. He glanced back at the door. The clones watching from the doorway both took a step into the room. He put the board back on the table, slow deliberate movements.

"Is she okay?" he demanded, voice quiet and controlled.

"Sit down, Zach."

"Is she okay?

"She's fine. Now sit down or the twins over there are going to get jumpy."

He sat down.

She caressed a finger across the screen of the data board and this time it replayed with sound. He stared at the image of Anya as she read out a statement, stumbling over the words and looking scared and alone. The recording was scratchy and broken in places but he got the gist of it. "This is a message for LC Anderton and Zach Hilyer. Please help me. Do what these people ask and they will let me go. I am unharmed. Please help me. This is a message for..."

It repeated, Anya looking scared each time.

Hil tried to remember the last time they were all together and safe but it was too far gone to come to mind. Mendhel hadn't betrayed the guild willingly. He'd really had no choice. And how the hell had these people found out about Anya and Mendhel anyway? It must have been someone in the guild itself. It was chilling to think someone could have sold them out. Suddenly Badger's message had a whole lot more gravity than he'd imagined.

"You don't know who you're messing with," he said quietly.

"You took a job. Finish it."

Hil tapped the side of his head in frustration. "That's the problem. I don't remember the job. I don't remember any details of the tab at all. I've had freaking concussion from you people shooting down my ship and screwing with my head. I don't remember a thing." He was lying, it was starting to come back to him but just in pieces.

"We didn't shoot you down, Zachary," she said. "You must have had a mishap on the way back to us. You were coming back to us, Zach, and you didn't have the package."

"Why kill Mendhel?" he said. "What the hell is this about?"

The woman smiled and looked across at her colleague as if fielding a question in a civilised meeting. His smirk deepened but no warmth reached those grey eyes. There was something about him that was chilling. Hil looked from one to the other, anger building.

"You really don't need to know what this is about," the man said finally. "And Mendhel? No loose ends. He was an easy kill, nothing at all like his reputation would have suggested. You people are over-rated. I was disappointed how easy he was. I put a gun to his head and he did nothing to stop me. The notorious Mendhel Halligan of the infamous Thieves' Guild and he rolled over and died like a stray dog." He leaned forward. "But not before he gave us everything we needed to know about you and Mr Anderton, Zach. Everything."

It was malicious taunting and there was no way it was true. Mendhel would never have given them up. Hil switched his focus to the woman and refused to rise to the guy. He was aware that the two thugs had moved in behind him, and felt them almost willing him to make a move, to provoke another beating. He sat calmly, pinning the anger deep inside and saving it. They'd pay.

The woman said, "And we want the job finished."

"You've got to be kidding me."

She smiled and shook her head. "Do you know the current bounty on your head, Zach? Twenty six million each for you and Mr Anderton. And that's just the open market. You don't even want to know what the Assassins' Guild has been offered for you. Work with us and we can pull strings to call all that off. Get the package and you get Anya back."

Hil stared at her. There was no way NG would've let him out if he'd known there was a contract out there. He thought of McKenzie standing there looking him up and down in Polly's bar. There was no way there could've been a price on him then. Sean would've known.

"I need information and all my stuff back," he said.

Anything to get away from here. If LC knew Anya was being held against her will, he'd be going after her. And LC had the package, somehow he had a feeling deep down that LC had the package.

They gave him coordinates for the drop and told him where to take the package once he had it. Then Anya would be taken to Earth and released. As much as he hated to, he couldn't help but think what the hell could be worth that much and why the freaking hell so many people wanted it. It had come from a lab, he could remember that much. And the security had been an absolute bitch to break. It had taken both of them doubling up, LC ahead and him on back up. He was starting to remember right up to the point where LC yelled for help. He could see the narrow accessways, could feel the growing unease and Skye getting frantic, and LC screaming in pain. And after that just flashes. He knew they'd gotten away with the package but it was not something he could grasp. He couldn't see it in his mind, couldn't remember the feel of it. He just knew they'd managed to get away with it. At least now he knew why they'd gone after it in the first place.

It was only once he'd been taken to another room and locked in by himself, while they made preparations they said, that Genoa contacted him, a tentative querying reach, softer than he'd ever heard her before.

"Zachary, if you can hear me I need you to respond. Wherever you are in there, you have to get out as fast as you can. Zachary, please respond."

"Genoa?"

"Zach, get out of there. There are gunships moving in on your position. I'm in low orbit and we have teams moving in. Are you able to extract?"

The room was sealed like the last one but he tried the door anyway.

"No, they've got me locked in a damn box. Where the hell are gunships coming from?"

He used a fingernail to ease the lockpick free from the band on his wrist and, leaning close to the door, he tried to identify any kind of mechanism he could play with.

"I don't know where they're coming from but they are headed straight for that building and I don't think that's a coincidence, do you? I can't pinpoint your exact location, Zachary. What kind of place is that?"

"They've got some kind of shielding. Can you get any fix on this room at all?"

She went infuriatingly quiet. Skye always gave him a running commentary, reassuring and always there for him. He concentrated on the door, finding the sweetspot, losing it, thumping it a couple of times then shaking his hands loose to calm the jitters. He tried again and almost had it. It was a complex magnetic encoded lock. His right hand cramped and he lost it, leaned his head against the door and swore softly. The building shook suddenly with the shock of explosions outside.

Hil jumped back. "Genoa?"

"We have a problem out here, Zachary, just get the hell out of the building."

There were more blasts and his hands were shaking as he tried again. He was about to kick the door when it clicked and swung open.

He ran out.

14

"The corporations," the Man said with a hint of disgust. "The balance of power between Earth and Winter tips precariously on the whims and the greed of men."

NG set his goblet on the desk. This was dangerous territory for a discussion with the Man.

"We take from and give to every corporation," the Man said, "on both sides of the line. They squabble and manoeuvre, they deceive and scheme. They are our lifeblood. It is an indisputable fact that there is no real art in their guile. These entities born of pure unadulterated greed are not driven by the same basic veneer of philanthropy that holds governments in check. But it is their innate drive for self-preservation itself that has dealt us a situation like this. Could we have anticipated that one corporation's aim for competitive advantage would send us to the brink of war?"

The Man poured the last of the jug into his own goblet and drank deeply. There were no clocks or timepieces in the Man's chambers and NG had the vague feeling that more time had passed than he realised. He'd glanced at his own watch a few times but it was frozen at the exact time he'd stepped over the threshold into this room.

He leaned back, trying to clear his head.

"Be assured," he said, "we would never have taken this job. Somehow, they found the chink in our armour and pushed it to force our people to act outside any boundaries we could have predicted."

Another explosion took out the lighting and must have knocked out the gravity compensation as well because Hil staggered against the wall as the floor rumbled and it felt like his weight increased a notch. Emergency lights flickered on and klaxons began to wail, like they really needed a warning of the shitstorm descending on them. There was no one around so Hil ran as fast as he could, knees complaining and legs feeling like lead. Each blast now brought down a showering of sparks and dusty debris. He covered his head with his arms the best he could, trying to keep going and find a way outside. It was typical, just as they were going to let him go, someone else moved in. Twenty six million. No surprise that he was mister popularity. Another blast sent him to his knees and he had to scramble backwards to avoid a section of wall that collapsed inwards.

He curled into a ball and let the debris rain down, taking a couple of knocks in the back and one to the back of the head that sent his vision spinning.

"Genoa, I'm getting bombed here. Any chance of some help?" He got to his feet and pulled himself along, coughing, climbing over the rubble and through into another dark nondescript and equally deserted corridor.

"Anything?"

Nothing. Either the connection was lost again or the ship wasn't wasting time feeding him information she didn't see as relevant. In that respect, Genoa was very different from Skye. Skye would have reassured him constantly, gentle nudges of contact to keep in touch. With Genoa, there was simply cold efficiency.

The emergency lights were struggling and patches of the way through were completely dark, just to add to the atmosphere of it all. Hil checked his wrist band, paranoid suddenly that the air could be contaminated. It was all clear so far.

Another blast hit somewhere up ahead. How far would someone go to collect on twenty six million? That woman hadn't said whether that was dead or alive. But presumably he was worth more alive so dropping a building on his head wasn't that smart. Hil stopped running and took time to gather his bearings. If he was getting bombed, so were they. And he wanted that data board.

It took a while to find a corridor that looked familiar. With the lights on, they'd all looked the same. Hil crouched and stared at the figure lying in rubble close to where he reckoned the interrogation room had been. It was the woman. Dead, as far as he could tell from here. He crept forward and reached out a hand to check her pulse. Nothing. Glancing over his shoulder to make sure they were alone, he searched her pockets, as much as he could reach in amongst the rubble. No ID, no personal effects, nothing. He pressed his hand against her neck, feeling the tell-tale chill of an imbedded chip.

Hil stood up and another not too distant explosion sent him staggering aside. Dust and debris tumbled down onto them. He looked down at the woman. That chip could contain information about who these people were. It took him about half a second to make a decision and thirty seconds to cut out the implant using the knife he pulled from his boot. She was dead, it wasn't like it could hurt. Even so it still made him feel queasy to slice into her flesh. The tiny implant wasn't far beneath the surface but he was careful not to damage it or trigger any protections. He wiped the chip and the knife on her expensive suit, put the knife back in its hiding place and pocketed the implant.

He stood back and looked around, blinking dust out of his eyelashes. The data board had to be somewhere. Another blast sounded closer and sent ceiling tiles crashing down. He ducked and backed off, and heard gunfire and shouts. The implant would have to do. He stared at the woman for a second, then turned and ran.

It was quieter further into the building. And darker. Hil began to think he was walking in circles when there was a shaft of light up ahead. He looked up, a deep down instinct holding him in check. He hugged in close to the wall. The shaft became a beam cutting through the dust and bobbed in the way searchlights do. It was joined by others and they scanned the corridor. Hil shrank back, seeing the shadows behind the beams, the outline of helmets and weapons and the cold efficiency of military teamwork.

He crept backwards quietly, thanking every single second spent in the Maze. The lights flashed in an arc over his head and over the floor to his right. They were coming this way. One silent step at a time, he backtracked to an open door he'd passed, staying just ahead of the lights, hearing now the soft mechanical hum of motors and actuators. If it was a rescue party they'd be yelling for survivors, if it was the guild they wouldn't be wearing heavy combat gear. He slipped into an adjoining corridor and ran and almost yelled out loud when a voice sounded in his head.

"Hil buddy, where the hell are you?"

"Kase! Shit! I'm in the goddamned building. Where the hell are you?"

"We're taking heavy fire outside, Hil. We can't get anywhere near the building. I've got two teams coming in from orbit who are going to take the roof but that's going to take a few minutes. Can you get up there?"

A beam of light flashed by and Hil winced, ducking down to crouch behind a pile of rubble. What? The roof? If he could have, he would have but it wasn't like he had much choice. "Yeah, I'll be there."

He sat still as the beam withdrew and the sound of footsteps and armour passed by. He looked around. There had to be stairs somewhere or an accessway through the ceiling.

There were two more massive blasts in the time it took him to find a stairwell, both close and at one point he could hear the tinny wheezes of voices through helmets, fading as he turned and slipped away in the opposite direction. Finally, he gently pushed open a door and saw with relief that it opened onto a narrow stairwell with steps heading up and down. There was a chilly breeze blowing down from above, but up it was.

He clambered up the steps, on all fours sometimes, breathing laboured. Two flights up and he could hear the rain outside. The stairs ended abruptly. Whether this was the roof or the top floor or what, it was impossible to tell. Twisted metal and prefab panels blocked the way.

The rubble was unstable but it extended up beyond a pile of ceiling tiles. Pipes and wires trailed down, sparking and leaking fluids. Rivulets of water streamed down from above.

Hil climbed up carefully and warily eyed the gap up to a maintenance gantry that had been exposed by the collapse. He took hold with his left hand and hoisted himself up, feeling the weakness in his right arm and ignoring the pain that shot up to his shoulder.

He pulled himself onto the mesh walkway and rolled, the sudden vibration from his wrist band giving him a shock that almost sent him tumbling back down. The display in the band lit up, figures scrolling. It was at maximum, overdose levels, and Hil looked from his wrist up into the jagged edges of a broken conduit that shone with a sickly green glow. It was hard not to gag. He turned away and fumbled with his sleeve. He could imagine the hoards of tiny electrobes swarming into his eyes and nose and ears and felt his chest restrict with panic at the onset of the poisoning.

He cried out softly and covered his mouth and nose with his sleeve, scrambling to get away. The gantry was more stable up ahead and Hil kept his breathing as shallow as he could, breaking into a light run. The band throbbed against his skin, only beginning to ease off once he'd made a decent distance. It didn't stop though, there were electrobes still present even if in lower concentrations.

It was awkward to climb in the increased gravity anyway never mind having to use one hand, with the other still throbbing every time it even bumped against anything, but he found a ladder and climbed slowly up to the next level, muscles screaming at him by the time he reached the top. It was cooler up there and the band calmed down to a vague tingle. Hil coughed and his lungs felt hot, his eyes were sore and he could already feel a trembling in his limbs that had nothing to do with the climb.

Bastard freaking electrobes.

He coughed again and looked around. It was a roof compartment, pipes and vents leading up. The rain was still pounding down, pouring in through rubble strewn holes in the flat roof, puddling and ponding and bouncing off the floor tiles. It streamed in rivers towards him, racing down any channel it could find in the irregular and broken flooring. It looked dark outside, searchlights panning across the building. He could hear the roar of gunships flying overhead and gunfire echoing.

"Kase, I'm up near the roof."

"Keep your head down, Hil. We're too far away. Whatever you

did to upset these people, they're serious. There's a whole damned army out here."

"I'm coughing up lungs full of electrobes here, Kase, where the hell are you?"

"Shit. Give me a minute."

It felt far longer than a minute and Hil jumped again when the connection flared to life. "Okay, get out there," Kase sent, sounding stressed as hell, "we're moving in fast."

Each breath was getting harder. Hil resisted the urge to sit down and flake out and climbed up onto the roof instead. It was flat and wet but vents and pipes gave him cover at least. He crawled out and peered over the edge. Figures were darting between the small buildings and vehicles out there but his eyes were watering and he couldn't make out who was who or where the guild teams were.

"Kase..."

"Hil, hold on."

He held on. He didn't feel like he was worth twenty six million. He felt cold and wet and miserable. It felt like his chest was caught in the grip of a vice.

"Hil, there's a tower at one end of the building. The ship is inbound now but she won't be able to stick around. You'd better be there, bud."

Hil squinted through the rain at the tower. It looked miles away.

"I'll be there," he sent and started running.

Halfway there, another blast shook the building and Hil staggered from the shock, trying to keep on his feet. He fell, rolled and tumbled and getting up was even harder. Coughing hurt. He scrambled forward and tried to see the ship. It wasn't on the roof yet and it could have been any one of a number flying low over the building. He stayed close to cover and picked his way across, splashing through puddles and avoiding the gaping holes and rubble. Twice he thought he heard someone behind him and the third time, red laser sights darted across his line of sight and shots sparked off a pipe ahead of him. He hit the floor and scrambled away, barely squeezing underneath a bent and twisted conduit. There were yells from different directions as if they were separating and spreading out to angle round on him. He stayed low and glanced about, and saw a grenade skittering across the roof towards him. In a painfully slow movement that should have been a graceful and sweeping kick, he managed to lash out with one foot and nudged it away. He didn't wait to see where it went. He turned and crawled frantically away and caught the edge of a concussion blast, nowhere near full force or he would have been out for the count, but still it sent his senses awry.

"Hil, buddy, the ship is moving in. Where are you, bud?"

He tried to respond but he couldn't manage to speak out loud or via the connection hardwired into his brain. He gasped and shook water from his eyes and tried to be as small as possible, tucked up inside a tangle of pipes as red dot laser sights and flashlights scanned overhead and the mechanical crunch of boots and armour sounded closer and closer.

Martha was the last person he wanted to hear but true to form, there she was. "Hil, this is the second time we've saved your ass. You want us to come in there and haul your butt out like last time or could you manage to walk it this time, do you think?"

He thought he sent, "I'll be there" with a touch of irritation and more than a hint of belligerence, she always brought out the best in him, but she snapped back at him, swearing that if he didn't want to bother he could go screw himself, so maybe he hadn't said it out loud.

"I'll be there," he sent again.

"Good because the ship is not going to wait for your sorry ass."

If anything, the rain seemed to get heavier and he envied the soldiers in their snug full-on body armour. The powered exoskeletons gave them an advantage in this gravity and a couple of times, he was spotted but he slipped away before they could pinpoint him. He was cold and wet through but agile as hell, despite the cough and pathetic weakness that was making him want to curl up in a ball and die.

He made it to the tower before anyone else and definitely before any ship. There was a flat intact expanse of roof, unbroken by any bomb holes or interrupted by any pipework so he could see why they'd chosen this as the RV. He hunkered down by the base of the tower.

"Any time now, guys, would be highly appreciated," he mumbled.

"We're taking losses down here, you little shit," Martha snapped back, "you'd better be worth this."

"Twenty six million," Hil muttered and sat back to keep watch, wondering if there was any way he could collect on that himself.

He was woken up by a sudden yell inside his head.

"Hil!" Kase screamed, "get away from the tower. If you're at that fucking tower, get the hell away from it!"

What? Hil shook his head and looked up, scrambling to his feet as he stared up at a fireball spiralling towards him. He ran, slipping and scrambling. The blast lifted him off his feet and threw him sideways into a wall. He hit hard and blacked out.

15

The Man finished his wine and set his goblet on the desk. "Another sterile holding facility? Forgive my arrogance, but why did it take so long to identify this corporation? We have agents and operatives, allies and informants on every world. How did this one corporation defy us?"

NG breathed out slowly. "They knew more about the guild than any outside organisation ever has. And they knew that complete anonymity was the only way they could challenge us in this way and get away with it."

"You said that you would never have considered taking this job? Yet, it must have been known that only the guild could succeed in such a venture. It is encouraging that outsiders believe so. Our very reputation, that brought us to this predicament, is also our saving grace." The Man sat back. "This corporation has dealt us a great compliment."

NG sat quietly. It was easy to consider so in the quiet calm of these chambers. He knew what his people had been through, the extraction teams and the field-ops that had been caught up in all this, and it wasn't easy to justify their pain. It had been a close call, from beginning to end, and there were still loose ends that were unresolved.

"You care," the Man said. "Don't lose that but do not forget what is at stake."

"I know. We deserve the reputation we have. Our people are good and they make their own luck. It's hard to stand by and watch when that luck fails us."

Hil could smell oil as he came to. The type of lubricant the grunts used on their hydraulics. He heard the whirr of an actuator and opened an eye in time to see an armoured hand sweep in for a malicious backslap across his cheek.

"You walk," an electronically-enhanced voice instructed and he was pushed upright and thrust forward.

He staggered a few steps and fell to one knee, expecting to be hauled upright again. He wasn't, he was kicked while he was down and the guy wasn't compensating for the increased gravity and increased momentum and increased son-of-a-bitch pain that his goddamned armour could inflict. They must want him alive, Hil decided smugly, otherwise he'd be strung up dead over someone's shoulder already. He stayed down and then they hauled him up and pulled him along between two of them, each holding his arms at the shoulder socket too tight to show any concern for his wellbeing. Alive, but not necessarily in one piece, he thought dismally. The pain in his right wrist had increased by several levels of magnitude to almost unbearable – whatever damage had been caused in the crash had been aggravated, when he hit the wall probably. It hadn't done his head any favours either.

They took him over the roof, past the burning wreck of a ship that was mangled in the remains of the tower. He couldn't help but stare and wonder which ship it had been and who else had bought it down there because of him.

They stopped at the edge of the landing zone and left him propped up by only one guard. There wasn't much he could do though, the guy's grip on his arm was backed by the power of hydraulic actuators. Hil managed to stand without wobbling and kept his head down.

"Kase? You there?" he sent tentatively, not completely sure they didn't have hardware that could overhear.

"Hilyer, tell me you are worth this." Martha sounded more pissed than he'd ever heard, pissed and disconcertingly upset.

"Someone thinks I'm worth it. What's happening down there?"

"We're getting our butts kicked," she sent quietly. "We've lost three ships and we haven't managed to regroup. There's four of us down that I know of and Kase is in a bad way. They're pulling back for some reason. I sent a team to the roof a while back, are they there?"

Hil kept his head down and tried to look up, eyes stinging and eyelashes dripping with raindrops.

"No," he sent through the connection. "But I know why these guys are pulling back."

She must have sensed something in his tone and it snapped her back to her usual charming self. "Oh, don't tell me. No, wait, you don't need to, we can see you. Well, isn't this something? You don't look so good, sunshine."

It had been humiliating enough the first time when he'd had concussion. Now he felt so wretched, he just wanted her to waltz up and whisk him away to a comfy bed. They'd been a cute couple when they'd been an item. He felt almost nostalgic.

"Hil," she sent quietly, "don't move."

It was hard not to tense as soon as she said it but his body was well trained, abused though it was at that moment.

He stood motionless and didn't even twitch so much as a single muscle when the guy holding him suddenly let go and fell to the ground.

It was timed immaculately. No other soldiers were looking in their direction.

There were only three people in the guild who could have made that shot, a high velocity armour piercing round, from god knows what range, through the weak spot between the visor and neck guard of the helmet. The guy hadn't had a chance and Hil was sure he could bet his twenty six million on Martha having taken it.

He ducked down and quickly checked the guy's armour for insignia, rank, anything that could reveal where they were from. There was nothing. The armour was like nothing he'd seen before. It was a translucent black brown and glistened in the rain, smooth except for hinged joints. The pistol the guy had been holding to the back of Hil's neck lay discarded, half submerged in a puddle. It was flashing a half charge.

Hil grabbed it and ran.

He made it into cover before any of them noticed but getting away completely was seeming more and more difficult.

A wracking cough sent him to his knees, clutching his chest and feeling like every spasm was going to make his head explode. He tried to keep quiet but the more effort that took, the more he ended up retching in agony, spots behind his eyes and oblivious for a time to anything around him.

He fell more than walked into another tangle of pipes and sitting tight, nestled in close to a valve that was venting steam and keeping his back warm, Hil watched the flashlights dance in a coordinated, precise pattern.

The pistol was cold to the touch, intricate machining and elaborate mechanics. He was no weapons expert but it was unlike anything he'd seen or fired before. The grip was too big for him, designed to be used with armour, but he reckoned he could fire it if he had to. It was a weapon at least.

Whoever these guys were, they were well equipped and well trained. The guild was a formidable organisation, but they were getting their butts kicked and he could hardly keep his eyes open, let alone make it out of here on his own. And he had a ticking time limit that the tightness in his chest wasn't going to let him forget.

Martha was quiet despite a couple of attempts he made to talk to her. Genoa wasn't there for him and god knows what had happened to Kase. He felt bad about that. But at least he knew now why this was happening, even if he didn't understand what it was about. And as much as he couldn't put any of it right, he knew how to get Anya back. And even LC maybe. If he could just get off this goddamned roof. He glanced at the band on his wrist. If he could get off the roof before it was too late.

Another loud explosion jerked him awake again. He gasped and held his head, willing the pain to stop.

"Hil," Martha broke into the private party going on in his head. "There's an escape ladder on the far side of the landing pad. Can you get down to ground level?"

He closed an eye and tried to focus with the other through the steam. "Yep," he sent back confidently, feeling anything but. "What then?"

"Just get there."

He could see the ladder and he could see a way to it.

Lightning was flashing across the sky by the time he made it to the escape. Twice, he'd frozen, lit up as if he'd been caught in the beam of a searchlight. It was the worst freaking thing to do. Freeze and you die. It was something they trained for, time and time again, taking a beating from the grunts every time the wrong instinct kicked in and you didn't move fast enough. Move, you stay alive.

He moved, anger at himself fuelling a forward momentum that got him to the other side of the building. Martha was yelling at him by the time he made it. He tucked the pistol into his waistband, made a left-handed grab onto the handrail and swung over, half falling down to the first level, feeling exposed on the open gantry. Shots pinged off the rail and he dropped down another level, pausing when Martha screamed at him to wait, nearly yanking his shoulder out of its socket when she yelled at him to move. Each rung was an effort and every breath was a fire-laced agony of wheezing. Eight or nine rungs from the ground and a spattering of shots sparked off the ladder.

Hil curled in tight and yelped as he felt an impact hit his back, jarring his right shoulder. All feeling in that arm vanished and he dropped. He hit the ground and rolled, kicking out as he sensed more than saw a body close by reaching down to him. They were too fast and before he knew where he was, he was being hauled aside, gloved – not armoured – hands holding him tight. He felt a sharp pain in his neck.

"Hold still," Martha hissed at him. "Quit fighting me, you moron. If we get out of this alive, I swear I'm going to kill you."

She was an angel at times. She pulled him to his feet and slung an arm around him, about all that was keeping him upright. A minute later, he felt a flood of warm strength tingle through his muscles. He'd never had a shot of any of the crazy drugs they used on the dark side – he'd never had to, field-ops didn't need to – but feeling the clouds clear inside his head and a bounce come back to his knees, it was hard not to wonder why they didn't. He muttered a thanks and managed to stay standing when she spun him around and started prodding at the sore spot on his back.

"Thank me when we're safely on a ship out of here," she said. "How bad is the poisoning?"

He checked his wrist and coughed. "Bad enough that if I don't get a shot of antidote within about thirty minutes, you're going to have wasted your time coming down here for me."

She glared at him and grabbed his wrist to take a look for herself. The numbers scrolling on the band were still higher than anyone ever wanted to see.

She cursed and grabbed his shoulder again. "Well, whatever they hit you with, it hasn't penetrated. They want you alive. Pity they're not so concerned about the rest of us chumps who are stupid enough to be out here trying to save your ass."

"What happened to Kase?" Hil asked. "Is he alright?"

She glared at him, then glanced out suddenly as if she was listening to something. She crouched and pulled him down.

"He broke cover to shoot a guy that was taking a bead on you," she sent through the link.

Crap.

"I don't know how he is because I'm here with you and he's over there, bleeding onto the goddamned tarmac. The whole situation has gone to crap. I don't believe it. You really screwed us up going solo like a fucking rookie up there on the orbital. Who the hell are these people?"

"They have Anya," he said abruptly, out loud. It felt like he should explain, like someone should know. "Not these people, the ones that took me on the station."

Martha had her gun up. She kept her aim steady but turned her head to look at him. "What?"

"Mendhel's daughter," he said and tried to stifle a cough. "That's why we took the tab."

"For fuck's sake, Hil, I don't care why you did it, or what you did. I don't care who these people are. Just shut the fuck up and try to stay alive for me. Can you do that?"

"I don't…"

She cut him off with a hiss, eyes now firmly fixed on whoever it was she had in her sights.

She took the shot, stood up and grabbed his arm. "C'mon."

He ran after her, feeling like his legs weren't his own. They ran faster than he could coordinate and he felt invincible, chest on fire and vision down to a narrow tunnel edged with black, but feeling like he could run all night.

They splashed across an open area and made it to a small group of buildings that were shrouded in darkness. They cringed in close to a wall as a searchlight swept past. A ship flew close overhead.

"We're screwed," Martha muttered out loud.

They could see the end of the runway from where they were. There was one ship there, listing to one side with smoke streaming from it. He could just make out figures guarding it. The main building was shielding their view of the rest of the runway, but they could hear shots still, distant and echoing in the night air.

"Are they guild?"

Martha shushed him again and stood head cocked to one side like she was listening to someone. Presumably she had a link with the other teams that she hadn't included him in on. It was probably best, he couldn't handle another voice in his head right now. The drug was wearing off already, he could feel the edge of it slipping away. His fingertips were tingling and it was getting even harder to keep his eyes open.

Martha swatted at his cheek.

"Stay with me, sunshine," she said. "We're going to make a run for it. They're going to give us a diversion. I've told them they can have a share in your twenty six million. Think you can make it?"

Hil blinked, not entirely sure he could even if he tried.

"Oh for god's sake," she said and another sharp pain hit his neck. "Hil, listen to me."

She gripped his arm tightly. "Another one of these will kill you – if the electrobes haven't already. Do you understand? We have to make a run for it. They can't hold much longer. Ready?"

Another surge of warmth blossomed through his limbs but this time his head didn't clear, it began to pound in time with his heartbeat.

"C'mon." She pulled at his arm and they broke cover. As they ran, the sky beyond the building lit up with booming explosions. He could see the ship up ahead and that became his whole world. One foot after the other, cringing each time there was another crash of thunder or bomb detonating around them. Ships screamed overhead and shots began peppering the ground around them. Martha held onto his arm and pulled, stumbling at one point so it was him pulling her along. If they didn't want to kill him, someone hadn't got the message.

Halfway there, the ship ahead of them erupted in a ball of flames.

16

The Man stood up and walked round to the cabinet on the far wall.
The flames of candles flickered frantically, dancing for survival, as he
passed. He took out a bottle and walked ponderously back to the desk.

"How wise," the Man said, "was it to send so many extraction teams
into such a volatile situation?"

And there it was. Again, with hindsight he should have known.
NG shook his head. "It wasn't. We lost some good people." What else
could he say considering what happened?

The Man picked up a pinch of black powder from a small round
pot and sprinkled it into the empty glass jug. He poured wine from the
bottle into the jug and swirled it as the reaction of the liquid and the
powder heated the wine and steam began to circle upwards. He filled
both goblets.

"I was trying to limit the damage already done," NG admitted.
"I could have sent the guild's entire security forces to get Hil out of there
but at the time we were still trying to play down the situation and I
wanted to know who they were. I decided that a contingent of extraction
teams could do the best job of running a discrete operation. I was wrong.
I just didn't realise why. And I didn't anticipate the size of the force
they'd be up against."

Hil threw a hand over his eyes, feeling the heat even at this distance.
Martha didn't slow. She changed course, dragging him with her,
away from the runway and back towards the darkness they'd left.
In his periphery vision, he could see the red pinpoints of laser
sights closing in on them.

Then with a thunderous roar, a mass appeared above them and
they both fell to their knees as the massive weight of a ship swept

in from behind them, too close overhead, displacing the air with a violence that left them gasping. It landed and skidded, metal screeching, sending shrapnel flying, sparks flashing. Wire fences crashed and tangled, lines breaking and whipping loose.

The ramp crashed open before the ship had come to a stop, scraping across the ground as the vessel slewed off ahead of them.

"Get down," Martha yelled at him, pulling his arm and throwing them both to the ground. He covered his head with an arm and put complete trust in her, lying there and waiting.

A burst of energy rippled out in a ring from the ship. He felt the heat from it as it raced over their heads and spread out behind them. He heard yells and screams some distance back, and looking back over his shoulder he could see figures caught in an agonising pulse of static time and energy before disintegrating in a spray of molecules.

Then Martha was up and dragging him to his feet and they were running towards the ramp.

The landing gear was trashed so the ramp was skewed at an angle, and rain was flooding down it, so they had to slip and scramble up into the ship. Martha punched the button to close the ramp and yelled at him to get inside as she guarded them, rifle barrel scanning the gap as the ramp rose and slammed shut.

Hil stood shaking and shivering, rooted to the spot. He didn't know which ship they were on and any fight or flight instinct he had left was in such conflict that he began to shut down. He looked at the band on his wrist. It was the longest and worst he'd ever been exposed. They'd all heard horror stories of electrobe poisoning and they laughed in the face of it but right now, as breathing got harder and the weight pushing against his lungs got heavier, he gave up, sagged and closed his eyes.

"No, you don't," Martha snapped and pulled him along towards the bridge. "Genoa, where the hell do you keep the medical kit?"

Martha pushed him into a chair and gave him a double dose of antidote. She thrust the medical kit into his hands and waved another pack of something he couldn't make out in front of his face.

"Take these when you wake up," she said tucking the pack in next to him and firing another shot of something into his neck. "Genoa, get him out of here. I'm going back for Kase."

And she ran out.

Genoa flew them up into orbit, taking a couple of hits along the way that knocked them sideways and at one point threw them into a dive that felt endless before she managed to pull up.

Hil sat and shivered, soaking wet and chilled through, feeling his eyes get heavier and heavier. Extracted for a second time sucked worse than the first time. He sat with the massive pistol resting in his lap and persuaded himself to reach a hand into his pocket to feel the cold outline of the implant there. At least this time, he had something more substantial than a concussion to show for his efforts.

He must have flaked out. Regaining consciousness in the middle of a fire fight was a new experience. Hil felt his stomach lurch as the ship dropped and rolled and he almost called out to Skye before his brain caught up with the fact she was firing weapons so it was Genoa, not Skye. Proximity alarms were screaming then she pulled a manoeuvre that almost made him pass out again. She accelerated then jumped without warning. They jumped twice more and each time, he felt like his head was going to implode.

It was only when they hit deep empty space and Genoa indulged him with a long, gentle drift that he began to feel like he might live.

He had no idea how much time had elapsed and as soon as he could move without feeling like he was risking an aneurism, he took a look at the pack wedged down by his leg, which turned out to be one of the general emergency catch-all medication packs the extraction teams used. He swallowed down the three pills in it and almost choked.

He coughed. "Any chance you could turn up the heat in here?"

He felt a subtle rise in the temperature as Genoa said, "Welcome back to the land of the living."

"Where are we?" he asked. He fumbled to unfasten the restraints, trying to avoid using his right hand at all, and stood up, grabbing the packet and taking another paranoid look at the label to see what he'd just taken.

"Sit back down," she said calmly, "we're going to make jump again soon."

"Genoa, I'm soaking wet. Give me minute, will you?"

He ducked out to the tiny cabin he'd thrown his gear into. He put the pistol into his bag and shrugged out of his wet coat and shirt. His right arm was mottled black and swollen, from his elbow to the fingertips. He prodded a couple of sore spots on his side and tried to twist around to see his shoulder. He was in a real state. The band on his left wrist was dark blue, data flashing on it that he couldn't focus on to read. It wasn't black any more so he took that as a good sign. He left the brace on his wrist even though it was tempting to take it off and relieve some of the pressure. He gently pulled on a dry shirt and wandered back to the bridge, ignoring the thought that he could snuggle down on the bunk back there and sleep. If he'd been with Skye, he would but Genoa was too much of an unknown.

"Where are we?" he asked again. "What are we doing?"

"We're not safe yet," she said.

And he saw the numbers flash up on the screen, counting down to jump. He heard the subtle change in the pitch of the engines and sat down quickly.

"What?" he said belligerently, irritated that she wouldn't explain. "What's the problem?"

Without any further warning, she threw them into jump and for a few seconds he couldn't see anything except flashes.

The pain in his head spiked and by the time they came out of jump, he was soaked in sweat and had one hand on his chest and another clutching the back of his head.

"Genoa, ease off on the jumps for a bit, will you?"

She must have sensed his distress because the temperature

warmed up another notch and she kept them on a steady stream for a while.

"Talk to me, Genoa. What's happening?" he said, trying desperately to keep his irritation down.

An image appeared on the main screen in front of him.

"Do you recognise that?" she said curtly.

He still couldn't see straight, couldn't quite focus. "No, what is it?"

"One of the ships that descended on that planet not long after you arrived there. The same ships that I'm trying to lose in jump. How did they know we were there? No one else knew we were going there."

He leaned forward and squinted at the image. "The people who sent in the tab knew we'd be there," he said.

"Yes, Zachary, they were the ones who took you from the station and had the crap pounded out of them by the army that descended in these ships. We have no intelligence on the group who sent the tab and we have even less on this new, rather well equipped, military who seem even more intent on getting their hands on you. They've followed us through jumps that no one should have been able to."

Hil sat back and closed his eyes. He was sore and tired and starting to feel like nowhere was safe to run to. They were supposed to have been watching his back on the station. Every tab he'd ever worked for the guild, the extraction teams were there, a safety net he'd never needed, but there and always, always, the best. He'd never doubted them before and it felt crap now to think in this massive mess of a situation his world had run to, that those guys could be on the other side.

Genoa threw them into another sharp manoeuvre that set his head throbbing.

"Zach, your stats don't look good. Zach?"

"I know," he said quietly, still uneasy, not sure if the queasy feeling he had was from a deep down distaste at going rogue from the guild, Genoa's flying or the drugs Martha had given him.

"Where do you want to go, Zach?"

Skye would have high-tailed it out of there and taken him somewhere safe, no questions, no doubt and let him deal with the fall out afterwards. Genoa had pulled an impressive stunt back there but while she wasn't blindly heading for home, she wasn't decisively taking care of them. She wanted him to make the call. When all he wanted to do was sleep.

"I don't know," he muttered.

"I'm low on fuel and I need repairs. And Zach, you need medical attention. Do you want me to try for the Alsatia?"

Yes.

"No," he said. He needed some time to think. It would look really bad not to go straight home. He'd had no choice last time and once there, they'd set him up. If he was going to clear this up, he had to do it on his own terms.

"I can take you anywhere, just tell me where," Genoa urged softly.

"Aston," he said. "We'll go to Aston."

17

"You knew," the Man said, "the ferocity with which the item was sought
by several parties?"

"I did," NG conceded.

"And yet you let Hilyer go running off on his own? Did you know
that Legal lodged a motion to have you suspended?"

"You'd never let that happen," NG said.

The Man smiled and pushed the goblet forward, motioning him to
pick it up. They both drank, the hot wine burning its way down to
NG's stomach.

"After the fiasco on Abacus," he said, "I decided that the best course of
action was to give Hilyer space. If I'd hauled him back here straight away,
we would have lost a chance to track Anderton. Hil was our best bet.
Legal doesn't always understand the subtleties of how the field-ops work.
And she was having trouble coming up with answers. She tried to interfere
and I reminded her of that. Being shown up never goes down well."

"And to your credit, there were others in Legal who backed you.
Is the matter resolved now?"

"Every family experiences disharmony at times. It's not often we
quarrel outright. We can look back now and see more clearly how
difficult the situation was." He took a sip of the wine. "We're fine."

"How fickle," the Man said, "are the affairs of men when a galaxy
is at stake."

Hil was sure he was being followed. By the time the subway train
came, he was shivering despite the humid heat, huddled into a
corner, glad he'd kept on the coat and seriously needing somewhere
to sit down. He stumbled onto the train and walked through three
of its rickety carriages before taking a seat and settling in.

The drop down from the station had been an uneventful trip crowded in with dock workers headed to the planet for downtime and city folk returning after trips to wherever on whatever business or pleasure had taken them away. He'd kept his head down and blended in, the pistol heavy in an inside pocket. There was no customs or security, no questions asked. If you had business on Aston, no one was going to stand in the way. You simply paid the going rate for an entry visa, referred to as an 'administration fee' at Aston immigration, more commonly known as a bribe on most other worlds and thanked every sense of paranoia that kept an unregistered credit chip in your pocket.

Genoa was tucked safely into a repair yard up on the waystation in orbit. Aston was one of Skye's favourites and Genoa would be fine there. He'd initiated a phony ID that had no connection to the guild. It hadn't started up any alerts and wouldn't leave any trace for the guild or anyone else to follow.

He left the tube train a station ahead of his destination and ducked off the main concourse into a maintenance tunnel. The idea of climbing the fifteen levels to the surface was more intimidating than it had ever been before. He had to stop regularly and at one point lost track of the time, sitting perched on a beam and resting his head against the cold metal of the structure, feeling the vibrations of distant trains.

It was hot there under the city. Aston was one of Winter's oldest settlements and its age-old infrastructure was crumbling as fast as the technology it was renowned for was speeding into the future. Dust flaked down each time a train came close.

He had three vials in his pocket. Two days of sleep and another shot of the guild's antidote on the way here had done nothing to ease the aches in his chest and the pounding in his head. He'd found the vials in the emergency kit and ignored Genoa's insistent nagging that he'd had too much already. Martha hadn't skimped at giving him the stuff when he needed it. And right now, he wasn't entirely sure he could manage the rest of the way to the surface without something.

He took one out and fingered it uneasily. It had been days since the last one. And if he just used it to get to Pen's, he'd be able to get help and he wouldn't need the others. One shot surely couldn't do any harm.

But needing anything was a difficult emotion to handle. You didn't get to be number two in the guild by depending on anything or anyone. If LC could see him now, he'd get the piss ripped out of him. He swore softly and put the vial away, hauling himself to his feet and making it up another two levels with excruciating effort before he passed out and came to sprawled in a heap.

The sting on his neck was cold but the warmth that spread across his shoulders down to his fingertips was welcome. He took a deep breath, feeling the pain fade into the distance, and half ran the rest of the way up, senses on maximum, taking detours to avoid any sounds of voices or activity that echoed his way. It was only when he reached street level and stopped to lean against a wall to catch his breath that he realised his heart rate was fluttering. It was seriously good stuff in a fix but crap, he had to remember not to use it.

It was starting to get dark as he made his way into Pen's district, taking it easy because he was feeling the burning in his chest reignite with each breath of smog-filled air. The city lit up and traffic got heavier, music drifting through the winding streets. Aston worked hard and played hard, in a citywide culture of decadence, crazy innovation and recreation bordering on insanity that somehow fuelled the awesome leaps its inhabitants made in pushing the limits of physics and engineering. They'd had good times here and those memories kept Hil going forward, sure he could trust the place and the people he was headed to.

He tried to walk steadily along narrow streets that were beginning to become crowded with market stalls, and tried to take his time and not panic. But the drug had set his nerves on edge and his sight was going. His memory was goosed again. Images of Martha and Kase, LC and Anya, fleeting thoughts of danger and hazards, the crashing force of impact and explosions, Skye and safety all merged together and left him twitching like he'd lost it. Like he'd never, ever been before. LC was the best operative the guild had because he flew on pure instinct. In contrast, Hil knew he was good because he trained and worked his ass off, and stayed in control. His head hurt and it hurt worse because he didn't have control.

An uneasy sense that he was being followed tickled at the back of his neck constantly. Turning round, even slowly and casually, made his head spin. If someone was following him, Pen's guys would deal with them as soon as he got close enough. He just had to get there.

He reached the main street, glad that it was dark, trailing a finger of his left hand against the walls and windows of shops to keep a grip on his balance, grounding himself against the old brickwork. He kept his right arm cradled up against his chest and concentrated on walking.

There were enough people on the street that he had to hustle his way through a few times. Someone bumped into his arm with enough force to make him gasp and cringe away, and as he moved he felt a sharp jab in his ribs, the hum of a gun powering up, and the someone moved with him, pushing him forward and grabbing hold of his arm in a grip that sent hot needles of pain shooting into his elbow and fingers.

"Keep moving," a voice whispered harshly.

Pure instinct kicked in and Hil reacted, dropping his shoulder and throwing a wild backswing, using the full weight of the brace on his wrist, ignoring the heat of the pain that erupted in the joint as his clenched fist made contact with the guy's face, blood spurting from the nose. Hil twisted round and pushed, hooking a foot behind the man's ankle so that he fell awkwardly backward. The gun discharged, sending a bolt close enough to Hil's shoulder that it tingled with the charge. He ducked, caught his balance and followed up quickly with a kick, catching the guy in the centre of the chest and sending him sprawling into the road.

He was vaguely aware of people shouting and bodies closing in. And as he turned to run, an arm grabbed his neck from behind and squeezed, pulling him in tight, punches landing hard against his kidneys. His knees buckled and as he pulled the second attacker to the floor with him, he curled up and rolled his shoulder, throwing the weight of the body behind him up over his head to slam into the pavement in front of him. He staggered to his feet, coughing, and turned to push his way roughly through the people standing watching.

He ran blindly into the nearest alleyway, hearing footsteps behind him. If they hit him with an FTH round, he was done. He veered into an open doorway and clattered through the back rooms of an electronics chopshop, components scattering as he crashed into tables and shelves. He ran through and into the front of the shop, ignoring yells to stop. The adrenaline rush fuelled by the last remnants of Martha's drugs caused a pounding in his head that drummed out the pounding of footsteps closing in. Whoever they were, he wasn't interested in stopping to talk. No one was going to get their hands on him that easily.

He swerved past the counter and was running for the door when he was tackled by a massive body slamming into him from behind. The momentum sent them both crashing through the glass door, shards exploding out into the street.

Hil curled up and tried to protect his arm as he hit the road, the shock of the impact almost jarring him senseless. Splinters of glass rained down. Cars swerved to avoid them and drivers yelled obscenities, the harsh glare of the headlights sending spikes lancing into the back of Hil's eyes. He rolled with it and almost managed to stagger to his feet when a hand grabbed his ankle and twisted hard. He was thrown around onto his back. The heavy weight of the gun inside his coat banged against his ribs. He kicked out at the hand holding his leg but it held firm and pulled.

No way were these assholes going to get him. He fumbled inside his coat, and as a figure loomed over him, kneeling and pinning him to the road, Hil managed to pull out the massive pistol and stuck it in the face of his assailant.

A hush fell around them.

He held the gun steady and said softly, "Back off. You've got the wrong guy," trying to focus the blurry image of the man in front of him. The gun was heavy but he aimed it without shaking, taking its weight with his left hand and shutting out the agony yelling at him from his other wrist. He was very aware that there was a second guy somewhere and he couldn't move, abs tensed in the half sit up position he was holding.

"The bounty said dead or alive, Hilyer," the guy hissed, "the only reason you're still alive is that I can't be arsed to carry your deadweight back to my ship."

"You've got the wrong guy," he said again quietly, slowing his breathing to ease the pressure in his chest. "Back off."

There were people watching and this guy's partner could be anywhere.

"We know exactly who you are," the man said, pulling his silver ID badge from a chain around his neck. He held it out for Hil to see then flashed it to the crowd. "I'm licensed and you're coming with us, pal."

Hil smiled and waved the gun slightly. "Get off me." He dropped the smile. "Now."

The bounty hunter looked around, for his partner probably, or expecting help from the crowd. But the atmosphere around them had changed. Hil used the opportunity to shift his weight and sit up, relaxed but keeping the gun pointed. The guy backed off, rocking back on his heels, fury sparking in his eyes. No one would help a bounty hunter on Aston. He'd made a mistake by identifying himself and he knew it. He stood up and took a step back.

Hil kept the gun's aim steady and got to his feet. He stared the bounty hunter in the eyes for a brief second, then backed away and pushed his way through the crowd.

No one tried to stop him and he didn't look back.

Approaching the market across the square from Pen's place, Hil shrank back against a wall and tried not to look a freaking mental case. The shakes had set in once the adrenaline rush and Martha's drugs had worn off. Way too many people were beginning to know his name.

Being late evening the market was at its busiest and the narrow lanes between stalls were bustling with people. The smell of spices, fried food and hot sweet doughnuts drifted across and almost made him gag. The noise and heat was cloying. They'd always raid the market at midnight when he stayed with Pen, cooler, less people and more opportunity to savour the array of products on display and browse the latest technologies before they reached the rest of the galaxy. Half the gear the guild acquired from various sources ended up here at one time or another. LC always found it hilarious to watch the prices the merchants charged for stuff they'd gotten their hands on months earlier. Winter was desperate for Earthside biowares. And a lot of the gear here was a freaky mix of stolen Earth technology and Wintran hardwired mech-tech. The market was the humming heart of a city that couldn't get enough of anything.

The building of the Merchant's Guild towered above the square, lights in every window. Hil couldn't afford to be recognised. He squinted through heavy eyelids. If someone else attacked him now, he was done. He had no fight left. He couldn't see straight for one thing and he wasn't sure his limbs would obey anything other than the basic stand upright and try not to fall over instructions his addled brain was sending out.

Pen's building was opposite. If he kept to the edges, he'd have to negotiate the tables and chairs set out in front of restaurants but heading straight through the market was not on. There were too many people in there that knew him. He thought of the look on Tavner's face at Polly's place and shivered. He felt that sinking feeling weigh down his stomach and forced himself to move, taking the edge route, muttering apologies to the people he bumped into and using the backs of chairs to lean on as he passed.

His vision was narrowed to a dark tunnel straight ahead. He got half way and slunk back into an alleyway between buildings, trying to focus on what he thought was Pen's place. It would just take a minute to catch his breath. Pen's place was warmth and safety. And that thought was the only thing stopping him from falling in a heap.

The scent of spices and burning oils mingled in the warm evening air that drifted in with the chatter of voices bartering.

He leaned against the wall and closed his eyes. And the cold steel that was the unmistakable barrel of a weapon touched the back of his neck.

18

"Men scurry like ants across the face of their planets," the Man said and flicked at a dust mote on the desk.

NG didn't follow the line of reasoning of that random statement so he sat quietly, waiting for the next question.

"The bounty?" the Man said eventually.

"We found out about that at around the same time we realised Hil had gone to Aston," NG said. "Word of it went round far quicker than anyone here had anticipated. I didn't appreciate how much we missed Badger. And as much as Sean O'Brien was sending word back on anything she was hearing, and the extraction teams were reporting in any rumours they encountered, we were all jostling on a back footing, trying to catch up and not really understanding why we weren't at the forefront any more."

And while no one had so much as a lead on LC, bounty hunters had closed in on Hil.

The Man looked up. "Did you consider how close we were to losing him?"

"Hilyer has proved he can look after himself before."

"Not with a price on his head."

No, he thought, and it still irked that someone had contempt enough to cross the guild in that way.

"Out loud, NG," the Man chided in response to his thoughts and nudged the goblet across the desk again. "The games we play with these pieces we move around our board are complex and it should not be unexpected to us that they may bite back every once in a while."

He froze.

"Losing your touch, Hil?"

It took a second to place that voice and in that brief time, it felt like he was balanced on the edge of a dark abyss. He teetered then his memory sparked and Hil relaxed at the sound of a voice that was exactly where it should be. He turned and the guy that was standing there smiled and pulled him back into the shadows.

"Hil. Man, you look like shit," the guy muttered. "Come on inside. Pen's been expecting you."

It was hard not to grin like an idiot at seeing Yani. The gun disappeared and Yani pulled a silver hip flask out of his pocket, thrusting it into Hil's hand and steering him with a firm hand against his back out into the market.

Alcohol probably wasn't a good idea but what the hell. The liquid burned his throat but it felt good. It felt very good.

He couldn't recall how but they reached Pen's door without incident. Yani disabled alarms and security by remote as they walked in, all the systems clicking back on as they passed.

Pen was waiting and waved a welcome towards his den, a low lit comfort pad of sofas and armchairs. Candles flickered around the edges of the den. High and low tech mixing in the absurd contradiction that was Aston.

Pen grabbed Hil in a bear hug as he walked in. Pen was a big man, the complete opposite of Mendhel, but the dark eyes were identical, and it was hard not to lose it completely.

Hil pulled away before the lump in his throat could bring tears to his eyes. "Pen," he said and faltered, not knowing how to say it.

Pen shook his head and said, "We know, Hil, we know and we have people on it." He steered Hil towards the den where three more of his men were standing. It was warm and in a strange way Hil felt the most safe he'd been since the crash. Pen controlled Aston's underworld and he inspired a fierce loyalty in his men. To be welcomed here was an honour that Hil didn't take lightly, especially in these circumstances.

Yani took up position at the doorway and Pen took two beers out of a noisy fridge unit in the corner and handed one over, saying, "Make yourself at home," like he always did.

Hil sank down onto a fat chair piled with shabby cushions. He raised the beer bottle in a wave. "Cheers, Pen."

Pen raised his back, returning the salutation. "Here's to twenty million and whatever the hell it was that you two maniacs managed to get your hands on."

Hil should have known word would have got back here. "Twenty six million, last I heard," he said.

"Ye gods. I always knew you two would hit the big time." He came and sat down across from Hil, and one of the guys set a tray of nachos and tapas on a low table between them, backing off respectfully.

"Hil, what the hell is it that you're into here? Do you know what happened on Earth?"

Hil closed his eyes and felt himself begin to sink down into a hazy void.

"Hil?" Pen said again, louder.

It took effort just to form words. "Would you believe me if I said I didn't know?" he said, hearing the words slur.

"No."

"We've been seriously screwed, Pen. I'm sorry, I don't know what happened to Mendhel."

Pen nodded grimly. "I've got people working on it but Earth's difficult for us at the moment. I've been told it was a professional hit but the Assassins won't admit to it so I'm inclined to think 'professional' is an overstatement. What does the guild think?"

"The guild won't tell me anything. Have you heard from LC?"

"No," Pen said and Hil wasn't completely sure that was an honest reply but he didn't care. If LC had been here, Pen would tell him in his own good time.

Pen leaned forward suddenly. "Shit, Hil, what the hell has happened to you?"

Hil blinked, having trouble focusing on anything. "I banged my head," he said, tiredness creeping deeper into his voice. "And there's a couple of other things."

"What?"

Hil reached out his left wrist, fist clenched, band facing up. The numbers were still higher than he was happy with and the guild antidote was taking its time.

"Shit, you don't do things by halves. Okay, I know someone who can help with that. What else?"

Hil reached into his coat and pulled out the pistol. He went to place it on the table and misjudged the weight of it and the distance. It clattered with a noise that made him wince.

"Holy crap, Hilyer." Pen leaned across and grabbed it. "This isn't your usual style." He peered at the weapon and hefted it from hand to hand.

"I need to know where it's from," Hil said. "And I need something smaller. It's too big."

Pen shook his head. "I've never seen anything like it. Where did you get it?"

Hil shrugged and downed the rest of his beer. He put the empty bottle on the table and grabbed a handful of tortilla chips, the room beginning to spin as he leaned over.

Pen sat back and held up the intricate weapon. Hil could just about see the light from the power cell winking on the back.

"It's beautiful," Pen said, no doubt weighing up its value. "For something so hefty, it's got an incredible balance."

It was a pistol, blinking a half charge. Hil didn't see the attraction. He'd hoped Pen would be able to identify it and give him an idea of where to head next.

Pen must have seen something in the look on his face. "Is this from the bastards that killed Mendhel?" he said. "Dammit, I knew he shouldn't have stayed on Earth. I tried to tell him. I tried to persuade him to…"

"No," Hil interrupted. "No, it wasn't them."

"So who was it? And where did you get this?"

Hil rubbed his eyes wearily. He was having trouble focusing. If he could trust anyone, it was Pen. The guy was Mendhel's brother. He was fairly sure this was the first place LC would have run to.

But it was still hard to say anything.

Pen frowned. "Hil, look, I need to know what you're into if I'm going to be able to help. I've heard there's a bounty out on the two of you, that you have something that, from what I can tell, half the galaxy is after, but that's just it – there's no details. What was it?"

"I really don't know," he said. "But someone took Anya to make sure we'd go after it. I don't have it. I need to find LC."

"What's happened to Anya? What do you mean – took?"

Hil described the recording he'd seen, described the people and the base they'd taken him to and the forces that had appeared after them.

"Bloody hell, Hil. Where's the guild in all this?"

"They don't know I'm here and I don't know who I can trust there. Someone's involved. There's no way anyone could have even known Mendhel had a daughter unless it came from inside." He didn't go so far as mentioning Badger and his warning.

Pen sat back and aimed the pistol towards the door, closing one eye to aim along its length.

"You know, you have other options than the guild," he said casually.

They'd been down this road before. Pen was not, and never had been, guild. He was one of Mendhel's closest contacts outside of the guild and being on the Wintran side of the line, was one of the most useful. Pen couldn't always understand the blind loyalty they all had for the guild and they'd stopped trying a long time ago to explain it.

Hil mumbled, "Don't go there, Pen." He wasn't up for an argument.

"You've been with them what, since you were fifteen? And LC since he was thirteen? You're institutionalised, buddy. Break away, come live in the real world. They're not doing you any favours."

"Pen…"

"I know, I know, they look after you. But ask yourself, Hil, is this really how you want looking after? Who's handling you?"

Hil groaned. "Quinn." One word answers was about all he was capable of.

Pen snorted and talked through a mouthful of corn chips and tomato salsa. "That's never going to work. Quinn will never have the patience to put up with you. Man, you should take a look at yourself. The guild has sent out an alert on you both. I've never seen anything so extreme. They're pissing themselves over this.

What are they so afraid of? If you want to leave it, leave now and don't look back. I can sort you out."

That's what he needed to hear. The last bit. Leaving the guild wasn't an option, no matter that someone had sold them out, but he had the mental capacity of a screwdriver at the minute so the debate would have to wait.

"Is it still NG in charge up there?" Pen asked without waiting for an answer. "I've got to tell you, Hil, the guild isn't what it used to be. There are mutterings that private contractors could do what you do at half the price and without the strings. I've heard it. I've even heard that the Merchants are saying they could set something up that would put your guild out of business. You know, you'd have one helluva career out here in the private sector."

It was tantamount to treason to even listen to this. Hil shut it out and felt himself drifting again. He closed his eyes.

"Pen, don't go there. I just want to get my life back," he said. "I need to find LC. He has whatever it was we took. We screwed up, Pen. Screwed up badly. We split. We didn't even make a plan to meet up. I took off back to the guild with a phony package just to get them following me so LC could get away. Well, it worked. They followed me, shot me down and did god knows what before the guild got there and got me out."

Pen was quiet. He knew when to listen.

"Skye was damaged. She's back at the guild. I'm here with another ship, Genoa, and at least two bounty hunters know I'm here."

"What was it, Hil? What was the tab?"

"Pen, I said, I really don't know."

"Have you got anything? I'm good, Hil and miracles are my speciality but for god's sake, give me something to go on."

Hil pulled the implant out of his pocket and held it out. "This is from a woman who was with the people who killed Mendhel. They're corporation, I'm sure of it. They have Anya."

Pen took the implant and wiped it on his trouser leg, shaking his head. He stood up. "I need to get some people in on this."

"Pen, nobody can know I'm here."

"Chill out, Hil. You're here because you trust me. Trust me, trust my people. We'll look after you even if your precious guild and the whole of the galaxy is after your ass."

Pen left the room and as much as Hil tried to stay awake, he felt himself slipping, nodding awake with alarm each time his eyes closed. For all he knew, Pen could come marching back in here with a bunch of bounty hunters. Maybe he'd already collected on LC. Pangs of guilt followed that he could even think that about Pen. Then more pangs that he was a sitting duck here. It took some effort to get the pistol off the table but holding it loosely in his lap made him feel better.

Pen came back with a tall thin guy that Hil hadn't seen before. He tried to stand up but the room went spinning away and he sat back, squinting, trying to focus on the man.

"That's the pistol," Pen said to the guy who nodded and reached over to take it from him. Hil offered it up reluctantly, not able to lift the weight of it to any height. The man smiled as he leaned down to take it and Hil waved apologetically, letting his chin sink down onto his hand, elbow resting on his knee.

"It's a nice piece,' the guy said, turning it round. "Where did you say it came from?"

Hil didn't hear Pen's answer because the room greyed out for a moment. He jerked awake as a hand touched the back of his neck and another hand took up his wrist, feeling for the pulse there. He turned his head slowly to see a woman perched on the arm of his chair.

"Pen, what on earth are you doing?" she was saying, the words soft and accented. "He needs serious medical attention and you're keeping him here talking about guns."

She put a cool hand on his forehead and he leaned into it, eyes closing. She was Pen's favourite medic and he almost grinned, impressed with himself for recognising her. She was from Earth and she'd crossed the line for the big man. Hil didn't remember her name but he knew she did good work.

"I know, I know," Pen said. "It's just a slight electrobe poisoning problem he has, a broken arm and god knows what else he hasn't mentioned. You can use the pod in the iso-lab, it's clean.

Hil sat up then, jerking awake and pulling back. "No, wait," he said. He didn't need an iso-pod. That would mean being out of action.

"Hil, relax," Pen said. "You're too valuable to me for me to let anyone get their hands on you for a measly twenty six million."

"Hil...?"

The voice was soft and feminine.

"Skye?" he muttered, feeling pain-free and comfortable. Soft, clean sheets and pillows that weren't guild so maybe he was at a Wellbeing somewhere. He couldn't remember booking in.

He almost yelled as tape was ripped off his hand and a cold sharp jab hit his elbow. This was eerily familiar.

A soft hand touched his cheek gently. "Hil, we need to go."

He opened his eyes to a dark room, the face leaning over him lit only by the faint light from the iso-pod. It took a moment to place her as Pen's medic from Earth and he had a pang of displaced confusion before he remembered making the decision to run to Pen.

"Where am I?" he said. "Where's Pen?"

She put a finger against his lips. "We're still at the town house. Pen's busy."

She helped him sit up and handed him a bundle of clothing and gear. "Get dressed and be quiet. Keep the patch on for now. And hurry. We don't have much time."

He instinctively reached up with his left hand to feel a bandage on his neck. His right wrist, he realised, was encased in a clear lightweight cast and felt numb. He could see and the pounding in his head had abated to a dull throb.

"How long have I been here?" he whispered.

"Not long enough but it will have to do. Get dressed," she said and turned abruptly, leaving him alone to find his bearings.

His clothes and coat had been cleaned, two knives and a small handgun added to his gear. The two vials he'd taken from Genoa were missing but everything else was there. He dressed and placed everything back in their usual pockets and hiding places, feeling twitchy about the abrupt awakening and wanting to get to Pen to find out what was happening. He saw with relief that the band on his wrist was dormant. He took a deep breath just to test it and sucked in cool, clean air that freely and easily filled his lungs and sent him slightly light-headed again.

He stood and stretched, feeling his muscles protest with a stiffness he wasn't used to. The woman reappeared at the door and beckoned to him.

"We're going out the back way," she said quietly. "Stay with me. I shouldn't be moving you but it's not safe to stay here any longer."

"What's going on?" Hil whispered to her back as he followed her through the house. It was dark, no lights, all of Pen's work stations off and strangely inert without power.

He caught hold of her arm and pulled her back. "Tell me what's going on," he said too harshly, but rattled again. He wasn't about to walk blindly into a trap. Pen liked this woman but Hil didn't know her well enough to shake off a growing sense of unease and distrust. Pen's stuff was never powered down.

She shook off his grasp and pushed him against the wall. It was shocking how easily she overpowered him.

She leaned close. "You've been here for three weeks. I've treated the electrobe poisoning. It was a new strain, that's why your antidote wasn't working. I neutralised the drugs you had in your system and I set your arm. I've stabilised the head injury but it hasn't totally healed yet."

She reached up and gently caressed his forehead and sent shivers of pain sparking behind his eyes.

"I still need to repair the damage to your neural interface but we can't stay here. You have to trust me. You need me. Don't fight against me."

"Where's Pen?" he asked again, softly this time, feeling helpless and like he was going to throw up. A lot could happen in three weeks.

"He's with LC," she said and let him go.

19

It was surprising to see the bottom of the goblet again so soon. NG eyed the jug. Placing his empty cup on the desk would invite another top up, so he kept hold of it, balancing it on his knee and feeling the warmth seep through.

"Tell me, NG," the Man said softly, "why did you not mobilise the instant you discovered Anderton was right there on Aston?"

Lying to the Man was suicidal, professionally and very probably literally. NG didn't even blink before replying.

"We did," he said. "But Pen Halligan has an extraordinary network on that planet. LC vanished before we could pinpoint his exact location. Pen outsmarted us, I'll admit that. We think Mendhel was good, but remember he always had the full support of the guild. Pen might be even smarter than his brother and he set up that network alone, based on integrity not fear. His people are tremendously loyal. We couldn't get through that in the circumstances."

It wasn't easy to admit that the guild had been outwitted.

The Man didn't react instantly – that was a good sign and NG didn't have to read his mind to know what he was thinking. An asset like Pen would be of infinite benefit to the guild. He'd tried before to persuade Mendhel to bring his brother in but he'd always laughed off the idea. The fact that LC and Hil had both run to Pen, rather than the guild, once Mendhel was gone spoke volumes. And that wasn't something he would openly admit to anyone.

The woman turned and walked away, heading for the back door.

Hil stumbled after her. "What? LC's here?"

She didn't break stride, her tall figure disappearing into the darkness ahead. He cursed under his breath and paused.

He couldn't believe that LC was here. But as he tried to think, a vague recollection surfaced. He had a faint memory of half waking in the iso-pod and hearing LC speaking with someone, but he'd brushed it off as a dream or muddled recall, confusing memories from different times. LC had asked if he was okay. He'd heard him, right there by his side, heard him say that they shouldn't have split up. Oh crap. His stomach back-flipped as he remembered. He reached up to his neck where a dressing hid the sore spot of the implant. He'd called out to Skye, telling her that LC was there but she hadn't replied because it was Genoa, not Skye, that was waiting for him at the orbital. And he'd not been able to stay awake.

He turned to look back into the house, unease at faint sounds that didn't belong. There was a tap then the crash of breaking glass was followed by a hiss and a loud bang.

He turned and ran.

Half way to the back door, there was another loud crash ahead of them. The woman swore softly in a language he didn't understand and grabbed his arm, pulling him sideways into the kitchen. They ran silently through the narrow room, hearing chaos erupt behind them. Pen's place was a warren of twisting corridors and steep staircases. In the dark that meant both hazard and safety, depending on whether the jerks breaking in had low light equipment. Hil's eyes didn't take long to adjust, he hadn't been awake long and he'd woken to the darkness. But the odds were that the intruders would be kitted out to the hilt. No one just broke into Pen's place. So they were up against it.

They dropped down two levels and ran through the cellar, hearing the distant sounds of voices coordinating the search. This was the one place that should have been safe.

The woman paused at a door and listened. Hil backed up close to her and watched both directions of the tight corridor. He had the gun out, held loosely in his left hand but the headache was back so he didn't reckon much to his chances of hitting anything.

"This is it – it leads down to the tunnels," she whispered. "Can you open it?"

He glanced back over his shoulder. The door had a keypad that was probably one of Pen's originals and probably rigged with a trap. "What? You know the way out but you don't know the code?"

She shook her head. "It's not working. Whoever they are, they've tripped out the whole system."

Hil pushed her out of the way, thrusting the gun into her hand. She took up his position keeping watch and he was sure she whispered 'be careful' at him.

It was awkward working the lock with a cast on one hand and nerves that were twice as jittery as they had been because they felt they'd been conned into a false sense of security. He leaned against the door and tried to remember everything Pen had ever bragged about. He was depending on the fact that they were breaking out, not breaking in so any defences that he did trigger should be aimed away from them. If anything, there should be an easy trip to it to get out if Pen had ever considered the possibility of circumstances like these.

The lock was stubborn, but then he wouldn't have expected anything else. Footsteps echoed down towards them. His heart rate upped a notch and he had to pause and concentrate to chase away the panic, thinking that no one should have been able to follow him here. He clicked into a connection and tweaked as delicately as he'd ever managed, and was rewarded with a soft hiss as the door catch released.

They slipped through and pulled the door closed behind them, abandoning Pen's place and on the run again.

The sun was coming up by the time they emerged from the tunnels. Hil was exhausted and stubbornly hiding it from the woman whose name he still hadn't remembered. She had led them on a winding trail through the city's underground, mingling with the late night crowds at the pit's nightclubs deep under the centre of Aston's spice quarter and smoothly blending in with the shift changers coming and going from the subways.

The day was dawning hot and humid, only the slightest hint of sea air on a faint breeze giving any respite, even this early.

Hil waited in the cover of a doorway and watched her scout out the street ahead, resisting the urge to sink down and sit on the dusty floor. She crossed to a building on the other side and waved him over. He didn't know exactly where they were but the buildings were even more decrepit than around Pen's place.

She pushed open a heavy metal door that had seen better days and stood aside, waiting for him to go in. It was good to get away from the street but there was still a nagging doubt about this that wouldn't let him settle. He hesitated.

She glared at him and muttered something that sounded like, 'oh for god's sake', and strode into the building, leaving him at the door.

If she was going to hand him in, there'd have been no need for the night long dance through the city. He tried to get a grip on his paranoia, closed the door and followed her inside.

"This is another of Pen's safe houses," she called back to him. "Make yourself at home. Give me a minute, I just need to get some things together."

Hil wandered through into a sitting room and ignored the lure of a sofa to follow her into what looked like a lab. He needed some answers before he was going to be able to settle anywhere.

"Where's Pen?" he said. "And LC? You said LC was here?"

"Not here," she said. "But yes, he's on Aston. Pen's with him and from what I can tell, he's in a worse state than you are."

"I'm fine," Hil said defensively, lying but not about to give in yet. "Where are they?"

She ignored him and rummaged in a cupboard.

Exasperated, Hil moved in close and said again, "Please, I don't think you understand. I need to go find them. I've been out for three weeks? You've got to let me know what's going on."

She stopped and looked at him, cold eyes half closing in a calculated squint that made him want to cringe away. He held firm.

"I know what it's like to be running for your life," she said and pulled a bag from a shelf. "Believe me. Pen has asked me to take care of you. I intend to do that before I let you go running off again. I don't think you understand the danger you're in."

145

She pushed him away gently and steered him towards a flat bunk pulled down from the wall.

"Sit," she said and started pulling medical kit out of the bag.

Hil knew when he was defeated and wasn't too stupid to admit he didn't feel great. He sat.

"Have you seen them?" he said and paused. "Has LC got the package?"

She didn't answer straight away and he thought she was going to be evasive, but just as he started to gear up for an argument, she said, "Yes. Yes, he has."

"I need to talk to him," he said and made a move to get up.

She stopped him with an outstretched palm. "No, you don't. Keep the patch on, whatever you do. This building is shielded, well shielded, but we don't know who we're dealing with yet. Pen has people keeping watch. Whoever raided the town house, they shouldn't have been able to find us and they shouldn't have been able to get to us without more warning than we had. Take your coat off. This isn't going to take long but you might as well get comfy. I'll finish up with you as fast as I can."

"Does Pen know we're here?" he said, shrugging out of the coat.

She caught hold of his arm and pushed up his sleeve. Seeing that she was readying a shot sent the paranoia spiking again. He wasn't ready to let go again yet. She must have felt him tense because her grip tightened.

"Trust me," she said. "You need to get back up to speed and what I'm going to do will help you. Your guild is in trouble, LC is in trouble and now Pen is caught up in it. We'd never turn you away, Hil, you know that but I really wish you hadn't come here."

He hadn't thought much past finding LC and getting Anya back. He realised with a pang of guilt that he hadn't considered the consequences of getting Pen involved. Pen's place on the edge of the market was probably trashed. First the guild, now Pen – the integrity of all his comfort zones was crumbling, any sense of security anywhere trampled from all directions. And he'd been out of action again for three weeks?

"I wish we'd never left Mendhel," he said, feeling guilty but irritated that she was blaming him. "We should never have agreed to it. If we'd all pulled back to the guild, none of this would have happened. They would have helped us get Anya back and screw the people who did it. I don't know what we were thinking. I don't remember what we were thinking. That we could pull it off? I'm sorry I pulled Pen into this but where was I supposed to go? The guild tossed me out to the wolves and for all I know, half the guild were in on it in the first place. Whatever is in that package, LC had better be taking good care of it because half the galaxy has gone nuts over trying to get it off us."

"You don't know half of it," she said.

"So tell me."

"Pen said he'll explain everything when he gets here."

"Pen and LC are coming here?"

She gently pulled open his shirt and attached a monitor to his chest. The quiet beeping was too fast, his heart rate was never that fast.

"Lie down," she said and nudged him, taking up his arm again. "I'm going to make this light. We don't know when we might get company again."

"Hey, bud."

Hil felt a hand hold and shake at his ankle. He felt better, startlingly better, and hoped it hadn't been another three weeks. He was still fully dressed so that was unlikely. He took a mental inventory of himself. He felt rested and his head felt clear, more than clear. She must have repaired the damage to the implant. The connection felt muted so he was still shielded but it was a cleaner contact than he'd ever had before.

He opened one eye and wiggled his hand. The cast was gone thankfully and it felt tender but he could move his wrist without a twinge for the first time in a long while.

Pen was wearing travelling gear, still dusty, and he looked more tired and strained than Hil had ever seen before.

"Elenor said you should be okay to move. You fit to go?"

Hil lifted himself up onto one arm. He did feel okay. He swung his legs round and perched there on the edge of the bunk, testing his balance.

"Pen," he said. "Where's LC? Is he okay?"

"No, he's in the shit. We all are. C'mon, we have to go."

Pen walked out of the lab, his shoulders hunched, fists clenching and unclenching. Hil caught up his coat, eased himself off the bed and followed Pen through to the main room. Elenor was there waiting, arms folded and looking as tense as Pen.

"Where's LC?" he said again.

Pen waved to the sofa. "Sit."

Hil sat down, looking from Elenor to Pen. It wasn't surprising they were pissed at him.

Pen sat down in a chair opposite and Elenor came and perched next to him. She set a bag down between them.

"I've sent LC somewhere safe," Pen said. "For the minute anyway."

"I need to see him," Hil protested.

Pen shook his head. "No way. There's no way I'm putting the two of you together. You don't know what's happening out there, Hil. I've never seen it like this before. LC has fucked up big time."

The big man rubbed his eyes and squinted hard at Hil.

"The bounty on you both has doubled. And your guild has sent out an all-points alert. Every team is out there looking for you. But at least they want you back alive. One rumour is saying there's a hit out there, dead or alive, they don't care, someone just wants you both that badly."

"It's not a rumour," Hil said. "I'm sorry. I shouldn't have come here." Now he could think straight, it was the worst place he could have come.

"Be serious. Where else could you have gone?" Pen said. "The problem is that LC is making mistakes. He's not concentrating, and physically, he's a mess."

Elenor shifted uneasily. "You should have let me look at him," she said.

Pen shrugged. "He wouldn't let me. He wouldn't let me anywhere near and he freaked when I said I could get you. What was I supposed to do?"

Hil felt cold. LC never freaked out about anything.

"You should have kept him here," Elenor said.

"How could I?" Pen said. "Half the galaxy's bounty hunters are right on his tail. I don't know how he managed to stay clear of them long enough to make it here at all. Aston is teeming with them. It's costing me a fortune to keep their attention diverted away from us. Our other problem…"

He took the massive pistol from his pocket and placed it on the armrest of the chair. "…is this."

20

"Profit and gain," the Man said. "We ply our trade across the galaxy and hold seats on every council. We send our operatives far and wide to bring information and technology and history back to our fold. And all for what?"

NG tried to keep his mind in neutral. The Man had never spoken so openly about the guild and its purpose. He felt strangely unnerved to be hearing this now, in these circumstances.

The Man beckoned for NG's goblet. "To save a civilisation that has not the wits to realise it is under threat. Countless species have come and gone, flourished and died throughout the universe. What makes this one worthy of redemption when others have floundered? Their greed astounds me."

NG leaned forward and placed his goblet on the desk. He'd never drunk so much of the guild's famed wine before, and never heated like this. He was sure the curious reaction in the jug was increasing its potency.

He didn't want to advocate on behalf of the human race, not any more, but that was his place here so he felt the obligation to speak up.

"Aston is especially decadent, anyway," he said. "And the amount of money on offer for our two operatives was obscene. People change when fortunes are to be made. Money and power. Ultimately, that's all we care about. What else is there?"

The light that had been flashing was dark, the pistol lying inert. The memory of a roof in the rain was somewhere Hil didn't want to go.

Pen picked it up and waved it at him. "This is from Earth. Special Forces, advanced tech that is beyond anything we've seen out here.

Bio-feedback, dna-tagged, nano-actuators. Ye gods, Hil, do you want to know what even having this here has triggered?"

No, obviously. Hil felt cold deep inside, thinking that those guys had been from Earth – the Earth military had sent in a Special Forces team after him. That elevated the whole situation beyond crap.

"Half my contacts want to get their hands on it to pull it apart," Pen said, "because they've never seen anything this advanced and the other half are backing away from me like I've got the plague, like I'm in league with Earth all of a sudden. Winter does not want a direct conflict on its doorstep right now. We've just disassociated ourselves from a hundred rebellions in the Between – we don't want to bring Earth forces trekking all the way out here because the Thieves' Guild screwed up. The odd piece of scrounged technology is fine, even the odd defection across the line," Pen looked at Elenor, "but waving a red rag at an Earth force kitted out with equipment like this, it's making a lot of people uncomfortable."

He put the gun down. "Anyway, that answers your question about who the assault forces were. What their interest in all this is, is anyone's guess. The other question, about the people who gave you the tab, is more complicated. The implant you retrieved has ID codes on it that we're still trying to crack. We managed to get past protections that were pretty sophisticated but we're still a way off learning anything useful. You were lucky not to blow yourself up getting it."

"I was blown up getting it," Hil said, "or at least she was."

Pen smiled grimly and looked at his watch. "We know it's a corporation – which ties in with your description of their set-up. Which one, we don't know yet but I have people working on it."

Pen paused and looked straight at him, unnerving intensity that he wasn't used to from Pen. "You realise, don't you, that Anya is probably dead."

It wasn't good to be confronted outright with that, but it had been playing on his mind. He'd spent three weeks in an iso-pod at Pen's place, days running before that, an indeterminate time at the guild and at least a week someplace after the crash so yes, he was aware that the time was probably long gone for a serious attempt at a rescue. He just didn't want to face it.

"I know they killed Mendhel," he said. "I hate to say it but yeah, I know, I wouldn't be surprised if they'd killed Anya too. We should have called for help. I can't remember why we didn't."

Pen looked at his watch again. "We don't have much time. Ele?"

Elenor opened the bag and picked out a handful of vials. "Antidote, in case you run into that strain of electrobes again. Stabilisers for the fractures, you could do with another week's worth. And these…" She held up the two vials he'd taken from Martha. "Don't use them."

It sucked to need to take meds and it was disturbing how relieved he felt to see the last two again, but he took the vials, putting those two in a separate pocket.

"What now?" he said.

Pen stood up. "It won't be long before the hooligans who raided the town house get around to checking the rest of my properties. We need to get you out of here. First though," he took a package out of his pocket, "LC asked me to give you this."

"You're kidding me," Hil said, almost snatching the package. It was small and heavy, neutral seals intact on its edges. "Is this it?"

"You know what LC's like. He wouldn't say. He did say though that you had to open it."

Hil stared at the package. He couldn't place it, couldn't dredge up any recollection of seeing it before. He tried to place it back in the mess of memories he had of fleeing the lab, helping LC out and desperately trying to make it to Skye before the building exploded behind them. There was nothing.

He tore open the seals and shook out the contents. A module not much bigger than his palm tumbled out. It was an AI memory back up module, which explained the weight. He tried again to place it, but if this was what they'd taken from the lab, that chunk of his memory was still missing, goosed from the accident.

He looked up at Pen. "I've never seen it before."

"There's an ASM over there. You can hook up on remote. We're shielded so don't worry about taking off the patch. If you want to be alone, I'm not going to argue. You've got five minutes then we're gonna have to go."

Pen picked up the pistol and walked out, followed by Elenor, who went up close and put an arm around the big man's waist as they walked.

The thought of hooking up with a module of uncertain origin gave him the creeps but why would LC say to open the package if he wasn't supposed to tie into the thing? It could fry the implant but that wasn't anything new these days. But worst case, it could kill him. A few weeks ago, he wouldn't have dreamed of doing what he was about to do. He peeled the dampening patch away from his neck. The skin beneath was smooth and cool. He could feel the outline of the implant embedded below the surface. The module was inactive. All he needed to do was drop it into the access machine and it would fire up. He had nothing to lose. If it screwed him, it screwed him. He was screwed anyway.

He watched the ASM accept the module and power up then settled on the sofa, head resting on a cushion at one end and feet up at the other. When he searched out and allowed the connection, it sparked into life with a jolt and a buzz that made him wince. There were a few seconds of static that rose in pitch to a point that was almost unbearable then a sudden quiet before the data stream kicked in.

The information that flooded into his mind was overwhelming at first. Star charts, calcs, lists of numbers and images flashed in front of his eyes at dizzying speed. He gasped and clenched his fists, the urge to disengage overcome by the need to know what it was. He couldn't comprehend it all straight away but the data would be there in his memory to be accessed.

Eventually, the flow of data slowed and the connection became passive. He began to probe gently, searching through the stream, looking for any sign of identification or source code, anything that would explain any of this mess. He reversed the direction of momentum the way Skye had shown him and started to query the module itself. It was tricky and dangerous and she'd always warned him away from trying it with an unknown in case of tripwires that would send a spark back at you that could kill, but in the circumstances he didn't care and took as much care as he could manage while working as fast as he could. There were barriers but he eased through and, with a jolt, realised the identity of the AI. She gave him access to a stream of images, himself and LC seen through the eyes of security cameras mounted outside the ship, running. It skipped to a scene inside the airlock, an argument, images of LC that matched the flashes of memory he'd had. He'd won the argument and, as if his brain had been cleaned out with detergent, he knew what was coming, knew why and watched with fascination as the scene played out from the AI's memory as clear as his own.

The stored data stopped abruptly and Hil lay quietly, keeping the connection neutral and open, letting it all absorb. A tug on his ankle brought him back to the moment and he disconnected, feeling the emptiness like a loss.

"We have to go," Pen said gently.

Hil opened his eyes and sat up. He retrieved the module and dropped it back into the packet.

"It's Skye," he said. "It's all on here. What happened, why. She erased it so the guild wouldn't find any of it. LC must have had this the whole time. Did he talk to you about any of it?"

Pen shook his head. "No, but c'mon we really have to go."

"I can't let anyone get hold of this," Hil said, holding up the package. "It's got everything on it, coordinates for the drop, everything."

"Well, give it here and I'll find out who the bastards are," Pen said.

"No, you don't understand. I can give you the coordinates but this…"

"What else is on it, Hil?"

There was no way he could say. But an idea of what he had to do was beginning to form. He'd risked everything to give LC a chance to get away and now he knew why. It was time to finish this.

"Pen, I need you to help me," he said.

"Ye gods, Hil, what do you think I'm doing? Come on, we can talk on the way."

The all-terrain jeep parked outside had its engine running. Two of Pen's guys covered their exit from the building and Pen pushed him inside.

It seemed to take forever to get out of the city. The sprawl of low buildings stretching out from the edge of the city boundary gradually thinned until they were driving through mostly deserted scrubland. They drove along the coast for a while then took a sharp turn inland.

No one said a word, the hum of the air conditioning in the jeep almost hypnotising him into sleep. Elenor had slapped the patch back onto his neck before they left and he had the feeling that everyone else was shielded too.

They switched vehicles twice, one time in an underground garage in a small mining settlement just outside the city – a quick exchange with little ceremony. The second switch was outside on a desert road. Another jeep overtook them in a cloud of dust, swerving in front of them so that both vehicles careered off the track. Pen swore and yelled at them to stay inside. He jumped out and ran to the other jeep.

Hil watched, using every ounce of restraint he had not to push open the door and rush over there. Elenor put her hand on his leg, calming. Pen looked pissed, leaning on the open window and talking heatedly with the driver. The guy gave him an envelope. Pen opened it and pulled out a data board, glaring at it angrily, turning to glare at Hil and turning back to speak to the driver again. Finally, Pen waved to them and Elenor gave him a shove.

The heat out on the road was stifling. And the glare of sunlight from the pale rocky surface made his eyes sting. They ran to the other vehicle and Pen held open the door without a word. Hil tried to stop and stand there, wanting to know what was going on. Now his head wasn't pounding, his temper was finding its feet again.

"Pen," he said, wanting to argue and make a stand.

"Get in."

"At least tell me what's going on."

Pen pulled the data board out of the envelope again and held it up. "Recognise these two?"

Oh crap. It was a still image taken from a security camera, not a great picture but obviously Pen's pad at the market place, two people captured on visuals entering the den. Two people who shouldn't have been there. His world took another tilt.

"I take it you do. Hil, get in the jeep."

It was hard to argue with Pen at any time, when the big man was angry it was impossible. And Hil felt like he'd been punched in the chest. He bit his lip and climbed into the jeep. Pen jumped in beside him and slammed the door, yelling at the driver to go.

"Who are they," he demanded as they skidded off the verge and took off.

Hil looked at the picture again, resting it on his knee. "That's Kase Wibowski," he said. "And that is Martha J Hetherington. They're guild extraction agents."

21

They sat in silence for long minutes. NG felt a trickle of sweat run down his ribs. It was hot anyway but to sit there under the gaze of the Man sent his internal temperature soaring.

"The guild," the Man said, "has never before in its entire history been betrayed." He let that well known fact settle like thick fog between them before continuing. "Guild agents working for a Wintran corporation against Earth..."

NG sat quietly. There was no need to emphasise the damage that had been done. Media had been working overtime to mitigate. And he would swear Legal were enjoying it. Sometimes the best results come out of the worst situations.

"Explain to me how you missed it, NG."

The Man was playing games with him. He knew fine well exactly when NG had found out and how but he was pushing him to admit it out loud.

"And your decision to tip off Jameson," the Man said, "giving information to him about the request to send Hilyer to Abacus."

NG nodded but kept quiet.

The Man poured more wine, filling the two goblets to the brim. "Do you defend that decision?"

"I do. Under the circumstances I considered that I had no other choice. They contacted me as soon as they realised their facility had been infiltrated. Jameson was furious. It didn't take much to work out that it must have been our people. There's no one else capable of it." He paused, then reluctantly added, "I didn't anticipate the strength of the force they would send to Abacus."

"This is a dangerous game you've been playing, NG," the Man said, throwing his own thoughts back at him.

"Isn't it always?"

They were wearing full assault gear. And Kase looked very much alive and well.

"You're shitting me," Pen said and grabbed the board. "That's Martha? Man, LC said you were nuts to let her go."

"I was nuts to have ever gotten involved with her. It was Kase and Martha that extracted me after the crash."

"Yeah, well it looks like they've got ulterior motives."

"How did they find me? I didn't tell anyone where I was going."

"Your ship," Pen said and took another document from the envelope. It was a tatty piece of plastic sheet, the type they printed out invoices on when someone wanted more proof than an electronic record. "You said you didn't know who to trust at your guild, well you were right to be paranoid for once. Your ship's up there for repairs, right?"

"Not my ship," he protested.

Pen glared him to shut up. "You said she was in for repairs? Major repairs, you said. Life support, shields, jump drive. You said she'd taken direct hits when she got you off that planet? She lied to you."

Hil looked at the invoice. It was a dockyard inventory, the type of anonymous ID guild ships used when they were out on a tab but it was definitely Genoa. And it was for a simple refuel and restock, minor repairs to the landing gear.

"I don't understand."

"Damn right you do understand, bud. You told me all along. You don't know who to trust at the guild. Well, I'm telling you, you can't trust your ship and you can't trust those two extraction agents."

"Genoa's not my ship," he said again, holding onto the window ledge as they swerved to take a side track off the main road.

"Whatever she told you, she was lying," Pen said. "Did you contact her from my house? The house at the market?"

He had that vague memory of half-waking and telling her that LC was there. He nodded, feeling stupid and ticked off that he'd been so stupid and was still being stupid. He'd thought he was calling out to Skye and he'd trust her with his life, but even so, even knowing the guild had been compromised, he would never have thought to suspect a ship.

Pen handed him the board. "Look at the rest of the footage," he said.

Hil flicked it on. The film started out hazy from the smoke and tear gas they'd thrown in but the image cleared up as it dissipated. He looked at the faces of the people scouring Pen's place, a meticulous, fast-paced search, coordinated with precision. He watched, detached, watched himself and Elenor run for the basement a fraction ahead of the intruders who went efficiently from room to room, guns up. Kase and Martha weren't leading the mission. They followed in last, at a distance, almost casually.

The jeep was picking up pace, Pen leaning over to speak to the driver.

Hil ignored them and looked back at the board. He tracked back to the beginning and watched, freezing at each face as they passed the different camera angles. Something was niggling and it wasn't just that Martha was there. He didn't recognise any of the other faces. If it was a guild operation, he should have known some of the other agents. He didn't know all of them but he would have thought he'd see some he knew. Kase and Martha were the only two who were obviously guild. So who the hell were they working with? It clicked into place as soon as he thought of it. He back tracked again and let it play, freezing on a face with piercing grey eyes.

Elenor was watching. "Who's that?" she asked softly.

Hil stared at the still, chill settling in his stomach despite the heat. "He was one of the guys that picked me up on Abacus. He said he killed Mendhel."

Pen snapped his head back towards them. "It's him? You're sure?"

The sense of betrayal formed like a physical lump in Hil's throat, anger seeping through every cell. His voice was strained. "Martha's been working with them the whole time. She rescued me from them after I crashed."

"And Genoa," Elenor said, "the ship? She's been feeding them information?"

Pen took the board. "Okay, this changes things."

Hil stared at the board. He'd been warned not to trust the guild and he'd known. Deep down he'd known. That it was Martha hurt but his grief over Mendhel was still tied firmly in anger so he wrapped Martha up in with that and controlled his breathing carefully. "It doesn't change anything."

"Yes, it does." Pen tapped his knee with the board. "Now we know who they are and where they are, we can find out what they are."

By the time they pulled up at the gates to the encampment, the sun was setting on the desert horizon. Pen had spent the rest of the journey giving urgent, succinct orders to their driver. Hil had let the time drift by, playing games with his breathing and heart rate, and working on his plan. Coming up with the plan took about two minutes. Refining it took about thirty seconds. He told Pen and said he'd need the big pistol back, and Pen said he was mad. He slept the rest of the way.

It was late when they stopped outside tall metal gates which opened for them without much of a delay and they drove into the shantytown. He'd heard about these places but had never been out here before. Pen gave directions and the jeep navigated a winding route through narrow, crowded streets, bumping over potholes and swerving to avoid desert mongrels that ran out in front of them.

"Here," Pen said abruptly, tapping on the back of the driver's seat. "You guys get inside. I'll be right there."

From the look on Elenor's face, Hil guessed she hadn't been out here either. The jeep pulled up and they climbed out. Yan was there holding open a door. He nodded at them and muttered, "Straight down the stairs."

They pushed past a dusty brown curtain and Hil followed Elenor down the steep steps and into an almost exact replica of Pen's den in the city. An array of monitors flickered around the perimeter of the small room, casting white light onto instrument panels and benches piled with tools and unfamiliar equipment. The centre of the den was filled with Pen's favourite type of chairs and sofas, low tables and candles. Elenor slumped into a chair and covered her face with her hand. He was hit by another pang of guilt that he'd brought this to them and lurked by the doorway feeling awkward and intrusive.

It didn't take long for Pen to come crashing down the stairs.

"Okay, we're covered," he said. He brushed past Hil and tossed the heavy pistol at him. "There you go, bud. I still think you're mad. Sit down, you're making the place look a mess."

Hil caught the gun and let a faint smile creep across his face.

"What about the other thing?" he said.

"That'll take a while to organise. In the meantime, stay here, stay shielded, whatever you do – don't contact Genoa, I don't want this place trashed as well, and we'll try to track down these corporate bastards. Are you serious about this?"

"It's more of a plan than I've had so far," Hil said and wandered across to the sofas. "And LC gets away. That's the point, right?"

It took five days for Pen to get everything he needed. Hil used the time to run and stretch some flexibility back into his muscles. The desert air was dry and Elenor chided him for pushing his lungs to their limit each time he returned coughing but it was working. He wasn't back to the level he'd been before all this kicked off, but he was starting to get close again. Two of Pen's guys fancied that they could race him but he outran them each time. They beat him in bare knuckle but not without a fight every time, and they all ended up with scuffed knees and elbows from the desert floor, and as Yan taught him a few pointers, they had to up their game to stop him winning. Elenor hated it and Pen laughed a lot. Until they remembered why he was there.

Fighting released some of the tension that was building with being stuck in the desert and running was the only way he could clear his mind. Pen warned him not to go too far outside the safety of the compound but once out there he couldn't help but push it and two days in, he pushed it too far.

He set himself a target of a ridge across the floor of the desert and ran. It was hard not to dwell on Martha and wonder why she'd done it. Their break up had been painfully vindictive on both sides but he couldn't believe that all this was a result of his insensitivity.

She'd betrayed the guild, not just him. And as much as she could be irritatingly superficial at times, it didn't fit with the woman he'd known that she'd do this for money. However high the price on their heads had gone, Martha just wasn't driven by that. At least he thought she wasn't driven by that, but as he'd found out, he hadn't really known her at all.

He picked up the pace, angry with himself for not seeing it, stumbled on a patch of loose stones and turned his ankle. He tumbled and ended up in a heap, breathing hard. He hugged his knees and looked around, exasperated, trying to breathe in air that was too hot and clear the fluff out of his mind. Elenor was going to be pissed.

He tested the ankle and decided it would hold his weight. Standing up proved him wrong but it wasn't so bad that he couldn't limp his way back, ticked off and tired.

Half way back to the compound, a trail of dust appeared on the horizon. He stopped and squinted at it. Vehicles. There was nowhere to hide so he limped on, wishing he'd brought a weapon out with him. He had the dampening patch on still and as tempting as it was to break cover and yell out, he didn't want to expose Pen and his operation, whoever it was approaching him.

Worst case was they could be Martha and her new buddies, slightly less worse would be bounty hunters.

He kept a steady pace and one eye on the road veering in from his left. The compound was still a way off by the time the dust cloud turned into discernible vehicles, jeeps he thought, and three of them. They roared up and careered past without stopping. Hil flinched away from the debris they kicked up as they passed, blinking his eyes clear of dust and feeling both relieved and deflated that they hadn't stopped for him. Maybe the universe didn't revolve around him after all.

He'd taken two more steps when one of the jeeps hit the brakes, spun round in a swirl of red sand and headed back towards him.

22

NG took a sip from his goblet, keeping his emotions in check.

"Don't be too hard on yourself," the Man warned again. "There are thousands of individuals in this guild of ours; you alone cannot touch each mind every minute of every day."

NG looked up and those dark glittering eyes were focused directly on him. "I should have known."

The Man shook his head. "You're not perfect. And as far as I am aware, the minds and thoughts of the machines developed by man himself remain closed even to us."

The room seemed darker and it took a moment to realise some of the candles had gone out, extinguished by a breeze NG hadn't felt. It had been a disconcerting time to lose control over his domain, to realise that rogue elements were shifting circumstances without his knowledge or influence. He'd always had such an indisputable insight to the workings of the guild that it felt like he'd closed his eyes and opened them to see that everything was different.

He took a deep breath.

"Evolution can take unexpected leaps at times," the Man said softly. "No one, no matter how strong, can control or prevent that. We simply need to be aware enough and lithe enough to adapt and grasp the reins confidently again to move forward. There will always be danger while we deal with these irrational and self-centred beings."

Hil stopped and waited, eyes narrowed, weight on one foot. If they had guns, he didn't have a chance. If they went for hand to hand, he'd give them a fight. As it was, the jeep veered off and pulled up with another handbrake turn to stop next to him. Yani leaned out of the driver's window and yelled him to jump in. There were two guys in the back, another in the passenger seat and all of them were cradling weapons.

Hil paused with his hand on the door. "Yan," he said, "what's going on?"

"Hilyer, get in. You shouldn't be out here alone. It's not safe."

"Yani, what's going on?"

The glare made it obvious he had no choice. He yanked open the door and squeezed into the back, slamming it shut as Yani pulled the jeep away in a squeal of spinning tyres and a cloud of dust.

They accelerated fast to catch up with the jeep ahead of them. Hil held onto the window frame as the vehicle bounced and lurched. "Yani?"

"Hil, don't ask."

He didn't push it any further. He appreciated the lift back and Pen could tell him or not when they got in.

Back at the compound, Hil jumped out of the jeep and stood leaning on the open door. Pen was waiting and started directing the guys from all three vehicles, loading and unloading kit, everyone dressed for action.

Yan went straight to his boss and the two men looked over towards Hil at the jeep, Pen looking unimpressed. Hil couldn't hear what they were saying but it looked like he was the source of the problem. Yan laughed and turned to go, patting Pen on the arm. Pen shook his head and strode over to Hil.

"Hil, get inside the house."

"What's going on?"

"You don't need to know. This doesn't have to involve you."

Pen's guys were hustling. Hil had never totally understood everything Pen was into and most times, he knew better than to ask. Sometimes it conflicted with the guild, often it was Wintran business and always it was illegal but there was something about the look on Pen's face that made it obvious that this did involve him. Pen hadn't been expecting him back so soon and if he had stuck to his plan, he'd still be out there running until it got dark. And they'd be gone.

"Is this…?"

Pen cut him off, raising a hand. "Hil, just go inside."

Pen was not a man to argue with, especially not in front of his men, he'd learnt that the hard way. But after feeling so helpless and hurting for so long, being wired to breaking point and being just about fit enough at last to do something about it, it was impossible to back down. Something clicked inside.

"Pen, I want in," he said simply.

Pen lowered his hand and stared, a crease appearing between his eyes and finally a shake of his head. "You're not fit enough yet, Hil. I know you think you are but we're going in fast. You won't be able to keep up."

It wasn't an insult, it was fact. But he couldn't sit back and watch. Not now.

"These people have trashed everything I care about," Hil said, not bothering to keep his voice down. "The whole galaxy is after me and I don't even know why. I'm sick of running, Pen. It stops here. I want in and I want a piece of them."

"They've had their hands on you twice," Pen said much more quietly. "And I get the impression they're losing patience. You want to know who these people are? Let us handle it. I'll tell you exactly who they are and where they are, and what you do from then is up to you."

"Pen, these people killed Mendhel. Don't make me sit here waiting while you go after them. I want in."

Pen was a big man in many ways and when he made up his mind, he could be an immovable force but when he wanted to change his mind, it happened quickly. He nodded.

"We go in five," he said. "Be ready."

Hil walked inside calmly, ditched the running gear he'd borrowed and changed back into his ops kit, almost trembling. He took one minute of those five to just stand there, breathing slowly, getting his emotions back in line. He then stashed the knives, tucked the small handgun into the back of his waistband and shrugged on his coat. Elenor was standing watching as he walked out through the den.

She caught his eye and he stared, not sure what to say. She didn't say a word, just set her face like she was trying not to cry, then turned away.

Outside, they were waiting and Pen gave him an armoured jacket and waved him into one of the jeeps. The jacket was uncomfortable under his coat and hampered his movement, which was frustrating. It was tempting to leave it off, but looking at the hardware they were all carrying, it was more tempting not to be stubborn for once. It was weird going into an operation with other people. He wasn't a team player and it wasn't easy to let go and let Pen's guys run the show.

Pen gave him a hint of a briefing on the way out, just the basic plan and an emphasis on the need for Hil to hang back and not interfere. Like that was going to happen. He nodded anyway and watched the desert pass by and darken as the sun lowered and eventually the orange haze on the horizon ahead turned into the lights of the city.

The guy they were after, the guy with grey eyes, was staying at a private rented apartment on the shoreline, an exclusive beachfront establishment that Pen explained would be heavy on security. Fast in, fast out. Enough bribes had been paid to make sure local law enforcement would take a long time to respond, it was the guy's own contingent they were more concerned about. This guy claimed he had killed Mendhel and that would have been no easy feat so Pen was going in heavy and hard.

The jeeps split up once they were in the city, one taking a direct route to the rear of the apartment's walled grounds, theirs and the other going the coastal road to slip in to the building's courtyard from the front. The gates swung open for them as they approached, payoffs paying off and making their entrance nice and easy. Hil and LC had always known the level of control Pen enjoyed in Aston but it wasn't often it was displayed outright this way. Pen owned people throughout the city and they tended to be fiercely loyal. Quiet words with key people and their path to this guy was clear and carefully maintained. Hil had no doubt that if the guy had run, he wouldn't have got far before being brought down and brought before Pen.

The guild had something similar but spread wider and therefore not always guaranteed. That tended to work in their favour. If you trusted no one in the outside, you weren't often let down. Problem was now he couldn't trust anyone on the inside.

Tiny lights sparkled along the driveway leading up to the house, scattered among well-tended shrubs that looked much too green for Aston. The jeeps crunched up the gravel driveway and pulled up at an angle, both noses in, at a front entrance that was dark but flickering with light from within.

Car doors were thrown open and they piled out, Pen's guys falling into formation around him like they'd done this a hundred times. It wasn't just practised, it was instinctive. Hil stood in the centre and felt the tingle of apprehension he always got before an op, nerves gearing up and reactions balanced on the edge. In the quiet before the storm, Pen stood, coat whipping in the sea breeze, and turned to him. "Stay close to me."

He nodded again vaguely and Pen must have seen something in his face because the big man leaned over and caught the back of his neck, pulling him in. "Stay close, understand?"

"I will," he muttered, eyes staring at the door, pulling out his gun with one hand and a knife with the other.

"If we don't know where you are, you'll get yourself killed. You understand?"

Hil nodded. He was back and it felt good. The universe narrowed to this moment in time and that doorway in front of them. No more running.

They went in fast. Pen was the eye of the whirlwind and Hil was a step behind. To both sides, as they pushed open the door and strode into the house, gunshots exploded out in all directions. Their footsteps echoed on marble tiles, plants and statues crashing to the floor as the corporate security realised they were being invaded and ran to defend their stronghold. Pen didn't stop and his guys spread out and dominated the entry. Up ahead more sounds of battle filtered back as Yan led the assault from the rear. The onslaught was relentless.

They turned into a huge open atrium in the centre of the building and came face to face with one of the huge twins, both arms up, two barrels held unwavering right at them. Pen didn't skip a beat. His arm swept up and the sound of the pistol firing was deafening. The ape dropped and more shots peppered the floor and walls around them. A massive glass sculpture shattered and Pen walked without breaking step, through the glass shards and towards a staircase that wound up from the centre of the hall.

Hil caught movement from the corner of his eye and turned his head slightly, trying to keep step with Pen and ignoring the pain from his twisted ankle. They were surrounded now by fewer of Pen's guys as the squads broke down into pairs and peeled off to search the ground floor. Yani and his guys were already upstairs. Pen took a step onto the first stair and a bullet ricocheted off the banister by his hand. He still didn't pause.

The staircase split half way up and Pen marched up to the right, reloading, as half his bodyguard peeled off to the left.

"With me, Hilyer," Pen reminded him without looking back. He hadn't seriously been thinking of sneaking off but the warning was well timed. It was taking every ounce of self-restraint that he had to stay in the open like this. These guys were insane. He'd never seen Pen in action like this before. Insane didn't quite cover it. No wonder no one crossed him.

They came up onto a wide landing that stretched out to the left and right, doors lining the corridor. Pen nodded left and waved his hand low down by his leg, fingers flashing in a signal too fast for Hil to read. Two of the guys still with them went right, leaving them to take the left-hand passage. Pen had two guns out and the two guys with him both had assault rifles. Hil spun his knife around the fingers of his left hand, watching the corridor and glancing behind occasionally even though he knew they were covered. The doors were making him nervous and like a self-fulfilling prophecy, one crashed open as he passed, a body hurtling into him and slamming him against the door opposite. They crashed through into a room and the gun went tumbling from his hand as he hit the floor.

Gunfire and yells erupted out in the corridor. Hil scrambled to his feet and saw it was the other twin, the massive guy lurching up and rushing at him, grabbing him in a tackle around the chest and throwing him against the wall. Wind knocked out of him, Hil fell back and the guy pounced on him, full weight pinning him to the wall, a huge paw squeezing him around the throat.

He couldn't breathe and instinctively Hil spun his knife into a backhand hold and swept it upwards, catching the guy with a vicious slash across his face, opening up a gash that cut through the eye and cheek. The guy roared and threw him to the side, turning and pulling out a gun, blood streaming from his ruined eye socket.

Hil rolled backwards, head over heels, as shots splintered off the floor around him. He stood, trying to scramble out of the way and took a hit high in the chest that took his breath and threw him back. His knees buckled and he fell.

The gunfire stopped abruptly and the room fell silent, the quiet broken only by footsteps getting closer.

Hil groaned and swallowed painfully, his chest feeling like it was on fire. He rolled onto his side and saw Pen and Yani standing over a body.

"He's still alive," Pen said, nudging the body of the twin with his foot. "Keep him that way. I can use him." He turned to Hil and grinned. "I thought I told you to stay close."

23

"I understand that we are still seeing the repercussions of this incident throughout Winter."

NG nodded. "It's always been volatile. And rather than contracting as alliances strengthened, as most people believed would happen, the Between is growing as more and more colonies begin to disagree which side of the line they feel most affiliated to."

The Man topped up his own goblet, frowning to see that NG's cup was still half full. "I also hear rumblings," he said, "that the activity of independent operators is increasing."

NG picked up his glass. "We actually have a theory that Hilyer might have been shot down by pirates when he crashed. We haven't been able to identify the ships that chased him and Legal is fairly certain that means they were independents."

"And Pen Halligan?"

"Is growing in influence," NG said, draining his goblet and placing it on the table.

The Man nodded his approval and filled it. "He's a good man and he is building an impressive empire. He handled Hilyer well by all accounts."

"Mendhel always said he'd make an incredible handler for the guild if we could ever persuade him to come in."

"Maybe so, but sometimes individuals can be of more value to us left to their own devices. We can take care to look after our own wherever they are, NG, whether they know it or not."

It felt like he'd been run over by a truck. Hil unfastened the body armour beneath his coat and felt tenderly across his chest.

"You'll be fine," Pen said and slapped him on the back. "It'll match your other bruises. Come on, we've got our man. They're waiting for us."

Hil reached down and picked up his gun, tucking it back into place. Out in the corridor it was quiet, two bodies lying sprawled in an open doorway. He forced a deep breath and followed Pen to another staircase.

Two flights up and the house was quiet and dimly lit, plush carpets with hidden lamps casting soft light. Faint sounds of music drifted along from somewhere. Three more bodies in expensive suits lay on the floor of the top landing, handguns left where they'd dropped. Two of Pen's men were standing by a doorway further along the hall.

They were waved through without a word.

The man from the surveillance tape was sitting in a chair that had been pulled into the centre of the bedroom, slumped to one side, clutching a bleeding wound in his right arm. He glared with arrogant disdain at Hil as he entered, grey eyes flashing just as he remembered. Yani and two others stationed themselves around the room, Yan at the door which he closed as they went in. A dampening patch had been taped to the guy's neck but no one had bothered to tend to his gunshot wound.

Pen wandered off to one side, casually looking around the room.

Hil stood back, watching, his heart rate refusing to settle. More bits of memory clicked into place as he stared into those grey eyes. He had seen this guy before, at Mendhel's safe house on Earth, right there at the beginning. He'd been there waiting for them, holding a gun to Mendhel's head while he explained what they had to do.

Hil pulled the gun from his waistband and held it calmly down by his leg. The guy was smirking.

"Hil," Pen said as he was twitching to take aim at the guy, "there's some of their kit in that room," and nodded towards an adjoining door, "go check it out. Go do your thing."

Hil held his breath for a second, still staring right into those cold eyes, then he nodded and slipped through the door, leaving them to it.

The other room was set up as a temporary office, terminals hooked up to screens and data boards strewn on a table that had been cleared of its usual bedroom paraphernalia. He gained access quickly and easily bypassed their security, working fast as he was trained to do and ignoring the thumps and muffled shouts coming from the room next door. Whatever they did to the guy wasn't bad enough.

None of the data he got to straight away had any ID codes at all, nothing to give away who these people were or where they were based. It was all superfluous junk and a lot of detail about him and LC which was disturbing to see. He lingered on a medical report that detailed his recent injuries and the electrobe poisoning. No one should have been able to get hold of this stuff but there was also nothing to give away the source of any of that information, nothing to tie it to Martha.

It was second nature to be patient though, and he'd hacked his way into some of the best systems around; this was very good but he soon had access to the deeper levels.

There was a stifled scream from next door and he couldn't help the small half-smile as he eased his way in and started to backtrack towards the corporation itself. Twice he nearly tripped auto-destruct alarm sequences and as soon as he got a feedback shock into his own implant that sent a searing probe crashing against his own defences, he knew he was nearly there. He got what he needed, got out and when he looked up, Pen was at the doorway watching.

"You have anything you want to say to this bastard?" Pen said quietly.

Hil nodded and pulled out his gun, following Pen back into the bedroom and walking straight up to their prisoner, pistol up in a grip that was aimed right between those grey eyes. The guy had been taped to the chair, arms, legs and chest, and was looking rough, eyes still glinting but hooded and swollen, blood dripping from cuts across his lip.

Hil stopped when the barrel of the gun was resting against the guy's forehead.

"Where's Anya," he said quietly.

The smirk widened and he said smugly, "You're assuming she's still alive."

One of Pen's guys slapped him across the back of the head.

"Where is she?" Hil said again, finger tightening on the trigger, every ounce of him wanting to squeeze it, for Mendhel, for LC, for Anya. He kept the aim steady, managing to keep the trembling he felt inside locked away.

The guy blinked slowly and casually as if he was bored. "She was easier than Mendhel," he said, staring Hil in the eye. "She begged me to do it. She screamed and screamed until I cut her throat."

The trembling threatened to surface. No one moved or said a word. He didn't believe it and looked into those eyes to see the lie, but there was nothing. Hard, cold malice and nothing else. Hil squeezed the trigger a fraction and abruptly let his arms fall to his side.

He turned to Pen. "I've got everything I need. I don't believe him but I have enough information on them to find her." He looked back at the guy and watched his expression change as he said, "It's Zang Enterprises and I know where they are."

Considering how hard it had been to break their system, it wasn't surprising to see the guy scowl.

"I know everything about them," Hil said coldly. "Do what you want with him."

Pen raised his eyebrows in an unsaid question.

"I'm not a killer," Hil said simply.

"No, but I am," Pen said.

Hil nodded and turned away.

"You killed my brother," he heard Pen say softly and he slipped out, leaving them to it, his heart hammering in his chest. As he walked away, the screaming began in the room behind.

A couple of days later word came through to the desert encampment that it was all ready. Pen went through the inventory then they sat outside and drank beer and toasted Mendhel and Anya, and downed one for LC as the sun set.

"Go finish this," Pen said, raising his glass.

Hil nodded. "Here's to Martha and whatever the hell I did that was so bad she turned into the double-crossing bitch queen from hell."

"You live in a den of thieves, what did you expect?"

Pen had always hated the guild. Hil bit his tongue as the urge to defend it automatically kicked in.

"I always knew your guild would tear itself apart," Pen said.

"Two people selling us out aren't going to tear it apart."

"The rot has to start somewhere."

Hil drained his glass and reached for another bottle. He'd lost count of how many they'd had and would feel it in the morning; Aston-brewed beer was strong, much stronger than anything the guild kept in the barracks for them.

"Well, this is where it ends," he said.

They were both quiet then. The sounds of the desert drifted across into the settlement on a breeze that was starting to get a chill edge.

Hil rubbed his forehead feeling the outline of the scar from the crash. "You know, that bastard even had medical notes on me."

"Zang is a big organisation. What else did you get from their files?"

"The place they gave me as the drop off is one of their facilities. Same type as the one where they took me after I crashed. I couldn't find anything on why they shot me down, it looks like I was on my way there. I don't get it. They kept me for five days. All that bastard had in his files was an entry saying I didn't have the package and they couldn't get anything out of me. I don't remember it."

He couldn't say anything to Pen but he knew now why he couldn't remember. The Chief had been right, it wasn't entirely down to the knock on the head he'd taken in the crash. LC had hardly been able to walk but they'd made it out and Skye had flown them to a safe haven, a place they only ever used when they needed to disappear, and they'd come up with the plan for Hil to take a phony package back to give LC time to hide until they figured out what to do. They knew a guy there who could come up with anything, no questions asked, and he'd delivered. He'd come up with a package and they hadn't asked what was in it. The seals on it were enough to fool anyone for a while. They'd laid low for days and the guy had managed to find painkillers for LC that were way beyond any legal spec, and even then didn't seem to have much effect, and some wacky substance he'd promised would wipe Hil's short-term memory. They hadn't asked him what it was. They just knew that no one could know what had happened.

Hil rubbed his eyes.

"They've increased the bounty," Pen said. "There are some big names chasing it. I wasn't joking about spending a fortune to keep them at bay."

"I don't understand why they didn't just pay the guild for the tab. That much money. We would have got it and delivered it right to them. Why all this?"

"Corporations like Zang are an entity unto themselves. What I don't understand is why the Earth military is so interested. That's what has blown the whole situation off the scale. You sure you didn't stick your hand into Earth's cookie jar?"

Hil shrugged. "I don't know where we went. It was a bitch to get into though, I can remember that now."

Pen leaned forward and beckoned for another beer, sitting with his elbows resting on his knees, head to one side looking intently at Hil. "Is there no other way?" he said sombrely.

Hil cracked open a bottle and slid it across the table.

"It's not just Kase and Martha," he admitted, opening up about the guild to someone outside like he'd never done before. He felt like he was the one betraying the guild. It was absurd. How the hell had things got twisted around like this? "I can't go back because I don't know how far it goes. There were things that were said when I was pulled back there after the crash, things that didn't make sense but now... Now, I don't even know if I can trust NG. And the guy that's supposed to be handling me over this..."

"Quinn?"

Hil nodded. "He set everything up so I was alone on Abacus. Kase and Martha were there but no other back up. How does that look now? Quinn must have known. He must have, which means he's in on it, and if he is, who else? Shit, Quinn always hated

175

Mendhel. He hated that we were always top of the standings. You could see him seething about it every time we came back. The son of a bitch."

Pen poured out a glass, slowly emptying the bottle. "Things aren't always as they seem, Hil. Don't assume you know everything there is to know about a person. People aren't always what they appear. You know, I was serious when I said about going private. You can stay here. You don't have to do this, bud. Stay here and work with me."

Hil was surprised to find his glass empty again and concentrated on that instead of letting Pen's words filter into any possible level of consideration. He set the glass on the table and reached for another bottle, the resolve to have another drink adding weight to his resolve to carry out his plan. "You know why I can't do that, Pen. It'll never end. They know I'm a link to LC. I can't go back to the guild and I can't stay here."

Pen understood because he let it go and let the conversation fade, both of them quietly drowning out any thought of tomorrow. The sun finally dropped below the horizon, an orange ball that took with it the last heat of the day. Lights began flickering on around them as the settlement prepared for night.

"I'm sending Zang a message," Pen said casually. "Their man should never have come here. His cronies will be going back with the clear understanding that whatever deals Zang has made don't carry here. I have people out looking for Anya and now we know it's Zang, we can make them pay. I know that doesn't solve your problem."

"I don't have any choice. They want the package. I need to take it to them."

"If you do find Anya alive," Pen said, "bring her back here."

"I will," Hil said, knowing fine well that Pen knew that was something he couldn't promise.

"Mend should've come out here. I always told him that guild of yours would get him killed."

"He was the best handler I've ever known," and that was an absolute truth. No one else was a patch on Mendhel. He'd been the only one who could keep LC under control. And the only one who'd stick his neck out when they screwed up, and give them space to screw up so they could learn. Hil missed him, more than he'd had time to realise.

They clinked glasses.

A door opened behind them and they both looked to see Elenor heading down the steps. She didn't say a word, just smiled at Pen and set a tall bottle of pale liquid on the table with two small shot glasses. She touched Hil's shoulder as she left, squeezing gently. He watched her go back inside. Martha had never been that gentle. They'd been a whirlwind together and he was honestly not sure what it had been that had torn them apart. Maybe he had done something but it sure as hell wasn't anything intentional. It was hard to think that things had gone so wrong she'd sell them out like that. She hadn't just betrayed the guild, she'd targeted him and LC for the suckers who would go running off to do their bidding. She'd known exactly what to do. Threatening Anya gave them Mendhel and LC, and Hil was a given after that.

"Pen, if you see LC again…" he trailed off, not really knowing what he'd meant to say in the first place.

"Don't you worry about LC, you have enough to worry about. Your plan sucks," Pen said bluntly, mostly the beer talking.

Hil shrugged. It did. What could he say?

He picked absently at a graze on his arm that he'd picked up courtesy of the desert floor in a sparring session with Yani. Elenor had refused to look at it at first, telling him it was his own fault and if he wanted to inflict more damage on himself she was having nothing to do with it. She'd folded and had cleaned it up for him. Pen was lucky, she really was good. His wrist had held up well and the headaches were mostly gone. Elenor was good for the big man. He could see it in the way they were together. Pen had rescued her and now she was holding him up. How did you find a woman like that?

"I'm sorry I've dragged you into this," he said. "You and Elenor, you don't need any of this mess."

"You didn't do this, Hil. You and LC are family here, don't

ever forget that. The bastards that killed my brother and took his daughter are the ones who did it."

Pen took the tall bottle and poured two shot glasses. He held one out. Hil took it and they both drank the whisky in one, a shot of hot fluid that burned its way down.

"Look after that woman," Hil said, gesturing back towards the building, the liquor igniting a spot of envy deep inside, thoughts of Martha mixing with images of Sean O'Brien.

Pen smiled. "You don't have to worry about me either."

"You're lucky, Pen. Every woman I've ever gotten close to either ran a mile or turned into a clinging harpy. Or stabbed me in the back."

"The one consistent thing in all those failed relationships, Hil, is you. Think about that."

Hil laughed and grabbed the bottle. He poured two more shots and raised his glass. "You're a good man, Pen. You'd be a great handler."

Pen nudged his glass with his own. "You take care of yourself, Hil."

They drank the fiery liquid and the rest of the bottle after that. Hil was having a problem focusing on anything and enjoying the fact that it was self-inflicted for once. He leaned on the table and felt his eyes closing.

Pen slapped him on the back. "Come on, bud. It's a big day tomorrow."

Hil sat up and rubbed a hand over his eyes.

Pen stood up and leaned forward onto the back of his chair. "What the hell was it that you went to steal, Hil?"

Hil stared intently into his glass.

He could feel Pen staring intently at him.

"You know, don't you?" Pen said.

"You don't want to know, Pen. It's best you don't know. It's best that no one ever knows. That's why I have to do this. I'm going to end it."

Damn right he was going to end it and he was going to take as many of them as possible with him.

24

"*Knowingly leaving Hilyer to run loose was not a popular decision,*" *the Man said. "Are you aware that Media backed Legal when they tried to lodge a petition to dissolve Acquisitions as an independent section?*"

NG paused, the goblet half way to his lips. He'd accepted the wine reluctantly and had been taking his time with it. He took a breath then took a long drink, feeling the hot alcohol hit his bloodstream. Juggling the four sections of the guild was a constant battle that he found exasperating at times.

"*Zach Hilyer is incredibly resourceful,*" *he said finally. "Ultimately he was our best chance of finding LC and that could only have happened if we gave him enough rein to run free. The Chief agreed with me that it was the best course of action and I backed him when Legal and Media started to give him a hard time. Acquisitions has to stay independent. Like it or not, the work they do is some of the most important of all four sections. It's the work of the field operatives that gives us our advantage. The others might not like it but they do know it.*"

The Man nodded slowly and leaned forward. "And while our people were squabbling behind closed doors, Earth dared put out a contract on two of our operatives and the Merchants' Guild moved to usurp our position in the open market. And the insolent corporation that defied us all to initiate this sorry affair quite arrogantly ran rings around everyone."

NG finished his wine with another gulp and placed the empty goblet on the table, wilfully courting another refill. "That's why Hil was the best person to throw out there to face them head-on. The eccentricity that's the very base of our power can be stifled in some circumstances. Sometimes, one wildcard thrown out of the pack is what it takes."

Hil strode through the station, chin up, shoulders back, and with the old cocky confidence he'd not felt since before LC had grabbed him that day and said they had a problem. He carried a bulky bag, borrowed clothes hiding the massive pistol which was deactivated and wrapped in a cloth.

He'd renewed the connection with Genoa as soon as he was clear of the planet. She'd gushed relief at hearing from him and he'd been impressed with his cool, calm front of innocent ignorance.

Pen had guys scattered throughout the station and Hil calmly reacted to their warnings, taking turnings, stopping and waiting when instructed, and was safely conveyed past any possible threat all the way to the dock. There was no sign of Kase and Martha or their ship. He wasn't sure what he would have done if he had seen them. Pulled out a gun and taken them both out probably, and enjoyed it. But it didn't happen.

The docks area was busy and as he approached, he could see the hauliers waiting with the crate by the entrance to the airlock leading to Genoa's berth. Pen was there checking documentation. He looked up and waved Hil over.

"Here's that stuff you asked Elenor to find for you," he said pulling out a small case.

Hil took it and opened it carefully. It was just big enough to hold three tiny auto-injector vials. Two of the spaces were empty.

"That's all she could get in the time," Pen said. "She says it will last for twenty four hours but don't depend on it past eighteen. And whatever you do, don't use it with that crap Martha gave you. Ele said that will be fatal however superhuman you decide you want to be."

Hil smiled and tucked the case away safely in a different pocket to Martha's vials.

Pen slapped him on the back. "You're all set and ready for go," he said and stuck out his hand for a handshake that turned into a bear hug. "Go get them, bud."

"Thanks for everything, Pen," Hil said, no need for any more ceremony, they'd said it all last night, and he went through to the ship.

"Zach, you won't believe how worried I've been since you lost contact," she said. "I've been scanning the entire planet."

I bet you have, he thought as he stashed the bag in the locker under the bunk.

"It's good to be back, Genoa," he said cheerfully.

"You're looking much better. I take it you found your friend down there. You could have let me know you were alright."

"I am alright and I've got the package."

She didn't react straight away and Hil smiled. Her massive ship brain must have been doing flips. He gave the hauliers the go ahead to start loading the crate into Genoa's hold and she took over, giving them instructions on storage.

"Here's the coordinates for the drop," he said, taking a seat in the bridge and noticing vaguely that it had all been cleaned. He'd been soaking wet and bleeding last time he was in here and tidying before he left had been the last thing on his mind. She'd had a complete scrub down.

Genoa took the data he input and started processing the numbers. She probably had it all prepared already, she'd know where they were going if she was in league with them. He had a brief flutter of concern, the thought that he was in all probability back in their hands, but he stifled it with resolve and a surge of belligerence. This time he knew what was going on and this time he was the one in control.

He checked that she had the numbers then jumped up. "I'm going to check on the package," he said and wandered nonchalantly out towards the hold.

Pen was still waiting dockside, talking to the crate guys. As he saw Hil leave the ship, he nodded to them and walked over.

"Well, if we weren't sure before buddy, we are now," Pen said. "You were right. She sent a tight-wire transmission long distance nano-seconds after you said it was the package."

Hil smiled. "I knew she wouldn't be able to resist. Half that ship's mental storage capacity must be taken up with her ego."

He took the band off his wrist and the knife from his boot and held them out. "Look after these for me, will you?"

Pen took them and caught him up in another hug. "Good luck, Hil. Come back, you hear me? That equipment is expensive, I want it back."

They got clearance and left the station with no problems. Hil avoided Genoa's attempts at small talk and used the time to sleep off his hangover until they were clear for jump.

With the course he'd set, it was going to take four jumps to get to the base. After the first one, he excused himself from the bridge and said he needed to check on the package again.

"It's fine, Zach," Genoa said. "I could monitor it for you from here if you didn't have it so well shielded."

Hil left the bridge anyway. "This is the most valuable item in the whole galaxy right now, Genoa. Humour me. I'm just going to take a look."

Once in the hold, he went straight over to the crate and opened up a panel on its side. He pulled out the control board from the massive device in the crate and began pressing keys in the sequence he'd memorised at Pen's place.

"Zachary, what are you doing?" Genoa said. "We need to make jump. I need you back on the bridge. So, Zach, was LC down there on the planet? Where is he now?"

Hil shook his head and had to bite his tongue not to throw back a sarcastic barb at her crass and phony curiosity and absolute lack of subtlety. She failed miserably at trying to fake concern.

"He's fine, Genoa."

He must have failed at trying to hide his lack of belief in her emotions because she dimmed the lights and her tone was harder when she spoke again.

"Zach, come up to the bridge."

He finished the initiation sequence, well aware that he had to move quickly. As far as she was concerned, she had him and the package. She could quite easily shut down life-support and jump. Dead or alive was the latest criteria on the bounty. He was sure they wouldn't care which they ended up with.

"Zach, what are you doing?"

He could almost hear her synapses sparking through the logic channel possibilities and had no doubt she'd reach a conclusion quickly that would not be in his favour.

She was starting up the jump drive and he felt rather than heard the slight change in the noise of the air-con. He punched in the code that Pen had given him and watched the lights on the board flash up green.

"Zach? How did Skye..?"

He input the final code and stepped back as the device fired up with a barely audible hum.

That had been the danger. Genoa was a smart ship, they all were. He knew it wouldn't take her long to realise that the crate he knew she would assume was the package was way too big to have fitted in Skye's hold. Skye was tiny, built for speed. It didn't often limit their capability to chase tabs but it had once or twice. If this had been the package, they couldn't have gone with Skye to retrieve it. Genoa had realised that just too late.

The ship powered down slightly, engines going to standby as the AI shut down. What he had just done was the equivalent of smashing a bottle over her head and somehow he couldn't bring himself to care. It was the only way he was going to be able to do what he had planned. He shoved the control board back into place and shut up the container.

According to the laws of Winter and some quarters within Earth's sphere of influence that recognised AI sentience, he was now guilty of kidnapping, but on a personal level and what bothered him more was that he'd effectively just hijacked a guild vessel. Now he hoped he could remember how to fly it.

25

"And of course," the Man said, lighting a long tapered candle on the desk, "the problem with a wildcard is that you have no way to predict the way it will fall."

The wick caught the flame and embraced the light, casting shadows across the wooden surface. The glow was mesmerising and NG felt his eyes drawn to the flickering halo of orange fire.

"Did you have any idea what Hilyer was going to do?"

NG tore his gaze from the candle's flame to the Man, the most powerful individual in the guild and possibly in human controlled space, sitting there opposite, and for the first time since NG had set foot on this massive cruiser, questioning his actions. It was hard not to be defensive, and with the liquor coursing through his veins and the darkness closing in, it was becoming hard to keep focused.

The Man didn't let up. "The furore that this item has generated suggests that it will have monumental consequences for the history of mankind," he said. "You, of all people NG, should understand the enormity of that. I worry at the timing of this development. It does not align with the timeframe for my plans."

Never before had the Man spoken so openly of such things. NG reached across and picked up the jug, filling both goblets with the last of the steaming hot wine. That the Man was worried did not bode well. For anyone.

"Again," the Man said slowly, "I ask, did you suspect what Hilyer intended to do when he left Aston?"

NG shook his head. "No, no I didn't."

Docking had never been his speciality. With no AI in control, the basic backup computer systems on any guild ship could handle a simple route with little input from a pilot. Hil's problem now was that he had to be careful exactly what he broadcast to the station before they arrived. He let the ship fly on auto from jumping into the system to a fair distance from the orbital but as soon as comms traffic started coming in, he disengaged everything and took manual control. It wasn't worth the risk that the automated systems would send some kind of signal that would give them away.

He strapped in tight because as much as he was trained to fly a ship this size, he'd be the first to admit he had no finesse. The mood he was in didn't help and he belligerently left it to the last possible moment to kick in the braking sequence and align for dock.

They scraped in, too fast and with station operators yelling warnings at them, but he really didn't care if Genoa lost a layer of paint or even an engine. The dock's safety systems were adequate enough to catch them. He ignored the warning sirens and powered down.

The welcoming committee dockside was a mix of emergency services personnel running to put out what looked like a fire Hil thought he'd probably caused with his stylish entrance, station security who looked pissed and the corporation heavies he was expecting. One of the uniforms was arguing with the suits but it was clear who had the situation under control.

Hil walked across the dock, no baggage, no weapons, pockets emptied. He scanned the group for familiar faces. He thought a couple of them had been on Abacus, but there was no sign of Kase and Martha. He was almost disappointed, but thinking about it, Martha wouldn't give him the satisfaction. She'd turn up on her own terms.

He didn't make it to the group before two of the Zang guys broke away and intercepted him.

As they got close he recognised one of them as one of the twins, looking like he'd had serious facial reconstruction, a deep scar crossing his right eye socket.

They frisked him roughly and didn't find anything because there was nothing to find. He took it calmly, trying not to smirk too openly. They weren't gentle and he wasn't going to give them the satisfaction of bitching about it.

They finished by slapping a patch on the side of his neck over the implant, that was expected, and restraining his arms too tightly behind his back, also true to form. What took him by surprise was the tiny device they stuck to the back of his neck. It adhered with a sharp pain like a needle going in deep and for a second he couldn't catch his breath. He gasped and the guy laughed and flicked the device, sending another shard of pain lancing through his spine.

Hil bit back a curse.

The guy with the scarred face shoved him back and grinned, holding up a small remote. With over exaggeration, he threatened to activate it. Hil stood his ground defiantly, keeping his balance, and keeping calm – until the guy hit the remote and an excruciating pain sent Hil to his knees, feeling like his heart was going to explode. It didn't ease up even when he managed to look up and see that the guy had disengaged the device.

"Not so cocky now, huh?" he said and hit it again.

By the time they pulled him up, Hil felt like his spinal cord had been ripped out, shivers of pain still darting in and out and sparks of light behind his eyes. That he hadn't been expecting but it didn't change anything. He wasn't sure what they thought he was going to try but he was going with them. He wanted to go with them but if they wanted to have their fun, then fine. He choked back what would have been a laugh if he could have managed it and the guy shoved him again but didn't activate the remote because a corporate suit was heading their way, frowning.

"Bring him over here," the suit said with disdain and Hil was pushed forward. "Where's the package?"

Hil smiled and shook his head. "I want to see Anya," he said. "Then I'll tell you where LC is with the package."

The twin with the missing eye moved in close and grabbed the back of Hil's neck. "You're not in any position to negotiate," he whispered harshly, holding up the remote again.

Hil kept the smug smile firm, keeping eye contact with the suit but answering Scarface, "Funny, but you're the second low life who's said that to me recently and the other asshole was wrong as well."

The man put up a hand, waving off his thugs. "We'll take you to Anya, alright," he said with a sneer. "Take him down to the base, and try not to kill him on the way."

The drop ship was the same type as last time, plush, reeking of money and still incapable of compensating for the vicious velocity of an emergency descent. With no watch or timer, Hil mentally kept a vague idea of how much time was passing.

There was a lot more corporate security once they landed and entered the corporation's complex of low, flat domes. He watched their systems closely as they passed through, playing games trying to figure out what plan he would've used if he'd been trying to break in. It wasn't impenetrable.

He changed his mind when they entered a wide, open, circular atrium that he could see was laced with bio-sensors. Corridors led in all directions like spokes, a guarded energy barrier across the entrance to each. To break in here, he'd need to infiltrate a bio-electronic security system that was at least as good as anything he'd broken before. He reassessed his opinion of the corporation he was dealing with. Not that it mattered.

They marched him across the open area, getting a mixture of indifference and curious stares from the corporate suits and lab staff they passed. He kept his head up and memorised every procedure they went through, only losing track a couple of times when Scarface screwed with the remote, giving him brief flashes of discomfort that verged on agony.

The whole place was bland, sterile bio-tech – corporation through and through but still nothing that would identify it as Zang. They reached a lift and the doors opened to an equally sterile and cold interior. Hil was pushed in and surrounded by his escort. The thugs stood to either side. He looked to one then the other and stared straight ahead, a slight smile twitching the corners of his mouth. He tested the restraints and reckoned he could get free when he wanted. The suit was standing with his back to him. He could break free and break the guy's neck before the scarfaced twin and his new buddy could move. But that wasn't the point.

As if they'd read his mind, they moved closer and a persistent throbbing emanated from the device, not enough to hurt but enough to take all his attention from anything but concentrating on staying upright.

They dropped down and leaving the lift, it was evident that security was tighter down here. They picked up another four guards who took them through more checkpoints.

At one, they shoved him into a cubicle and told him to strip. A more thorough search still didn't find anything. They gave him loose fitting pale grey pants and a matching oversized shirt to put on. They really weren't taking any risks and didn't even let him keep his boots. It was flattering in a way.

Then it was more cold corridors until eventually, they were led through into a large room with knots of people standing waiting. Hil scanned the faces and his stomach muscles tightened as he spotted Kase and Martha up ahead. He caught Martha's eye and she tensed, trying and failing to keep any emotion from her face. He smiled as he was led past. She stared without moving.

For once it was Kase who couldn't resist speaking up. "Hey, Hil buddy," he said. "Nothing personal, y'know. Just business."

If he hadn't been expecting to see them, it would have been near on impossible not to react. But he'd got all that out of his system at Pen's place with the help of a good friend and a bottle of whisky so seeing them now face to face, he could keep up the air of nonchalance, even though his eyes might have said different. Screw them all.

He stopped and turned to them. "Hey, Kase," he said, "heard from Genoa lately?"

The phony smile on Kase's face dropped and Martha's eyes widened a fraction. Hil was given a shove in the back and moved on before he could say anything else.

He heard Kase say to someone behind him, "Hey, get me a link up to security on the orbital. Now!" as Martha muttered, "What the hell?"

It was a small victory but sometimes that's all you need to keep going.

He was taken into a smaller room with a soft carpet underfoot. There was a small table and just one chair. He was pushed into the chair and they secured the restraints. He didn't resist. They gave him a short, sharp shock before throwing the remote down onto the table, laughing as they went.

He was left alone.

It was quiet, very quiet considering how many people there were in the hallway outside. He kept track of the time and kept his heart rate slow and steady. It was unfortunate that Elenor hadn't managed to get him two shots of the drug but he'd manage. He toyed with the idea of busting out of the cuffs but decided they were probably watching and he didn't feel like putting on a demonstration.

So he sat there. The longer, the better as far as he was concerned.

Finally, the door opened and he counted seven people as they trooped in and took up position around him. The twin, his new buddy and the suit were among them, as were Kase and Martha who avoided looking at him. The last guy to enter was an older man, much older and with an aura of power about him that made the room hush. He stood immediately in front of Hil, who resisted the urge to sit up straight under an intense gaze that was directed right at him.

"You're late," the man said. "We were expecting you days ago."

Hil stared back, eyes narrow.

The old man gestured. "Untie his hands," he commanded and Hil had to stifle a smirk as Scarface rushed over to release the cuffs.

Once his hands were free, he rubbed at his chafed wrists then slouched back even further and folded his arms, still staring at the old man, wondering who he was in all this.

"Where is the package?" the old man said quietly, his accent something vague, nuances of Earth mixed with subtle shades of Wintran.

"Where's Anya?" Hil replied defiantly.

The hush in the room deepened as if they couldn't believe he dared to speak to the old guy like that.

There was a moment then the man smiled, a wolf's grin that creased up his face. It vanished as fast as it had appeared. "Bring her in."

26

The Man stood and for a moment NG thought that was it. He'd never been in here so long and the thought of heading out to a cold beer and fresh air was suddenly very appealing.

But the Man leaned forward, resting his hands on the desk. "You lost him."

NG looked at the two empty goblets next to the empty jug. If the Man refilled the jug, he wasn't sure his bloodstream could handle much more. "There are occasionally times," he said, "in some jobs when an operative has to go deep. We don't always know exactly where they are all the time. Hilyer has been involved in that type of job several times. We trust our people and they repay that trust with loyalty."

He realised as he said it how shallow that sounded.

"We've seen how loyal our people can be."

"I know Hil," NG said. "I have no doubts – about him or LC. I might not have been able to reach every member of our crew but those two I did know. And if Hil had to go to extremes, then he did so because he believed that was the only way."

"It was a bold, reckless challenge that he threw down to the corporation."

"Hil thinks he knows his limits but when he's pushed, he tends to surprise even himself."

The old man broke eye contact and moved to one side to let one of the suits get to the door. Hil looked from the old man to the door, not sure what to expect. They'd decided Anya was dead. It sent a shiver through him to think she might be here. That she might still be alive. He'd have to change his plan.

The door opened and everything Hil had planned turned on its head anyway. Anya walked into the room. He sat up then and would have stood up if it wasn't for a heavy hand on his shoulder pushing him back into the chair.

She stood in front of the table and leaned on it, up close. He could smell her perfume. She looked older than he remembered and sharper. She picked up the remote, slender fingers immaculate and manicured.

"Hello Hil. My god, you've had us chasing all over the galaxy trying to find you."

Her voice was soft and seductive, more mature than he could have imagined Mend's little girl could ever be. They'd all protected her as she grew up. As they all grew up. Even when LC had been getting close, Mendhel had warned him off, 'keeping her safe from the hot-headed field-ops', he'd said.

It took everything he had to calm his heart rate as it threatened to race off with a surge of adrenaline. Anya was here. She was alive and well. And she sure as hell didn't look like a prisoner.

He cast a look over at Martha but her face was still impassive. He couldn't tell from either of them if they'd known. Probably, he decided while he was sitting there dumbstruck.

"It's good to see you again, Hil," she said softly. "Now tell me, where's our package and where's LC?"

Hil leaned forward so she was even closer. Whoever it was behind him, stepped in again with a hand on his shoulder. Anya glanced up quickly and that was enough for them to back off. She looked down at Hil again, fondly he could imagine if he didn't have a hundred different scenarios running through his head trying to figure out exactly how they'd all reached this point. She reached a hand up and stroked the hair back from his forehead, gently, reaching round to the back of his neck to touch the device there. She had the remote in her other hand, and for a moment he thought she was going to activate it. He tensed, as much as he tried not to.

Quiet seconds ticked past. And instead she waved dismissively. "This isn't necessary," she said.

This time the hand forced his head forward roughly and a spike of pain that seemed to last forever made his vision narrow to a dark tunnel. The device was pulled out and a malicious slap to the back of his head made his senses reel.

He took his time looking up and all he could see was Anya's face, the rest of the room greyed out. He tried to reckon how much time had passed since he left the ship. It was still too soon.

"Where is he?" she asked again.

Hil got his breathing under control, let every muscle relax and used every trick he knew.

"LC's dead," he said finally. "The bio-weapon you sent us to get, well we got it. LC got it up close and personal. He got infected. We ran into trouble before the lab was destroyed. One of the guys in there was crazy and there was no way he was going to let us get away with it. He had vials of the stuff ready. LC was careless and the guy managed to inject him with it. It was all we could do to get away."

He paused and had the feeling the whole room was fixed on him and every word he was saying. "There never was any package. LC was the package. Everything else was destroyed. We got away but it killed him. I killed him, Anya. He was in agony and there was nothing we could do because there was nowhere we could go. He begged me. In the end I put a bullet between his eyes."

He stopped and calmed his breathing again. He looked up at her, trying to focus with eyes that wanted to close.

Anya was looking at him with an expression that could have been pity, desire or distaste, he couldn't tell. She looked aside suddenly and cocked her head ever so slightly as if listening. She couldn't have had the implant long, that small affectation people developed early on was a dead-giveaway. A brief moment passed as she was obviously being fed information from somewhere outside the room, then she stared straight back at him.

"Hil, that's a very sad story, but you're lying." She stepped back and he got another slap to the back of the head. Crap.

"Where is he?"

Whatever sensors they had the room kitted out with were good, but then he hadn't really expected otherwise.

He looked hurt. "Anya, why are you doing this?"

She leaned back on the table so close he could have kissed her. "Why? Hil, I didn't do this. You did this. You and LC and my father. You and the guild. You all forced me to this."

Disturbingly then, Hil wondered about the sanity of his plan. She was mad. Mendhel's little girl had manipulated them all.

"I don't believe it," he whispered. "We protected you from the guild. Mendhel didn't want you anywhere near it."

"That was the problem," she whispered back harshly. "You shut me out. My whole life, all the people around me, the people I cared most about and was closest to, all part of your precious guild. All I wanted was to be a part of that. It was all I ever wanted. But now Hil, all I want is that package."

Hil shook his head. "I'm telling you the truth," he said. "LC was the package. You killed him, Anya. You sent him there and it killed him. Just like you killed Mendhel. You might not have pulled the trigger, but you killed your own father."

Her face fell and she stepped back. "What?"

Oh crap, she didn't know. Hil swallowed, trying to gather his wits. "Mendhel's dead, Anya." He glanced over at Martha and back to the woman Mend's little girl had become. She looked dismayed but there was a flicker of disbelief.

She shook her head and her eyes glinted. "You're lying. You're a cold bastard, Zach. I never trusted you. Why do you say things like that? Why do you think I would care?"

"These people murdered him, Anya. You've been used."

"I don't care. Mendhel was never a father to me," she said viciously. "He sent me away, kept me at arm's length all those years. All those expensive schools I was packed off to so he wouldn't have to deal with his unwanted daughter being around. And I worked so hard, tried so desperately hard to be the best at everything. Just like you and LC, just so I'd be noticed and accepted into your little world. You never understood."

"He sent you away to protect you, Anya. Your father adored you. You were always his little girl. The guild changes people. He just wanted you kept safe from all that."

For a long second he thought he saw doubt in her eyes, a troubled look flashing across her face. Then it was gone as fast as it came. She held the remote up between them. "We can make this easy or very difficult for you, Hil. Tell me where LC is and tell me where our package is."

"Anya," he said softly, trying desperately to think of a way to appeal to the young girl he'd first met all that time ago, "these people have used you. Come home with me."

Her eyes flashed with anger and he knew it hadn't worked. "Okay, okay," he said quickly. "I can tell you where the package is. But believe me, LC is dead. Otherwise he'd be here with me, wouldn't he?"

She looked uncertain then so he pushed it. "LC wanted me to find you. He asked me to take care of you, Anya. You don't need to do this."

She pushed back from the table then and took a step back, listening again to whoever was speaking directly to her.

"This is all very touching but he's stalling," the old man said. "The question is why?"

Hil looked across at him, weighing up how much time he needed. "You want the truth?" he said. "We want to negotiate. You gave us the job to do because you don't have anyone else capable of even thinking of trying it. We did it. LC has the package and he's waiting for me to contact him. As soon as we get paid what we want, we'll give it to you. Then we'll disappear and you'll never hear from us again. We don't care what's in the package but we want the bounty off our heads and we want fifty million."

Anya was still listening to someone but she glowered at him and glared at the old man. "He's still lying," she said. "I told you he was an arrogant, cocky son of a bitch."

She paused again then looked puzzled and said, "There's something wrong. There's a problem at the docks."

Hil flinched as someone grabbed the back of his neck again.

"Wait," Anya said.

Before she could say anything else, Martha exclaimed, "Oh my god, Hilyer."

All eyes went to her and Hil could see both Kase and Martha were agitated.

"Hil," Martha said, stepping forward, apprehension and confusion making her brow crease, "where the hell have you been for the past week?"

Genoa. The problem at the docks must have been Zang's security finding Pen's massive disruptor – Kase must have got his link. If she was back online, the first thing Genoa would have done would be to contact her partners in all this. She wouldn't know where she'd been, but she'd know there was time missing.

What happened next would all depend on the timing.

"I'm not lying," he lied. "You want the package, you have to trust me. I came here to you. I didn't have to. You want it? The price has gone up."

Kase stepped forward as well, looking angry. "What have you been doing, Hil? Where the hell did you take Genoa?"

"He did what?" Anya said aloud suddenly and turned on him. He thought she was going to hit him but she just glared, hands on her hips.

The old man held up a hand and everyone hushed again immediately. He turned to the suit at his side. "Fiorrentino, what is going on?" he demanded.

Kase and Martha looked to each other and over at Anya as if they didn't know whether they should speak. It was astonishing to see Martha stuck for words.

"Sixty million," Hil said just for the hell of it.

The old man turned and pointed straight at him. "Where's my package?"

Hil opened his mouth to speak and clamped it shut again as the door burst open. Anya spun around to face the newcomer who was two steps into the room and looking like he'd just drawn a short straw. "What now?" she snapped.

Martha grabbed Hil's arm. "What have you done?" she hissed at him.

Hil ignored her and watched the guy at the door, who brushed past Anya and went to the old man, leaning in close and saying something too quietly for anyone else to hear but the suit who was standing at his side. The suit turned suddenly, anger evident.

"Get those cuffs back on him," he growled.

"What's going on?" Anya said.

Someone grabbed Hil and pushed his face down hard onto the table. His arms were caught up and twisted behind him.

"Oh shit," Kase said. "Hilyer, you son of a bitch."

Martha must have received the same message. There was still a massive hand pushed against his head, but Hil could see Martha's face pale from his limited vantage point.

"What's going on?" Anya said again, too far down the food chain to be getting the updates the others were, and not linked to a ship which suddenly had all sensors up and active.

Tremors of a deep underground blast reverberated through the room, too distant to knock anyone off their feet but enough to send a clear message they were under attack.

"Three Tangiers Class battle cruisers just entered orbit," the suit said, heading for the door.

Another blast shook the complex. Shit, their timing was just about perfect. The whole situation had a hint of deja-vu about it, except Hil knew pretty much for a fact that the Earth forces that were descending in drop ships right now wouldn't try to take him alive this time, regardless of the deal they'd made. As far as they were concerned, they were here to pick up the package and eliminate anyone even remotely associated with it.

27

The Man narrowed his eyes. "You have a great belief in our people, NG. Yet, as we have determined, several betrayed us. And the initiator of that betrayal was, by extension, one of our own. How could such a deception have been perpetrated without your knowledge?"

There was nothing he could say. Mendhel had kept his family on Earth with full permission from the guild. They all thought they'd taken precautions to protect Anya after her mother died. He'd tried to persuade Mendhel to bring her in but a promise made long before had bound both of them. He'd had good people watching her and it had been difficult to confront the fact that their allegiance was now in question.

The Man frowned and wandered off in the direction of the wine cabinet, sending the candle flame between them into a frenzy of dancing light.

"Are we secure now?" the Man asked, his back to NG.

"Yes," he said then watched, keeping quiet, as the Man brought back a bottle and threw two pinches of the black powder into the jug.

"It never ceases to amaze me," the Man said, steam billowing up as he added the wine, "how destructive man can be when slighted."

The docking manoeuvre he'd pulled off at the main Earth orbital days earlier had been only marginally better than his entrance at the station above Zang's base in the Between. He hadn't set fire to anything that time though and he'd walked off the ship carrying Pen's holdall. Hil had re-engaged the power cell in the pistol before he'd docked Genoa and he could almost feel it emanating its pulse of energy as he set the bag on the check-in desk to be scanned. Earth still had the tightest security cordon of all the old planets. It was impossible to land anywhere on the surface of the planet without being tracked and every orbital had stringent security procedures that hadn't been relaxed since the colony wars centuries ago, and random rebel attacks through the decades had pretty much ensured a state of permanent high alert around the seat of empire.

It was what he was counting on. And if anything, it looked like security was tighter than the last time he'd been here.

He left the docks and joined a queue at arrivals. No one could enter an Earth orbital without documents and a baggage check and search. They were twitchy about bombs. Earth was twitchy about anyone trying to bring anything back to the home porch that could affect its security, ecosystem or economy.

So the queues took a while and armed security wandered up and down the lines. Hil stood patiently and shuffled forward with the rest of them.

At the desk, he pushed across the documents Pen had arranged for him and stepped into the scanning arch. Lights swept across him, lingering on his eyes, covering his whole body and the bag he'd dropped at his feet.

He watched the clerk cross-reference the bio-stats. It was easy to stay calm. He'd injected Elenor's single vial before he'd left the ship and its drug was now coursing through his system keeping every possible giveaway function steady and within normal parameters. He also had complete and utter faith in Pen so the papers would be fine. What was in his bag wasn't and it was just a matter of time.

The machine scanned him again.

The clerk apologised for the delay, then started to sweat and fluster, fiddling with his cheap earpiece. No high tech implants for the minimum-wage slaves. After all his years spent relieving people of their hard-earned wealth, be it mineral, animal or on one occasion even vegetable, Hil still found it astonishing that security personnel, employed to keep people's lives and inestimable wealth safe, were some of the most poorly paid and often inept employees in the galaxy. It was one of the great riddles of the universe.

He didn't react when he heard the frantic footsteps closing in from several directions. The clerk backed away from the desk. Hil didn't move as the sounds behind him got closer and he could hear the distinctive rattle of weapons being readied. The clerk ducked and ran.

Someone yelled, "Get down on the floor," in his ear and hands grabbed him, pulled him out of the scanner and forced him to the ground. His face hit the cold deck and a knee hit the centre of his back.

They'd found the pistol then.

They yelled at him to get his hands on his head and he played the perfect prisoner, lacing his hands across the back of his head and laying quietly. They yelled people to move back and the weight on his back increased as if they thought he might try to make a break for it. They were probably disappointed that he didn't. He stifled any cocky comments that came to mind and restrained himself from struggling as they frisked him, taking the small hand gun and his two knives. Then they twisted first one hand then the other roughly behind his back and lifted him up.

They kept at least three automatic rifles trained on him and it was almost amusing to give the orbital security a bit of excitement to liven up their day. They were twitching and hyper as hell so it must have been a while since they'd had an incident to deal with.

The people behind him in the queue had scattered and formed a circle of curious onlookers. He stood quietly, a security agent on each side holding his arms locked in a grip twisted behind his back so he shouldn't have been able to move an inch. It was a good hold, the guy on the left marginally better than the one on the right. If Hil had wanted he could have taken them both down, either incapacitated or dead, in seconds. It wasn't just the cold barrel of a rifle pushed against his jawline below the ear that stopped him, he wanted to speak to the people who owned the pistol and the bulky guy who was marching across the concourse towards them, flanked by two nervous looking security personnel, was going to make his introduction. More travellers backed off as they approached, torn between fear and curiosity.

The guy stopped just outside of arms' reach. His bearing and appearance suggested ex-military, his senior years and short greying hair suggested experience, the weary lines around his eyes suggested active service. His nametag said Dixon and he didn't exhibit any of the nervousness the rest of the security detail with twitching trigger fingers were. Hil decided he liked the old guy. He looked down at Hil with squinting eyes and a slight incredulous disbelief.

"Who," he said, "the hell are you and what the hell do you think you're doing?"

Hil glanced sideways without moving his head. The clerk had inched back into position, as if he'd never run away, and was watching. He shrank back again as Hil caught his eye.

Hil smiled and looked back at the security chief. "Run the serial number," he said softly.

The guy's eyes got even narrower and he nodded almost imperceptibly to his men. It must have been a sign to hustle because they hustled, clamped his wrists in a set of hefty cuffs, and got him below decks and in a holding cell with impressive efficiency. The door was slammed shut and a guard posted.

The cell was dark and bare except for a plain steel table and two matching chairs all welded to the floor. It was about big enough for him to pace three steps in all directions and was designed to be claustrophobic as hell. On some jobs he'd spent days living in ventilation shafts barely wide enough for him to squeeze into. The psychology wasn't wasted on him but the desired effect was.

"Well I don't know who you are," Dixon said, when he came back four long hours later, "but you've definitely got someone's attention. I don't suppose you'd like to tell me what the hell is going on?"

"If I did, the guys you've just been told are coming to pick me up would probably kill you," Hil said, a smile twitching at the corners of his mouth as he looked up at the security chief from his seat.

"How the hell did you know…? Never mind, I get the feeling this is way above my pay grade. I've been ordered to hold you until they get here. Anything you need while we're waiting?"

"No, I'm good," Hil said. He brought his arms forward and placed the cuffs, open, on the table. "You can have these back."

"How…?"

"Don't worry. I'm not going anywhere."

The safetycuffs were standard issue on Earth to the civilian police and security services. The Earth Empire, ever conscious of its public image, had introduced the first models years ago after a well-known and outspoken political demonstrator had died while restrained. Supposedly escape-proof, they contained bio-triggered release mechanisms – the idea being that if a prisoner was dying, actually about to die, the bio-feedback would release the cuffs allowing practical access for medics, something about public perception and human rights and all that crap that Earth allegedly still cared about. Mendhel had taught them all how to get out of them. It was one of his first tests for new operatives, figuring that if they couldn't get out of a set of these then they should maybe think about a different line of work.

It had taken Hil a while but he'd done it. The cuffs hadn't been fooled easily but he'd managed to slow his heart rate drastically enough, without passing out, that they'd just popped open.

Dixon looked at Hil and shook his head in disbelief. "I will be so glad when you're out of here," he said. "Yell if you need anything."

Two hours later the door opened and the old guy was back, this time flanked by two serious looking heavies in military uniforms. Dixon stepped aside and let the two soldiers past.

Hil stood up. He'd used the time to rest, not quite sleeping but not just waiting.

The soldiers took hold of an arm each and roughly forced him face down over the table, definitely military.

"You're getting transferred," came a voice from the doorway. Officer Hil reckoned and noted the lieutenant's insignia as he managed to raise his head slightly.

"Why is this man not restrained?" the new voice said condescendingly to the veteran security chief.

Dixon looked the junior officer up and down, and with a look of sheer disdain grunted, "You want him, you cuff him" then to Hil, "Watch yourself with this asshole."

And he turned and left.

Hil watched the interplay with interest and noted the subtle shift in the balance of power. He'd always been better than LC at reading people and he filed away the lieutenant's lack of experience in dealing with civilians and obvious discomfort for future reference.

He twisted one arm free and as the soldier scrabbled to secure him, the officer scowled, and shouted at them, "Get those cuffs on him."

They'd marched him back up to the dock flanked by the heavily armed soldiers with station security accompanying them the whole way. Hil had the distinct impression they were glad to be rid of him when they handed him over to a group with three more uniforms, who all looked even more pissed to see him.

They searched him again, like they didn't trust the orbital civilians, and took off the fancy safetycuffs, replacing them with the age-old military favourite, simple blade-proof plasticuffs securing his wrists again, to the front this time. To make a point, they secured a second set around his elbows and pulled his arms tight together. Once they had him safely inside a drop ship, they tied a third set around his ankles. He got the message loud and clear, plasticuffs were impossible to bust without a knife.

He wondered how much they knew or whether the ID on the gun had just triggered some general alarm. He was gambling that the unit sent to get him on Abacus would be the one to pick him up here, somewhere along the line. If he got dumped into a military prison, his plan was goosed. He was relying on someone somewhere identifying him from it, and wanting to talk to him enough not to just kill him outright or hand him over to the bounty hunters for however many millions the price on his head was up to.

He couldn't tell from these guys, apart from the young lieutenant, what rank they were. So he had to be patient, and hope the drugs would fool any bio-sensors long enough for him to pull off the scam and convince them he was telling the truth.

The ride didn't take long so they either docked with a battle cruiser or landed at a base somewhere. The deceleration didn't feel like it was a drop down planetside so he didn't think they were on Earth itself.

Once stationary, they pulled him up and freed his ankles so he could walk. His escort sloped off half way across the dock and were replaced by guys who were wearing the same kind of heavy body armour as the troops had on Abacus, and straight away Hil knew his screwball plan had worked, so far anyway.

The young lieutenant stayed with them and as much as the soldiers showed deference to him, there was an edge of tension. Judging from the silence, the guys in armour were talking to each other through implants and it was clear the young officer was not in their loop.

A couple of times heading through the base, Hil was shoved roughly. He tripped twice and knocked his head against a bulkhead, and to make it clear, one of them grabbed him around the neck and squeezed just enough to send his vision spinning off into grey before he was pulled forward again.

The lieutenant didn't notice or chose not to see. So that was the way it was going to be. He didn't know how many of the Earth troops Martha and the guild agents had taken down during that firefight, but he'd walked in here holding the weapon of at least one that he knew of.

They made it clear he was in enemy territory and when he was finally pushed into a cell that was smaller than the one on the orbital, it was a relief he didn't have anything worse than a few bruises to show for their animosity.

They sat him on a bench, tied his ankles again and locked a belt around his waist, securing it to the wall, all the while covered by two armoured soldiers with rifles aimed constantly at his head.

He could see tiny cameras in each corner of the cell and no doubt there were other monitoring devices present. Gravity was slightly lower than Earth normal but it didn't feel like they were moving, so they were probably on another orbital or a base somewhere. It was rumoured that Earth black-ops had a base on the dark side of the moon, but a no-fly zone was strictly maintained so no one he'd ever met had seen it. And if that's where he was, which was looking likely, he was the only guild operative ever to have had the pleasure.

When his escort were satisfied with his restraints, they backed off, one of them giving him a parting slap to the side of his head. He kept his expression neutral and his heart rate slow and steady.

They stepped aside, keeping their aim steady and one of them opened the door. The man who walked in looked more like he should have been at a dinner party than on a military base, wearing a black tuxedo that looked like it cost more than Hil made in a year and Hil made a lot.

The guy didn't say a word but the cell suddenly emptied so it was just him and the slick suit, bow tie unfastened and hanging loose around his neck, eyes hooded as if he'd had to sober up fast. He must have been pulled in from a night out. That didn't bode well.

The door was closed and the guy stood staring.

Eventually he spoke out loud, his voice clipped and heavily accented, old Earth through and through. "Give me one reason," he said, "why I shouldn't have you shot right here and now."

28

"Provoking Earth," the Man said, "was a dangerous strategy."

NG swallowed his mouthful of wine and blinked, trying to clear his mind. One by one the candles around the room were flickering and dying, snuffed out by a darkness that was becoming more and more dense and oppressive.

"Hil wasn't acting on a strategy," he said. "I pushed him to show initiative out there, alone, and he did – how can I fault him for that?" He paused and took a deep breath. "I really thought he'd go after LC. I can read minds but I've never claimed to be able to read the future."

The Man smiled knowingly. "There is no way you could have anticipated the likelihood of Hilyer initiating a direct confrontation with Earth."

There wasn't but he still felt responsible. It was beginning to feel like the whole universe was spinning around a point in space that lay directly between himself and the Man, close enough that he could reach out and touch the centre of all existence.

"Earth and Winter are powerful," the Man said slowly. "Innovation drives the very essence of man, in all directions and at every scale. We feed the escalation of that innovation and we control how and when man advances. We control the future, NG. We create the future, don't ever forget that. War is unpredictable. Tension and intrigue – they are our tools. We must take them to the brink, without pushing them over the edge. To allow, to precipitate, outright warfare between the two..." He shook his head. "There is too much at stake."

There was no way to know how much this guy knew. Hil gambled and went straight to the point. "I know where the package is," he said, "and I know where LC is. And if you kill me now, you'll never find him."

"What makes you think we don't know exactly where he is?"

As much as Hil knew that Elenor's happy juice was taking care of moderating all his vital signs, he still kept his gaze steady and his breathing slow and easy.

"Like we've known," the man continued, "exactly where you've been every step of the way."

Hil smiled. "No," he said smoothly. "You have no idea where he is. And if you want that package, I'm the only one who can get it for you."

The guy had no discernible signs of an implant, and Hil couldn't tell if he was getting input from somewhere.

"You're either very bold, or very stupid, delivering yourself to us like this, Mr Hilyer. NG said you were one of his best operatives. If you think you're good enough to trick us, you need to be better than good. We don't lose well."

At the mention of NG, Hil felt his resolve slip. He didn't show it.

"It's no trick," he said. "I'm offering to lead you right to him, and the package and the corporation that sent us to steal it, all delivered up in one go."

"And why should we believe you'd do that? The profile NG gave us on you doesn't suggest to us that you'd betray your guild."

The guy was trying to goad him into a reaction so screw it, Hil gave them one.

"I don't owe the guild anything," he said bitterly. "They tossed me out. Was it NG who told you I'd be on Abacus? I knew someone at the guild was selling me out. I want to make a deal. I give you everything you want and I walk away. That's it."

"You want us to believe that you'd give up a friend to save yourself? That's not very honourable."

Hil laughed. "I'm a thief. It's not a very honourable profession. I want my life back."

He had absolute faith that Elenor's drugs would show them he was telling the truth. But the way he felt right then, it wasn't far off. He'd known LC could never go back to the guild. He knew Martha, Kase and Genoa had betrayed him to Zang and had strongly suspected that others at the guild were in on it too, but to hear NG's name there in that context had been galling. He wanted to think this guy in the slick suit was fast talking to throw him but why would they even know NG's name? The Earth forces had found him on Abacus. If it had been NG that had given him to them, then he was more screwed than he'd thought. So what the hell?

"Kill me and you never find him," he said again. "Let me go, follow me to the corporation and I'll make sure LC is there with the package."

"Look at yourself, Mr Hilyer. You're not in a good bargaining position. Tell us where he is and we'll take it from there."

"You'll never get anywhere near LC."

The man paused, motionless, still no emotion on his face. He was either weighing up Hil's offer or listening to someone else weigh up the options.

"And you will?"

He had them. "LC trusts me," he said. "I know which facility the corporation wants to use for the meet. Those bastards set us up. I can get LC and the package and take them there. You follow and everyone will be there in one place."

"And what about you?"

"I want ten million and all hits on me called off."

"You expect us to let you walk away?"

"It's the only way you get the package."

The man was quiet again, his gaze intense and unwavering. "We can arrange that," he had said finally. "You give us Mr Anderton and the package. Then what?"

"I can take care of myself," Hil had said. "Just make sure your clean up crews know to leave me alone."

As if that was ever going to happen. He was past caring. The room shook with another blast.

The old man was shouting, thumping a fist on the table in front of Hil's face. "How dare you bring this down onto us. Who the hell do you think you are?" he yelled. "No one – no one deals with us like this."

There was another explosion that sounded a lot closer. He could hear Anya as well, shouting now at the old man, at Martha and Kase and him.

The old man was so close that Hil could feel his breath. "Where is my package?" the man hissed, each word forced through lips that were parched and withered. His eyes were old, far older than he looked from a distance.

The guy in the suit put a hand on the old man's shoulder, "Troops are landing, sir. We need to leave."

"My package!" the man screamed.

A bomb-burst somewhere in the complex made the room shudder. The lights flickered.

The old man's eyes narrowed and he stood back, glaring. "Kill him."

Hil felt like he was in the eye of a storm, still and deceptively tranquil. The cold metal of a gun barrel pushed against his neck, the hand still clamping him to the table. "Anya," he said softly.

She was standing just staring. He thought she was going to say something and he would have liked to think she showed some emotion, but there was nothing. The hand tightened on his neck.

"Dammit, wait," Martha shouted, coming forward. "He's our only way out of this."

The moment hung, the absolute silence in the room edged by the distant rumble of explosions. The old man looked around, incredulous that anyone would argue with him, but then he looked at Martha and she said again in that persuasive way she had, "I know him. Those troops landing are going to sterilise this facility. He has a plan to get out of this and that'll be our only guaranteed way out."

Hil looked up with a faint half-smile and let an expression of total indifference dance across his face.

Martha got the message.

"Oh shit," she said quietly, "he hasn't got a way out."

Everyone in the room turned to Martha. She looked at Hil with dismay.

"Sir," the guy in the suit said urgently, breaking the mood and taking the old man gently by the shoulders, "we have to go." He turned, pointed at Hil and said harshly, "Get that restrainer back on and bring him to the executive hangar."

They left then, hurrying out as bombs devastated their stronghold and troops descended, Anya and the other bodyguard scurrying after them.

Hil tensed. There was no way he wanted that damned device hooked back into his spine. The cuffs were pulled tight around his wrists and a hand was gripping his hair.

He shut it all out, judging his weight, the distance and exact point of balance. The hand tightened around his neck and Hil shoved the table, bracing his feet at just the right angle and throwing himself back. His head impacted with a face behind him and the chair went flying. It wasn't deft or as powerful as he hoped but it sent Scarface tumbling as he fell into him. The device went clattering along the floor and Hil went flying as the big man managed to grab a handful of his shirt and throw him against the wall.

The next blast took out the power and the room fell into darkness. Hil blinked, not sure for a minute if it was his eyesight that had gone. He shuffled along the wall, moving away from the sound of shouting. His own plan hadn't extended much past this point but there was no way he was going to die with his hands tied so he made himself some space in the darkness and began to work the cuffs free.

Emergency lights flickered on almost immediately, casting a blue tinge to the room. A hand grabbed his arm and pulled him upright before he could get free and the gun was pushed into the side of his neck again.

"You know," Scarface hissed into his ear, "the plan was to kill you later anyway. Give me an excuse. Go on, try to escape. Just give me a reason. The old man won't care."

"Is that all you've got?" Hil said back, trying to twist away to ease the pressure.

As far as he could see, there was no one left in the room but he was banking on Kase and Martha being there behind them.

"I bring a shit load of freaking bombs," he said, "flying into your lap, on top of us all trapped right here together and you threaten to kill me. Yeah, you'll have to beat them to it."

The guy didn't appreciate the irony and the pressure eased as the gun was pulled back and returned for a swift blow to the side of his face.

Hil staggered slightly and laughed. "This is what we do when people screw with the Thieves' Guild," he said, blinking blood out of his eye. "Enjoy."

He thought he'd misjudged then. Maybe they were alone and he thought Scarface was going to shoot him outright but Kase intervened, coming out of the shadows fast, pulling Hil away and aiming his own pistol unwavering in the guy's face. "Back off," Kase said, "he's ours. Go do your own job and get the boss out of here."

"The boss?" Hil couldn't resist saying incredulously, "excuse me but I thought our boss was NG, Kase. You that far gone?"

Kase ignored him and stared down the guy, both holding guns up aimed at each other, Hil in the middle, until Martha stepped up adding a third pistol to the equation.

"You heard him. Back off, buddy," she said. As stand-offs went it was impressive. The explosions were getting closer and the lights flickered like they were threatening to go again completely. Hil's hands were still tied and Kase still had a firm grip on his arm. If he broke away now, maybe all three of them would shoot each other. He twitched as if he was going to make a break for it and flinched as Kase's pistol fired up close to his ear, deafening, and Scarface dropped with a hole in his forehead to match that of his twin.

In a smooth motion, Kase shoved Hil away, and it was all he could manage to stay on his feet and look defiantly at the two people who were supposed to have been on his side. Kase switched his aim to Hil.

"You've played this all wrong, Hil," he said. "You stupid son of a bitch couldn't just do what you were supposed to do."

Hil looked from Kase to Martha but she'd switched her aim too. "What the hell are you doing Kase?" he said. "The guild is never going to let you get away with this."

Kase's eyes were alight with a fury he'd never seen before. "This is bigger than the guild," Kase said, his voice raising in pitch. "The guild's done. Finished. And this was our ticket out, except you've screwed it up for all of us."

His gun wavered and for a moment Hil seriously thought he was going to pull the trigger, but Martha said calmly, "Kase, Hil's our only way to the package. Think about it."

Kase started to nod, but then shook his head. "No, this bastard has done nothing but screw us around."

A blast close by shook the room and the lights dimmed. Kase swore and took a step forward, gun up and finger tightening. The lights flickered again and as Kase fired, Hil dived to the side too slow to avoid a burning hot graze to his arm. He fell and rolled, a second shot punching into the floor beside him. The third shot came nowhere near and after he'd rolled again and come up onto one knee, Kase had dropped his arm and stood, wavering, clutching at a hole in his chest. He staggered and dropped, gun spilling from his outstretched hand, eyes staring.

Martha lowered her pistol.

"Shit," she said and looked over at Hil with something that could have been sorrow but equally and more likely was disappointment. "Well, if you don't have a plan to get out of here, I damn sure do."

29

The Man poured the wine slowly, taking a deep breath and inhaling the fumes as the dark liquid splashed into the goblets. "Jameson has been a valuable ally. Can you say that is still true?"

It was a loaded question. When could they ever truly trust any ally?

"We have an uncomfortable understanding," NG admitted. "I'll be much happier when we find LC and I can return their property. As it is, we're maintaining a precarious situation between the two powers. And we're nurturing several breakaway factions. The situation is still volatile."

"Jameson was a fool to over-react with such vehemence."

"Earth is afflicted by pride," NG said. "They lost control of the colonies a long time ago and they still refuse to acknowledge it. They still think overpowering force is the only way to subdue a potential threat."

"And that very threat of force is exactly what fuels the stubborn defensive nature of the colonies and Winter. They are all fools."

The Man pushed one of the goblets across the desk. "Zang acted beyond any limits of treaty. I trust that we are wooing Ennio Ostraban."

NG almost winced at mention of that name. The man was an obstinate, pig-headed egotist. "He presumes to represent Winter and we deal with him as such, but there are numerous others that can claim equal if not more valid regard. The incident with Zang has made all of them nervous. And nervous doesn't suit these people — when threatened, they have a tendency to lash out."

"You didn't need to do this, Hil," she said when they were out in the corridor, klaxons screaming, broken intermittently by a recorded voice advising all personnel to evacuate the facility. Martha was pulling him along by the arm, keeping him close as if she was worried she could lose him. She'd taken off the cuffs and checked his arm, which was bleeding but really was little more than a scratch. He'd shrugged her off and demanded a weapon. She'd refused.

"You didn't need to betray the guild and sell us all out," he said, pulling back because he could hear footsteps. "Wait up," he whispered and backed up.

Ahead of them, doors banged and there were yells and screams of "Don't shoot," thin and scared voices pleading innocence that were silenced by sudden and unrelenting gunfire.

Martha cursed and they backed away, veering off into a narrow smoke-filled corridor. Another explosion sent them reeling into the wall.

"We have to go down," she shouted. "Find a stairwell."

It was hard to breathe. Down made sense because everyone else was fleeing upwards. He really didn't want to get caught up in any crowds, but down?

He hesitated and bent over coughing, and Martha grabbed hold of him. "I don't care what agenda you had coming here," she yelled at him, "but I'm extracting you. That means you're mine, you have no say from here on in."

Her eyes bore into him, close up. The smoke was sooty so something was on fire. It wasn't just dust. The facility was crumbling and burning around them.

Hil caught hold of her hand, bunched as it was around the front of his shirt.

"What do you care?" he said quietly, nose to nose.

She shoved him away. "You have no idea," she said viciously and grabbed his arm again, pulling him along, half running, half stumbling, each blast feeling closer and closer.

She pushed him through a doorway that led to a set of steep stairs. They teetered at the top, listening. Footsteps thundered above them, entire levels emptying of people as they tried to flee. Below them was a silence that echoed with rumbles of instability.

"Down," she said again, and propelled him ahead of her.

Hil caught his balance and jogged down the stairs. "When did you know about Anya?" he said, without looking back, raising his voice enough that she'd be able to hear.

"Not until we got here, Hil," she said, sounding even more pissed. "I swear. I didn't recognise her. I've never seen her before."

They reached the next level and he paused at the landing, not sure what she intended. It seemed freaking insane to keep going down.

"Down!"

Who was he to argue with a mad woman? He took two steps down then stopped as red dots danced up the stairs towards him. He backed up. The clatter of armour and weapons echoed up towards them. Martha grabbed him and pulled him back up.

"Shit."

They backed up to the landing and pushed through the doors into a level that was dark. No emergency lights and air that was still and warm.

"The central core," Martha whispered into the back of his neck. "We'll go down from there."

They moved quietly and fast, veering away from any voices, and twice running from sounds of gunfire and screaming. Hil kept moving from instinct more than any actual decision to go with her.

She led the way and watching her shadow up ahead, it was impossible to figure out what she was intending. It was tempting to stop, slide away and never see her again.

But there was something about Martha that messed with his head and there was a reason why she was going to such efforts to keep him alive.

"What are you in all this, Martha?" he whispered.

"You don't want to know," she whispered back, "just trust me right now."

"Not good enough."

"Hil, there's more to all of this than you'll ever know. The guild's in trouble and Earth's about to declare war on Winter. The guild has been acting as if it's oblivious to a lot of crap that's been going on and now it's all landed right on its doorstep."

She stopped suddenly at the sound of voices echoing from behind them.

"Give me a gun," he whispered.

"No way!"

They glanced back over their shoulders. From the sounds of gunfire, corporate security was trying to put up some kind of defence and they were caught in the crossfire. Two soldiers in corporate uniforms appeared, yelling and raising weapons. Martha shoved him and they ran, veering off through the nearest doorway.

They crashed through onto a balcony that extended around a massive conference hall. The emergency lights were flickering on and off, casting a flashing blue strobe effect throughout the area. As they ran round into the open, they were greeted by more shouts and gunfire that raked across the balcony's handrail and ricocheted off the wall.

"Go!" Martha yelled and sprayed a hail of bullets down towards the soldiers running across the hall towards them.

Hil kept his head low and ran, shots trailing him. There was another opening directly opposite the one they'd come from. He trusted that Martha was behind him and ran for it. There was a deep boom and the landing ahead of him erupted into a blaze of flames and debris. Hil staggered back from the shockwave of the grenade and flinched as shots homed in on him and something hot punched into his side, sending him spinning back, knees buckling.

A hand clutching the back of his shirt yanked him backwards and he stumbled, holding his side, fingers feeling hot and sticky. He was vaguely aware of another explosion on the balcony behind them then Martha was dragging him, screaming at him and firing, taking down the two soldiers who burst out through the door and hauling him past them as they fell. In the temporary safety of the corridor, she pulled him upright and hissed in his ear, "Don't let me down, Hil," and they ran and stumbled, falling through another door into a stairwell.

She dragged him down two levels before she let him sag onto a step and slump against the wall.

"Shit," he muttered, holding onto a burning stitch in his side, trying to breathe and calm his heart rate.

Martha knelt by him. "Let go," she said softly and pulled away his hand, pulling up his shirt to slap on a patch that stung as if she'd poured acid onto him. He recoiled and tensed, swearing, then relaxing as the heat eased and his side numbed. He let her tape the patch into place and watched her as she popped a couple of shots of meds into his side. He was shaking but she was as steady as if she'd just been for a stroll in the park.

"What do you want, MJ?" he said. "The twenty six million?"

She glared at him as if he'd slapped her. "No, Hil, I want you."

She stared and he stared back, holding in a grin that was probably more to do with the drugs than what she'd just revealed.

They sat there for a moment, then he said, "I don't get it."

"What don't you get, Hil?"

He waved a hand generally. "All this. I don't get it."

"No, you don't. This corporation decided it was big enough to take on both sides, and it thought it could ride roughshod over anyone that stood in the way. Bringing Earth Special Forces down on them isn't going to change anything, Hil. This is one facility out of thousands. You think this is going to affect anything they do? You've all been so superior in your cosy little guild, dabbling in this and that but you've been used to do their dirty work. Earth wants control of the colonies back and the Wintrans have just been stupid enough to give them a reason to do it."

"The bio-weapon?"

"Yes, the weapon you were sent to steal," she said. "I don't think Earth itself even knew exactly what their lab was developing but when a Wintran corporation took enough of an interest to send the Thieves' Guild in after it, a lot of eyes were suddenly looking in this direction. They nuked the lab you broke into, did you realise that? Earth destroyed their own facility, completely, razed it to the ground. Two thousands lives snuffed out in an instant just because they were in the wrong place at the wrong time. Earth were that desperate to cover this up. And you wonder why so many people want to find you and LC?"

She stood, pulled out her back-up pistol, checked its magazine and handed it to him. "Come on, we have to move."

The drugs had numbed his whole side. He prodded absently at the bandage. "I've never been shot before."

"Yeah, well welcome to the delights of the trauma patch. You'll feel it later."

They worked their way down to the next level and he waited while she checked the corridor was empty. After a moment, she ducked back into the stairwell and beckoned him to follow.

It hadn't slipped past him that she'd referred to the guild as his, like she wasn't part of it. He asked quietly as they walked, "Who are you working for, Martha?"

She ignored the question.

"Who was that old man back there?" he asked, starting to feel belligerent.

She stopped and turned, and said, "Hil," in that way she had that was always the start of an argument, but then she was cursing and her pistol was up and firing past him. He flinched away and shots from behind peppered the wall next to him. Red laser dots danced across the corridor. He stumbled and ran, catching up with her as she backed away, firing. A canister bounced past them, rolling against the wall and belching out smoke.

"Shit," she said and pushed him through a door. He took the lead then and, sensing she was right behind, he ran through what looked like a canteen.

"The kitchen," she yelled. "We can get to the maintenance vents from there."

The doors crashed open behind them and more canisters flew past. The smoke was acrid and his eyes were stinging, throat sore, before they managed to get through to the back of the room. It was dark but the assault teams would have infrared, low light and thermals so the advantage was all on their side.

The kitchen was warm and he bumped into hot surfaces that burned his fingertips as he half ran, half staggered through, not caring much beyond the need to get away. Martha pulled him sideways into an alcove and they dived through a hatch, slamming it shut as footsteps thundered into the kitchen behind them, pans clattering with the impact of high velocity rounds as bullets strafed across the room.

They climbed down another two levels before they stopped for breath. The narrow vents were smoky and noisy, and what little environmental control was left was working overtime trying to compensate for the damage to the complex.

They ended up over a massive circular maintenance area, below the atrium, he reckoned. It must extend down through the whole place, with these access areas in between each floor, shot through with tubes and pipes, a lift shaft in the centre, all lit by temperamental emergency lighting that was about to give up the ghost.

"You okay?" Martha asked walking behind him as he led the way for a while.

He was feeling hot and clammy but he wasn't going to admit that. He twisted around to see that she was checking a bullet hole in her armoured vest. "Are you?" he said.

"Bastard hit me but it didn't go through. I'm fine."

They walked on for a few moments, then she said, "Where's LC, Hil?"

He didn't answer. Didn't know what to say, and with her asking that, it was hard to trust her again.

"What did you promise them?" she said. "You, LC and the package all here in one place, a surgical strike to eliminate everything in one go?"

"Just about," he conceded. "It was the only way I could think to get rid of the price on our heads. If everyone thinks we're dead, why bother looking for us?"

"And LC walks away with the package? God, you people are obsessed. Can you never let one go?"

Hil smiled. Maybe once he'd been like that but that wasn't what this was about. Not now.

"That old man back there," Martha said, "is Zang Tsu Po, CEO of Zang Enterprises, one of the largest corporations in the Wintran coalition, and one of the richest men in the galaxy. He's left his fortified enclave on Winter only three times in the last five years and he came here today to see you."

"And what? I should be flattered?"

"Christ Hil! Do you have any idea what it takes to bring someone like that out of his rat hole? Can you try and get it through your thick skull how serious this is? He wants that package. NG wants the package and Earth wants it back. What does that tell you, Hil?"

"It's an important weapon, I get it."

"No, you don't. It's not the package any more. It might have been at one time, but now look at what it represents."

She looked at him like he was stupid, then said slowly, "Earth Special Forces have just openly attacked a Wintran planet. Going after you in the Between was risky enough but here…? You might just have started a war."

30

"Rumours of war are exaggerated," NG said.

"Even rumours have the power to bring down empires."

"Ostraban is claiming that Zang Tsu Po was working alone. It has even been suggested that he might have been acting against the interests of Winter purposely to incite aggression against Earth that would ultimately benefit himself. The Zang corporation is building a reputation as a cutting edge arms dealer; it would profit immensely from a war."

The Man shook his head. "These beings inspire me at times but so often exasperate. Everything that we have been working towards could be destroyed by one man's greed."

"The official Wintran position is that Zang has gone renegade. That in itself could be dangerous," NG said, reaching for his wine. "Losing face never goes down well. Whether his actions were justified or not, Hilyer caused him immense and costly collateral damage."

The Man picked up his own goblet. "Then we must ensure he does not have the time or opportunity to regroup and strengthen. We must force Winter's hand into discrediting any position Zang may retain. He murdered our best handler and blackmailed two of our best operatives, NG. That will not go unanswered. Hilyer may have been rash operating alone as he did but in many ways, he simply reacted naturally in the same way that we, as a guild, will continue. No one in this galaxy comprehends the true extent of our power. Zang will pay. And, as always, Earth and Winter will be unaware of our intentions."

"Heads up," Martha said quietly, "we have company."

She was looking away from the central core. He followed her gaze and could see the bouncing beams from flashlights and red lasers working their way through the maze of pipes and ladders.

Something she'd said registered with him suddenly. "The lab belonged to an Earth corporation?" he asked.

"It wasn't just an Earth corporation, Hil, it was a government research facility. Top secret. But yes, it was Earth. You just figured that out?"

So they'd been sent by a Wintran corporation to steal from the Earth government. No wonder the entire galaxy had erupted against them.

"We didn't know," he said.

"Hil, even we didn't anticipate that this could happen."

He looked at her, not at all sure who that 'we' was. But what the hell. She was either guild or not, it didn't matter. He'd had his moment of revenge. He'd brought fire raining down on Zang. And it was time to get out.

They moved quietly, Hil content to let Martha lead. He watched her up ahead, moving silently, equipment wrapped against noise, hips swaying, confident that he was behind her. The way she moved was hypnotic. And it was hard to remember how he'd felt when he'd found out she'd betrayed them.

They reached a ladder and dropped down a level and Martha led them round to the central lift shaft.

He could feel his temperature rising. "Is it getting warmer?"

Martha looked at him. "Environmental controls were fried a while ago," she said and swatted his neck. "Take the dampener off. I can hook up with you."

He'd forgotten it was there. It was funny how quickly he'd become used to being out of touch; after living in constant connection with Skye for so long, and remembering the awful torn feeling of losing her, it was strange to realise now that he was used to being alone.

"We need to go down," she said. "We won't have a chance up top. They're targeting the facility's entire infrastructure. The main hangar's been hit. We don't think anyone got away, but we're not sure."

There was that vague 'we' again.

He tore the patch off his neck and felt the implant engage and accept the connection.

She gestured with her pistol towards an access panel by the door of the lift shaft.

"Go to it, sunshine," she sent, her words soft inside his head. "We don't have much time."

"I don't have any tools," he sent back.

"What?"

He spread his arms, exaggerating the show of his current state of dress. "No tools."

She rolled her eyes and threw a tool kit at him, guild standard and nothing fancy but it would do.

"Where's your wristband?" she asked, watching him work.

"I left it with someone. These idiots missed it twice but I didn't think Earth would be as stupid."

She nodded and strode away to check that they were still alone.

He broke into the panel easy enough but the electronics inside were shielded and protected by barriers and codes, beyond anything a normal facility would utilise. He worked steadily and broke each level as he encountered it.

He almost jumped when Martha yelled inside his head. "Hil, you in yet?"

An echo of gunshots reverberated through the narrow space, some way off, but then the rattle of grenades bouncing along the metal walkways was followed by a loud curse from Martha and a series of explosions that rumbled through the platform he was standing on.

He was too close to getting through to look up and he was fairly sure that the footsteps running back to him were Martha's so he cursed, took a gamble on the last couple of connections and snatched his fingers away in case it blew up.

Whether it was luck or judgement, the hatch swung open as Martha ran round and pushed him down. They fell in and she slammed the hatch behind them, a resounding click resetting the lock.

The circular lift shaft had a maintenance cage around its perimeter, with platforms at each level and steep steps spiralling up and down.

It was dark and freezing cold, and as he gasped in the icy air, he felt the unnerving sting of electrobes hit the back of his throat. Crap.

"Don't breathe in," Martha warned, pushing him along the gantry, like he might not have noticed that the air was teeming with the little bastards.

He had too much first-hand experience not to have recognised it and he bit back a comment, glaring back at her dark shadow behind him. Behind her, there was a thump and sparks flew from the edges of the hatch they'd crawled through. They wouldn't waste time trying to break the lock and it didn't sound like it would take them long to break through.

Martha caught up with him and pulled him close. She held up a small round device that looked scarily familiar in the dim light and for a split second he thought he'd seriously misjudged her, again, and he flinched away, instinctively balancing his weight for a fight.

"Oh for god's sake, Hil, trust me," she hissed. "It's not the same. Look."

She pulled aside her collar at the neck and showed him an identical small circle stuck against the skin at the base of her throat. It was blinking green. "It creates a vibration that repels them and breaks down their cellular structure if they stick around too long. Trust me."

She wasn't having any trouble breathing and her eyes weren't watering so what the hell. He took the device and pushed it against his throat. It pierced the skin with the same vicious bone-deep pain he'd had from the other device he'd encountered on this planet, and a trembling spread down into his chest.

Sparks were still flying behind them, Martha silhouetted against the flashes of light. "It can take a bit of getting used to," she said.

"No shit!" Hil hissed back, doubling over as his lungs constricted and his vision swam. He felt like he was about to pass out when it began to ease.

Martha gave him a shove. "Come on, we have to go."

"Where the hell did you get these? They're not guild," he asked as they ran round towards the stairs.

"No," she said, keeping close behind him. "They're experimental.

We don't know how long they'll last, or what concentrations they're effective in. So enjoy while it's working."

Great. And whoever that 'we' was, they had access to kit the guild didn't – that wasn't encouraging.

Hil started down the stairs. The steps were steep and narrow, meshmetal cold under his bare feet. They didn't make it to the next level before there was a blast above them, the hatch clattering inwards, and shots began to ping off the railings. Martha returned fire and yelled him to go faster.

He jumped the last few steps, stumbled and cringed away from sparks ricocheting off the wall, running on and round to the next staircase. His head was pounding and a nagging ache had started to pull at his side. He was down to the next level before he realised it had gone quiet. He leaned on the railing and looked up. Martha was padding down the stairs towards him, gun in her left hand, her right arm held defensively up against her chest.

"Go," she shouted as she approached.

She was hurt and he wasn't sure whether or not to care. She'd probably saved his life back there on the balcony and it seemed cold to brush that off, but he knew she could look after herself and she'd be covering her back whatever she had planned for him.

"Go!" she said again as she caught up to him. It wasn't the place to stand and argue so he went, taking it a bit more easy because he was seeing flashes of light behind his eyes pulsing in time with his heartbeat. It was better than dying of electrobe poisoning but it was damned distracting.

As they went deeper, more and more rumbles echoed through the shaft next to them, groans and pangs of a substructure that was failing. But there was no one else shooting at them.

Eventually she called out, "Wait up, this is it."

He stopped, sitting on the bottom step to wait. His side was throbbing and he could feel it was bleeding, sticky warmth leaking through the bandage.

Martha sat down next to him. "Put pressure on it," she said and pressed against the hand he was holding there. "It's a good thing you guys don't get hurt often because you suck at looking after yourself."

He glanced round at her and saw she had a trauma patch of her own taped to her upper arm.

"I'm fine," she said in that tone that meant don't question me or I'll rip your head off.

He leaned back nonchalantly, trying not to shiver too much, and said instead, "So what's the plan?"

"There's an underground stream they pull into a water treatment plant down here to use for cooling and power. We get to the stream and follow it out."

"And then what?"

"We get off this rock."

"And then?"

"Hil, for god's sake, stop being so suspicious. I'm trying to get you out of here alive."

She pulled an auto injector from a pouch on her belt.

"Who are you working for, MJ?" he asked again, watching her fit an ampoule. He still had hold of the spare pistol she'd given him and as much as he'd seen her check the magazine, she could have been checking that it was empty for all he knew. He tried to gauge from its weight whether it was loaded. "It sure as hell isn't the guild so why should I think you have my best interests at heart here?"

She turned to look at him, then reached up and pulled him forward into a kiss. He didn't resist even though he knew it was dangerous and he leaned into it, not even sure that was what either of them wanted. A sharp cold jab hit the side of his neck and she pulled away, shooting a second hit into her own neck. "Time to go."

They listened at the hatch before opening it, the lock from the inside being a simple twist open, and climbed out onto a gantry that ran around the lift shaft. Below them was a tangled network of pipes and below that, lit by the few emergency lights still on, they could see water shifting around massive plant machinery and conduits. Half submerged, half broken walkways criss-crossed the area with ladders extending down into the dark oily water. An eerie silence was broken only by a gentle sound of waves lapping up against the heavy equipment.

"Shit," Martha said. "The tunnels are over there somewhere. We'll have to climb across and see if we can find one under the water. Go ahead, monkey boy, see if you can find us a way over."

Hil smiled, the drug giving him that warm feeling of invincibility. None of the extraction agents were ever allowed in the Maze but they knew enough about it to know what the field-ops could do. He climbed up onto the railing and jumped across to a narrow pipe that dropped slightly with his weight but held. He caught his balance and ran along to a section of walkway that had fallen to dip at an angle into the water. He reached across to test its stability, decided to risk it and swung himself up, climbing it like a ladder along to the intact section. Then he sat and watched Martha pick her way across. She was fine, it wasn't that difficult, but she was hampered by gear. Once she was half way, he climbed up and worked his way through the easiest route he could find to the centre of the room then waited again.

Neither of them saw the guy who fired the shot that hit her, its echo rebounding around the vast space as she fell, bouncing off pipes to hit the water and go under.

Hil jumped up and yelled, caught between looking for her and spotting where the shot had come from. He flinched back as the entire area lit up, flares landing on walkways and others splashing down to ignite the oily surface of the floodwater. The flames spread rapidly. He ran forward and searched frantically for Martha, firing at the shadows he could see flitting amongst the machinery.

Thick dark smoke began to fill the area and shots ricocheted off pipes by his head.

"Martha!" he yelled silently through the implant.

Nothing, then, "Hil! Get the hell out of there." She sounded pissed but alright so he backed off and ran, clambering over debris and machine blocks.

"Where are you?" he sent.

"In cover," she hissed at him. "The tunnels are over by the back wall, get your ass over there. I'll see you there. Just don't let these guys get a shot at you."

Hil ducked down and worked his way to the back wall, keeping tight and keeping his breathing shallow. The smoke was acrid but mostly hanging just above the water. He made it to an area where the walkways were pretty much intact and hunkered down low against the wall. "Martha?"

There was a pause then, "Give me a minute."

There was splash off to his left and he ran over to help her out of the water. She was pale and swearing and digging around inside her vest. "Bastards are using armour-piercing," she gasped. "Oh shit."

He helped her pull out another trauma patch and pushed it into place against her back inside the soaking wet vest.

She caught hold of his hand as he finished and looked square into his eyes. "You have to go," she said. "The tunnels are right below us. Dive down and swim through and you should find the river."

"I'm not going without you," he said before he realised he meant it.

"If we go together, they'll be right behind us," she said, wincing as she shifted her weight. "I stay here, I can slow them down."

"No."

"Hil, you don't have any choice in this. You go. I'll catch up with you later."

"No." He'd never been very articulate in arguing with her.

She reached up and gently stroked his cheek. "You have no idea, Hil."

"MJ…"

A flare landed next to them, and they lurched away as a hail of bullets impacted into the wall behind them.

"Go," she yelled and pushed him over the edge.

31

"*Martha Hetherington.*"

NG rubbed his eyes. "We don't know where she is," he said. He hadn't had much time to find out anything before coming in here but that was one thing he had prioritised. "Legal have been backtracking over her records and every log she ever filed with us. We can't find any trace of her original screening. Right now, we don't know how she was recruited into the guild, or by whom. I'm working on it. I'll have to interview all the field operatives and extraction agents personally, in fact every person with duties outside the confines of the Alsatia. Someone managed to plant an agent in our midst and I want to know how."

"*Wibowski?*"

"*Was clean. We have data on him and it's immaculate. He was turned somewhere along the line.*"

"*And the ship?*"

"*We don't know. Genoa's history appears to be clean but we can't deny that she actively and aggressively worked against us. Science are trying to figure out how someone could have reached her without setting off alarms. I should have realised we were vulnerable.*"

The Man swirled a hand over the jug sending the rising vapours dancing. "Investigate by all means and adapt if necessary, but do not dwell and fret, NG. Your efforts are concentrated rightly on progress. Paranoia is an insidious disease that I will not allow to infiltrate this guild. We are playing with high stakes. It is inevitable that there will be some who see the superiority of our guild with envious eyes and seek to attack us."

He hit the water and plunged below the surface as it erupted in flames. The icy shock of the freezing water almost drove the air from his lungs and it pierced the wound in his side with a ferocious sting. He fought disorientating confusion and kicked down, bumping against the wall and feeling along it until he swam up against an edge. The wall gave way to an opening and he swam forward for what felt like an age, chest beginning to burn and the weakness in his side sapping his energy.

He headed up and felt a pang of panic as his outstretched hand hit a ceiling above him, the tunnel completely flooded and no chance of air. He kicked forward again, slowing and with no idea of how far the tunnel stretched. Flashes of light stabbed behind his eyes and he started to sink, kicks getting weaker, when he felt a swirling current grab him and he was swept sideways.

The flooded stream was flowing fast, eddies and currents tumbling him through a dark tunnel. Hil made the surface and gasped in a breath, trying to keep his head above the turbulent surface of the water as it carried him along.

Martha's plan sucked worse than his. He tried calling through the connection but there was nothing.

It was dark and the swirling current battered him up against rocky outcroppings, a couple of times with the sickening snap of ribs breaking. There was nothing he could hang onto and each time he was swept away again, bobbing beneath the surface.

The effort to get back up to breathe was getting harder and harder until he was suddenly hit by a wall of freezing cold air and he was freefalling down, water splashing and spraying around him. He curled into a ball and closed his eyes, giving in to the fall, the way they'd been trained. Shit happens and if this was it, this was it.

It lasted forever and he zoned out every hurt, every ache, every twinge of panic and simply fell. The impact when it happened was a shocking splash into deep water that was even colder.

He sank, his entire body shutting down, until something sparked and that stubborn survival instinct kicked in, sending him fighting his way to the surface.

Breaking through, he shook his head and opened his eyes, blinking away the sting of the water. It was dark, but the dark of night outside not the pitch black of the tunnels, and the current was still strong. The stabbing pain in his side was either so hot it was cold, or so cold it was hot, he couldn't tell but it hurt like hell.

He let the river carry him away from the side of a ravine that was emanating rumbles and distant echoes of deep explosions from inside the complex and as soon as he felt the flow of water begin to slow, he kicked out and swam for the riverbank.

Dark shadows loomed up ahead and after a couple of bumps and scrapes, he managed to grab hold of a branch and pull himself up onto the muddy slope, spluttering and coughing up river water.

Whatever drugs Martha had given him were spent and he lay half in, half out of the water for a while, just breathing quietly, shallow breaths against the pain in his ribs, eyes closed, cheek nestled in the cool mud. Dying wasn't high on his list of things to do, but it was hard to bring any semblance of a plan to mind.

The voice that reached out to him was soft, far softer than Martha ever was. "Hil, honey, I know you're hurting but I really need you to start moving, hon."

Skye hadn't been with him for a long time, so he ignored the absurd notion that she was speaking to him as delirium. It was nice to hear her voice though even if she was a delusion.

"Hil, hon, you need to wake up."

He blinked.

"Hil, I'm coming in to get you but you have to move. There's a clearing a hundred and fifty metres east. You have to get there, I'm not going to be able to wait. Do you understand?"

His eyes were too heavy to keep open.

"Hil, I'm not going to let you die on me! I'm coming in and I'm coming in hot so you had better haul butt and get to that clearing, do you hear me?"

"Skye, what are you doing here?" he mumbled to humour his delusions.

"Hil, you've got a gun ship bearing down on your position," she yelled through the connection, "and I have three fighters on my tail. Just stand up and move or I am going to be so pissed at you."

This felt familiar somehow. "Skye?"

"Hil, just move!"

He pulled himself out of the water and tried to stand but his feet were so numb he couldn't feel them. He crawled up the bank, every movement sending shooting pains through his side, every breath catching in his chest.

"Skye, I don't know which way is east," he said on the verge of giving up or throwing up, he wasn't sure which would be worse.

"Keep going the way you are," she replied after a moment, "that'll do. But you have to speed up, honey."

He rested his head on his arms, took a breath and staggered to his feet. Clamping a hand around the soggy dressing on his side made it hurt more, taking his hand away made it hurt more than that so he opted for hurt he could control and hugged himself tightly, trying to will a bit of warmth into himself.

Each step was agony but bit by bit he moved away from the river, stumbling every time he stood on a loose rock or fallen branch.

"You're almost there, hon," Skye urged constantly.

He could hear a deep droning but glancing around he could only see distant lights up at the cliff top and ahead there was only darkness. The temptation to lie down was overwhelming but each time he faltered, Skye was there gently nudging him to take another step, one foot in front of the other, reminding him how warm and comfortable he'd be once they met up.

He concentrated on that thought and banished everything else until the droning behind got louder and a dark shadow appeared above the tree line ahead. He looked back and saw a set of search lights scanning over the landscape, some way back but catching up. The pain in his side was almost unbearable.

"Skye?" he gasped.

"Almost there, Hil."

He broke through into the clearing at the same that she landed with a roar, flames flaring into the undergrowth. The ramp dropped and he limped across the open area, expecting a gun ship to open up at any minute, staggered on board and made it to the bridge. Skye had the heating on full, and midway through fumbling to buckle in to his seat, she took off, accelerating hard enough for Hil to feel the effects as the artificial gravity struggled to compensate. He closed his eyes and passed out.

Respite was brief and he was jarred awake as she tilted hard up, leaving the surface and going for orbit. She pulled a couple of manoeuvres that were so extreme he was almost thrown from the chair as the AG gave up even the attempt of trying to keep up with the frantic changes in direction.

"Buckle up, honey," she warned, "this isn't going to get any easier."

He tried to grab the ends of the harness but his coordination was shot and he only managed to get one end. He'd forgotten how fast Skye could be.

She levelled suddenly and accelerated hard again, then braking and falling so fast the seat dropped out from under him. He caught up with a bump that sent a spike of pain shooting through his side, grabbed the harness and buckled in, eyes watering and a string of obscenities on the tip of his tongue. He bit them back because he was angry at Anya and the corporation, Kase and Genoa and Earth and everyone else in the universe, but not Skye and he wasn't going to hit her with the brunt of it.

She tipped again, almost vertical and picked up speed.

It felt surreal. She wasn't supposed to be here. Hil started to shiver uncontrollably.

"Skye, what the hell are you doing here?" he muttered.

She was quiet.

"Martha was right behind me – did you see her down there?"

There was an awkward silence.

"Skye, how much do you know?" he said, suddenly wondering how the hell she'd found him. "Thank you for the rescue and everything but how did you know I was here?"

Hil trusted Skye implicitly, there was no doubt there but he had no idea how much of all this she might know.

"LC gave me your memory modules," he said, knowing he was distracting her and feeling the pull from another bone-crunching reorientation. "I know what happened at the lab."

She still didn't say anything.

"We were set up. Mendhel's daughter set us all up and Kase gave us to them. Do you know all this?"

She wasn't giving him anything on any of the display screens but it felt like they were going for orbit. A deep unease fought all the aches for his attention.

"Skye?"

"Quinn sent me out after you, Hil," she said finally. "I don't understand everything but I know you spent time with Pen and I know you shut Genoa down with a massive disruptor. And I know you gave yourself up to Earth to provoke them into that attack down there. And right now I'm trying to shake off three Earth fighters that are trying to catch up to us."

There was something in her tone that was unsettling him.

She veered violently with no warning. Hil bit down a groan and tried not to pass out again. The baggy clothes were drying in the heat of the bridge but the damp patch on his side was seeping a chill through to his bones.

"Skye?" he said quietly.

She didn't reply but another voice that he wasn't expecting crept into his head.

"Zachary, what are you doing? Zach? Are you trying to leave without me?"

Oh crap.

He gave Skye access to the conversation, maintaining a private connection with Skye herself.

"Zachary, you hurt me. You had no right to do that."

Skye was quiet still but he knew she could hear Genoa and it finally struck him what may be wrong.

"Skye," he sent privately. "Genoa was working with the traitors. She was selling me out the whole time. She betrayed the guild. I had no choice doing what I did. I know how it looks, but…"

"She did what?" Skye interrupted and started flashing information up on the screens for him, pulling out of a steep dive and ramping up the acceleration again.

Genoa's voice whispered to him again. "I am going to find you, Zach."

"Genoa, you're finished," he said, too tired to argue with a crazy ship that had almost got him killed. "The whole thing is done and finished, can't you see that? Haven't you noticed what is happening down there?"

"She was working with Kase," he sent to Skye, switching to private. "I shut her down because she would have given away everything I was trying to do. Going to Pen's should have been the safest place in the galaxy but she led them there to me…"

He trailed off and leaned forward to squint at the image she was showing him on the main display.

"You ruined everything, Zach," Genoa said. "You've no idea how much damage you've caused by running to Earth. You really are more stupid than you look. How does Skye put up with you? How is she going to feel knowing how you violated me? How does she know you won't do that to her, Zach? She'll never trust you again."

The screen was showing real time footage of an outside view, close up, a ship that looked a lot like Genoa, undocking from the orbital.

"She's right there," Skye said, sounding angry now, more like the ship he knew. "And she doesn't know I'm here."

"She's talking to me, why can't she see you?"

"Quinn didn't give me time to get completely fixed but he did make sure I had full stealth up and running, and upgraded. She'll know you're onboard a ship but all she'll be seeing is the vague haze of a disruption field and the disturbance we're causing ripping through the atmosphere at this speed. That's how the fighters are tracking us – once we're in orbit I'll lose them."

She paused and changed course again, the motion making his stomach cringe.

"How can she ever trust you again?" Genoa said, spite dripping from every word.

Skye broke through into orbit and their flight eased into a steady drifting as she circled the station. He felt himself relaxing muscles he hadn't realised were so tense.

"Hil," Skye said, "what you did to her is impossible for me to understand but what she did, my god. I wish I'd been there for you. I'm sorry."

He didn't know what to say. The psyche of any AI was tremendously complex and he'd known exactly what he was doing to Genoa when he shut her down. How Skye would react hadn't even crossed his mind. But how she was reacting now on hearing that one of her own had betrayed them was fitting and if she had weapons, he'd join her in hitting the fire button without a second thought.

"Zachary, you're not going to get away."

He ignored her and said, "Skye, I'd never do that to you – you do know that, don't you?"

She was quiet again, but more charts and screens flashed up.

"Skye?"

She was easing round to intercept Genoa's flight path, the two ships on headings that would put them nose to nose.

"Honey, this whole situation has been hard on us all. I've missed you and it's been hard knowing what you've been going through and not being there for you. If I'd known what she was doing…"

Hil looked at the screens. There were two huge Earth destroyers maintaining orbit either side of the station.

Skye began to power down. "Hil, I'm going to sit here and drift for a while until they get bored trying to scan for us. If I warm up for jump now they'll be all over us like a rash before we can get away. Go and see to that injury, hon. And tell me what happened down there."

"Kase is dead," he said, easing himself up and limping to his cabin. "Martha killed him. I don't know who she's working for but it's not the guild and it's not Zang. She saved my life. She got me out of there."

He stripped off and pulled on soft dry trousers. He didn't bother with boots because his feet were too sore. He held a towel against his side without looking at the wound too closely and rummaged through their first aid kit, looking for anything that looked like the patches Martha had used.

"So is Genoa the only traitor left?" Skye said, a chill in her tone.

"I suppose so," he said. "The only one I know for definite. I don't know where NG is in all this. I think he's been talking to Earth, someone said something, but I don't know…"

She interrupted again, "Hil, hon, NG is the guild. Whatever he's done, it will have been for your own good, don't ever think otherwise. Genoa on the other hand…"

Hil found a trauma patch and took some painkillers, grabbed a shirt and limped back to the bridge. He sat and carefully pulled the towel away, stuck the clean patch in place and shrugged into the shirt, feeling sore in too many other places to care too much about anything other than sitting still for a while.

The view of Genoa still filled the main display. "I should have guessed," Genoa hissed in his ear.

The target warning light flashed. She'd tagged them with her missile system.

"Skye," he said, "what's going on?"

"I just told her I'm here. She's coming out to us. She can't afford to let us get away, Hil. She's going to come right to us."

"And we're going to do what?"

"We're not going to do anything. Sit back and watch."

The angle switched to a view of the orbital and the two destroyers flanking it.

"She'll run," Hil said.

"She can't see them. Thanks to Quinn, my upgraded stealth capacity extends beyond my own hull. Right now I'm blanket filtering Genoa's sensors. She's seeing only what I want her to see."

He'd never heard her sound so vicious.

Genoa was still sniping at him, "Zach, you're not going to get away with this. You don't know how far this goes, who is involved. We will find LC."

Skye cut in before he could say anything. "Yeah," she said. "Whatever you say. Goodbye Genoa."

Hil opened his mouth to comment and shut it fast, flinching away, the screen in front of him blossoming with brilliant light and Skye rocking slightly from the blast in front of them as Genoa's hull exploded into billions of fragments that billowed out into space.

"Holy shit," Hil said, "don't tell me you've got weapons now."

Skye laughed and there was an edge there he'd not heard in her before.

"It was the destroyer. They sent warning messages but somehow she didn't get to hear them or see the missiles they threw at her when she didn't respond and return to dock like they wanted."

Holy crap. It was shocking. But the painkillers were kicking in and his side was happily numb again. He almost felt like he could relax, like he was back in his comfort zone. Like it really was all done and finished, except, he thought with a sinking feeling, going back to the guild wasn't something he was eager to do and if he did go back, Mendhel wouldn't be there and nothing would ever be the same again.

There was also something else niggling at the back of his mind.

"Skye, why did Quinn send you out after me?" he said.

"Because he's a good handler, Hil. You don't see it because he's different to Mend, but that doesn't make him bad at his job. He was worried about you, he knew you weren't fully fit and he said you'd need me. He pulled strings to get me ready and told me where you were going. I haven't interfered because he told me not to unless you were in real trouble."

It took a moment to sink in. He couldn't imagine Quinn looking out for him.

"How the hell did Quinn know where I'd be?"

"I have no idea. But honey, if you know where LC is, we really need to find him."

It still all came back to the package. Hil closed his eyes. "Honestly Skye? I don't know where he is but even if I did, I don't know if I could go after him."

"He won't survive out there by himself, Hil. I know you've drawn a lot of heat away from him, hon, but look at yourself. It's over. We're going in and if you care anything for him, help us bring him in too."

She began powering up the engines. "Let's go home."

32

"Earth and its military are becoming increasingly bold," the Man said, pausing as he poured more wine. "Their action against Zang was a catalyst for more incursions into Wintran controlled territories. I am disturbed that they appear to be growing in impudence. You've spoken to Jameson, what fuels their aggression?"

"Jameson is furious." Deservedly so, NG thought. "He initiated the attack on Zang after our operative presented him with an opportunity, a meeting that Hilyer was lucky to survive by all accounts, and Jameson isn't convinced that we don't have the package here."

The Man placed the jug on the table. "I take it you calmed the waters."

"Jameson isn't easily pacified," NG said. "The old Earth Empire was looking for a fight and as much as it was Hilyer who went to them and incited further aggression, Jameson is the first to admit that they were looking for a reason to give Winter a bloody nose. Hostilities between the two have been escalating. The chase for this package simply ignited tempers and passions that were already smouldering. And what is absurd is that no one even knows what is in the package. Hilyer still has no intact reliable memory of it."

"Hilyer knows what was in that package."

"If he does, he's hiding it well."

Medical kept him for a week. Total lockdown and no access to anyone except NG who'd demanded a complete debrief. Legal were trying to get their hands on him but NG posted guards at his door and no one got through, not even the Chief. Not even Skye.

It sucked.

Hil lay down at the top of the Wall in the Maze, legs dangling over the edge, muscles complaining from the exertion. The first half had been easy enough, the overhang had almost killed him.

When they'd let him loose from Medical, NG had ordered him to go straight there. "Work out the knots," he'd said and cleared the rota so no one else could get in.

He'd been in there for five hours, easing back in then pushing it as hard as he could manage. The Wall had finished him off and he lay there, emptied his head of any thoughts of anything and slowed his heart rate.

He heard Fliss before she even entered the tube that led to the top of the Wall, almost silent footsteps that meant she wasn't being careful to be quiet. He didn't sit up, just tipped his head back over and opened one eye. She emerged from the shadows and knelt by his head, ruffling his hair.

"Hey," she said.

"Hey you," he answered back, welcoming the human company for a change.

She sat on the edge and he pushed himself up, awkward still, side aching in a reminder that he'd been through the wringer and his body wasn't going to let him deny it yet.

"How did you get in here?" he said. "I'm supposed to be quarantined."

Felicity smiled and put her arm around his waist. "NG sent me."

"To spy? To find out what else I know?" He tried not to sound too bitter and twisted. Fliss had nothing to do with any of this. "I don't know where LC is, Fliss, I swear."

She shoved him away gently. "He asked me to check that you're still sane," she said. "As sane as you ever were. But yes, everyone wants to know where LC is. I'm sure the Chief will grill you once NG lets you free."

She pulled him back close and ruffled his hair again, stroking the back of his neck like he was a child. "You're back on the standings board."

He laughed. "Where have they put me?" he asked, fully expecting to be down at zero.

"Top," she said, smiling. "They reinstated your full record. No one else is near, even though you've been out of action for months."

Top of the standings. It didn't feel the way he'd expected and it hadn't happened the way he would have wanted.

"Lulu and Sorensen have been vying for the top," Fliss said.

"They're welcome to it."

"No, they're happy enough for you to be back. Tabs are tough at the minute. Security's really tight pretty much everywhere. People are saying you've started a war."

"Yeah, so I've been told. Believe me, it wasn't intentional."

She grinned and prodded his side hard. "So where'd you get shot?"

He flinched away. "Right there, thank you."

"Everyone's shocked about Kase," she said. "Legal screened all the extraction teams and field-ops. The Chief went nuts when he heard."

"When he heard about Kase, or when he heard they were screening everyone?"

"Both, I suppose. He's been fuming since you left. There are rumours he had a stand up fight with NG over the screening – that wasn't a good time to be in Acquisitions."

"When I was out there, someone told me the guild was falling apart."

"Oh, we're not falling apart, Hil, we're realigning. Apparently Media thinks this whole war thing could be a real opportunity."

He turned to look at her, incredulous.

She shrugged. "Who knows?"

Hil lay back down and closed his eyes. She put a hand gently on his chest.

"How's it been working with Quinn?" he said.

"Didn't you hear?" She pulled up his shirt and played with the edge of the bandage wrapped around his waist. "We were all taken off Quinn and given to Addison. Quinn's been handling you, Hil, and only you. I heard it's going to stay that way."

He didn't know what to think about Quinn and the man hadn't been to see him since he got back. It didn't matter.

"I don't know if I can do it any more, Fliss." He knew he sounded tired and he felt tired. It was seriously tempting to take Pen up on his offer.

"Nonsense," she said, stretching out next to him to look at him face to face. "You're guild, Hil. It never leaves you, you know that."

Yeah, he did know and being back there was turning out to be a mixed bag of emotions that was a hell of a lot more confusing than he'd felt when he was with Pen. As soon as he was cleared, he had to go back to Aston to get his stuff back. Staying there was looking a serious proposition.

Fliss sat up and touched his arm gently. "Number one in the guild – it's what you've always wanted."

"What I used to want," he said. The truth was that competing with LC for every point in the standings was what used to spur them both into getting better and taking tougher and more impossible tabs each time. Fliss was right, it was what he wanted but not this way. It felt like a hollow victory and he knew he hadn't earned it. He didn't want it this way. If they couldn't both be there at the top, then he didn't want it alone. He didn't know if he wanted it at all.

NG didn't stand up when Hil entered his office, shown in by one of NG's staff. The room was warmer than usual and quiet.

NG was sitting at his desk and he waved Hil towards a chair opposite. He sat down, trying not to slouch but still feeling sore and strung out, and not sure what this was going to be about. He wasn't sure where he stood with the guild and he wasn't entirely sure where he even wanted that to be.

There was a wooden box on the desk and two glasses filled with amber liquid. NG took one and gestured to the other. "To the guild."

Hil reached for it and raised it to his lips uneasily. The whisky was good quality, the best he'd ever tasted.

"It's from a small island on Earth," NG said softly, "where the soil is black, where humans haven't forgotten who they are."

"To Mendhel," Hil said and waited for NG to nod and drink before draining his glass in one.

"We want you to stay, Hil."

And there it was, as if NG somehow knew how close he was to running away, for good this time.

"You did the right thing, staying with Pen." NG sounded strained. "I want you to know that we believe that. And I'm sorry that you were left out there not knowing who to trust."

"LC's still out there." It sounded more belligerent than he felt, if he was honest, but he still wasn't sure that the Alsatia was where he wanted to be.

NG poured two more glasses. "Please Hil, you don't have to fight against us any more. I know what you did to protect LC and we'll find him."

Hil took the glass and held it, swirling it round so that the liquid splashed up the sides of the tumbler.

"Badger is missing," NG said, "but he sent word that he was bugging out so I'm sure he's fine. And Sean is still working with us. We'll find LC."

Hil sat sullenly, not wanting to be persuaded. "I don't want to work with Quinn," he said abruptly. "And I want to know who Martha was working for."

NG stood up and wandered off away from the desk. For a moment, Hil thought he'd pushed it too far and he half expected NG to call in the Watch and have him thrown in the lock-up. Then NG turned back and perched up against the end of the desk, looking disturbed rather than angry.

He took a deep breath and said finally, "We don't know. We have our suspicions. We know it wasn't Zang and we know she was taking orders from elsewhere but…"

"Is she still alive?"

"We don't know," NG said again.

Hil downed his whisky. Any feeling that he could come back and feel safe here in the guild, the invincible Thieves' Guild, was fast evaporating.

NG walked back round to his chair and sat. "Hil, we've been

badly shaken by all this, I won't deny it. And I won't pull any bullshit morale boosting propaganda on you. We screwed up. But we don't sack it and close shop because some arrogant corporation thought it would try to pull our strings for its own gain. Zang is licking its wounds and we have ground to patch up with Earth. We're still looking for Anya. And we still have to find LC. But in the meantime, we're not going to fall apart. The guild is far bigger than any of the crap this has thrown at us. And we want you back."

"I don't know," Hil said, biting off the rest of what he was going to say, that he didn't know if he could do it, or wanted to do it any more.

NG shook his head. "We want you back up to speed and we want you to work with Quinn. I'm not going to lose you, Hil."

Hil put his glass on the desk and eyed the bottle.

NG topped up his glass.

"I can't work with Quinn."

NG stood up. "There are some things you need to learn about Mr Quinn." He opened the wooden box. It had a brass clasp and hinges that creaked. He pulled a stack of papers from it, loose leaf real paper. "This is from Mendhel's house on Earth. I think he would have wanted you to see this."

NG held out a tatty piece of paper with a picture on one side. Hil took it, carefully, feeling the rough edges and grainy texture. He'd only seen real paper before in Legal's library and that was all bound into books. He'd never seen a photograph on paper before, never held one in his hands, and a lump formed in his throat as he looked at it, and saw Mendhel sitting on the ramp of an APC smiling with his arms thrown around Pen and Quinn, the three of them in battle fatigues, looking younger than he could have imagined.

Hil stared at the picture.

"They've been friends for a long time," NG said.

"I didn't know." He didn't understand why Mendhel had never said anything, why Pen hadn't said anything when he'd been bitching about the guy. Thinking about it, he'd never seen Quinn and Mendhel together, had never seen them actually argue. It was the field-ops that argued and fought. He'd judged Quinn and got it wrong. Same as he'd been wrong about Martha.

"Pen should have this," he said quietly.

"He's going to get it. You're going to take the whole box to him on Aston. Then I trust that you'll be coming back."

NG took the picture and put it back in the box.

"Talk to Quinn," he said. "You might be surprised. The handlers are far better at manipulating their field operatives than you guys could ever guess."

He smiled and picked up his whisky. "You're guild, Hil. And now you're at the top of the guild standings. The Man is planning some special projects and he wants the best. Welcome home."

33

NG's goblet was almost empty and he was almost done. He forced himself to sit upright, stretching out a tension in the muscles across his shoulders.

The Man rested his elbow on the desk and leaned his chin into his palm. "The impact on the guild has been extensive," he said. "Losing Mendhel and taking Quinn out of Acquisitions severely depletes your stable of handlers, NG. We cannot afford to stagnate. But amid these scandals of betrayal, should we really be recruiting? It will be difficult for our people to accept outsiders."

"It's always difficult for us to welcome newcomers. Look at me, everyone still calls me the New Guy. But how else do we bring in new blood and expand our talent pool. It will be hard in the circumstances but we need to and there are good people out there."

"Find them," the Man said. "War is inevitable and I fear the pace to implement my plans must be hastened. We must strengthen our position amongst these splintered factions of man."

The last vapours of the remaining wine hung above the jug, slowly dissipating. Only a few candles remained lit. The Man looked at him with hooded eyes. "I ask again, where is Luka now?"

"We don't know."

"Find him."

The piece of junk in geostationary orbit around Sten's World was not the nicest of places to be running from a determined bounty hunter. LC fumbled another magazine into his pistol as he ran along the walkway between sectors. The incident in the bar had shaken his nerves more than he realised. He'd thought they were close again but not that close.

He ducked into the half cover of a doorway to catch a breath and let Thom, an acquaintance of only a few hours, catch up with him.

"This is crazy," Thom said, dropping in alongside him. "Have we lost them?"

"I don't think so," LC said, grinning. "These guys are some of the best. We should make it back to the ship though. Don't look so worried, kiddo."

Thom scowled. "I'm not that young."

LC smiled.

"Why is he after you anyway?" Thom said.

LC looked up from checking the charge on the pistol and shrugged. "Gambling debts. Don't ever play poker with the Gadini brothers." He nudged Thom with his elbow and snatched a glance back down the corridor. "C'mon."

As they left the alcove, LC walked backwards for a few steps. The walkway was empty but something didn't feel right. He stopped and edged against the bulkhead, motioning Thom to do the same. He stared at the access stairs where a tangle of pipes were hissing steam. A shadow moved where it shouldn't have done. Metal glinted in the light of the stairway lamp.

He cursed silently and lifted his pistol, aiming towards the stairs. He was greeted by a hollow metallic clatter and saw a small object tumbling towards them. He blinked, then yelled, shoving Thom off to one side, trying to get down himself as the blast threw him into the wall.

He almost laughed as sparks of sheer agony flared behind his eyes and his cheek and left arm crunched into the cold metal of the bulkhead. He staggered around.

It was a strange feeling to be looking down the wrong end of a gun barrel through the effects of a concussion blast and he couldn't focus, either on the end of the barrel aimed at him or the figure standing half in shadow behind it.

So this was it after all. He began to lift his hands in grudging surrender and flinched back, his knees almost buckling as a shot resounded in the narrow space. The gun and its owner dropped. LC took a step back, swaying, blotting blood from his cheek with the back of his hand, waiting for the second shot, not quite trusting that this was a reprieve.

The corridor remained quiet, his guardian angel anonymous.

LC stumbled backwards and stooped quickly to help the kid to his feet.

Thom was closer on his heels this time as they ran on towards the docks.